THE
FROZEN
GIRL

BOOKS BY ROBERTA GATELY

THE
FROZEN
GIRL

ROBERTA GATELY

Bookouture

Published by Bookouture in 2021

An imprint of Storyfire Ltd.
Carmelite House
50 Victoria Embankment
London EC4Y 0DZ

www.bookouture.com

ISBN: 978-1-80019-029-0
eBook ISBN: 978-1-80019-028-3

With love to my twin sister, Susan Richard, who has nurtured me, listened to me, and taken care of me since before we were born. Can't imagine a life without her by my side.♥

PROLOGUE

"Nine-one-one. This call is being recorded. What's your emergency?"

"Well, I..." and then the hum of traffic and car horns in the background muted all other sound. Then silence, as though the caller had put his hand over the mouthpiece.

"Nine-one-one. What's your emergency?" the dispatcher repeated, his voice a little irritable.

"Well, I'm not sure it's an emergency. Not anymore, at least."

"Sir, you can call your local station. This line is for emergencies only. Where are you? I'll connect you to the district you're in."

"This is sort of an emergency. I think it is, anyway."

This time the voice was a little warmer. "Sir, what is your emergency? Can you describe it to me?"

"There's a body here," the caller said slowly as if he wasn't quite sure of what he was saying.

"A body? Is the person in distress? Have you checked for a pulse?"

"No, but I can tell that whoever it is, is dead. The ice is breaking up here along the Neponset River under the bridge. The body, what's left of it, seems to have just floated up. But, it's... well, it's still under the surface of the water."

"What's your location?"

"I'm under the bridge, the Dorchester side."

"Neponset River Bridge?"

"Yes, by the pylons."

"I'm sending units now. Please don't touch anything."

"I won't."

"Can you tell me anything about the victim?"

"No, I can just barely tell that it's a body. From the clothes and hair, maybe a woman, but I don't know for sure." He paused then. "I think I'm going to be sick."

"You've done really well, sir. Help is on the way. Stay where you are. Okay?"

"Yes. I'll stay." His breath seemed to come in spurts as if he was running.

"Find somewhere to sit and put your head between your knees. What's your name?"

"Patrick. Patrick O'Hara."

"Okay, Patrick. Deep breaths. Are you sitting down now? A unit is almost there."

"I can hear them. I feel a little better now," he said, his words almost lost in the shriek of approaching sirens, and then the sound of voices and commotion.

There was a click, and silence once again.

CHAPTER 1

Day 1—Sunday

"Help! We need help!" a desperate voice called from the ambulance bay, his shouts almost drowned out by an ear-splitting volley of sirens. Jessie turned and saw a young police officer, the front of his uniform splattered with blood, motioning wildly toward the entrance. She moved instinctively, grabbing a stretcher, as she sprinted toward him. "Page the trauma team," she shouted over her shoulder. "And Dr. Merrick. Page him stat."

She abandoned the gurney and raced through the sliding doors, not sure if there'd be one injured or several. She only knew she had to act fast. Someone's life was in the balance. Four patrol cars, the glare of their headlights and flashing blue strobes almost blinding her, were parked helter-skelter, the officers surrounding the back door of one car. Jessie hesitated and blinked away the glare.

"Over here," one of them shouted, and Jessie ran to his side and reached in. A young policeman lay on the back seat, his blue shirt pulled open, his T-shirt splashed with blood, his hand over a wound on his upper chest. His eyes were filled with panic. "I've been shot," he said as though he couldn't quite believe it himself. "Help me." He gasped for breath.

"I will," she said calmly. "We'll take care of you." She turned and shouted for a stretcher. In minutes, the stretcher was there, and the policemen loaded the young man onto it as more sirens and noise filled the air. Out of the corner of her eye, she could see a crowd of blue uniforms spilling into the bay, nervous shouts creating an impossible din. Jessie ran alongside the stretcher and into the trauma hallway, pointing the way to Trauma One.

She stopped quickly to shout into the intercom for the trauma team, and to advise the policemen to wait outside. As the door slammed shut behind her, she pulled on gloves and turned to her patient, her stethoscope moving quickly as she listened for his lung sounds. Just as she began to cut away his clothes, the door burst open. "Heard the sirens as I was leaving. What do we have?" Tim Merrick asked.

"Gunshot to the chest, short of breath, absent breath sounds in his right upper lobe, a hemothorax, maybe. Just having a quick look to see if there's anything else, and to get his vital signs." As she spoke, another nurse, a medical assistant, and two resident physicians filled the room, each silently and expertly performing their assigned roles—starting IVs, calling for blood, hooking the man to a monitor—the hum of activity giving Jessie a chance to whisper to her patient. "I'm Jessie," she said. "We're going to get a few things done before we take you to the OR." His eyes still wide with fright, he nodded as she threw a sheet over him, and Tim probed his wound. "What's your name?" she asked, gripping his hand.

"Danny," he said, so softly she had to lean in to hear. "Danny Coyle."

"Well, Danny," she said, "you're in the best place to be if something like this happens to you. You're going to be alright. Do you have any medical problems or allergies we should know about?"

He shook his head. "I'm healthy. It was just a routine traffic stop, and instead of pulling out his license, he pulled a gun and shot me." His voice cracked as he spoke. "Will someone call my wife? I don't want her to hear this on the news."

"Yes," she said. "I promise." With barely a glance, she slid an intravenous catheter into his vein, withdrawing blood into color-coded tubes before connecting a bag of IV fluid. Satisfied that the line was good, she placed a second line before setting up the chest tube and drainage system.

"Blood pressure's one hundred palp, pulse of one fifteen," a voice shouted. "I'll check a hemoglobin and get this sample to the blood bank," another called. The team worked seamlessly. An X-ray technician slid a large metal cassette under the patient. "Everyone out," he said, and the team slipped into the alcove as the technician took the X-ray.

"Urine looks good," one surgical resident said as the other announced Danny's hemoglobin was eight, low but not yet critical.

"Blood coming," Jessie shouted, just as Tim Merrick slid the X-ray onto the wall-mounted reader. He studied the film. "Some blood right here," he announced, pointing to a dense white shadow on the film, "and a collapsed lung as well. At least there's no mediastinal shift—no imminent danger, but no time to waste. We'll get a chest tube in and get him upstairs. Can someone call the OR, and see if they're ready?"

Jessie barely had time to explain the chest tube to her patient before Tim had performed the procedure. Jessie slipped her hand into Danny's. "It's okay. Squeeze. This will be over with quickly." He looked utterly terrified.

Tim pulled off his gloves and turned to him. "That bullet went right through your lung, and this chest tube will drain the blood and reinflate the lung. You'll be breathing easier soon. We're going to take you to the OR to have a look and see if there's any other damage. Any questions?"

Tim was as brusque as ever. Danny shook his head, beads of sweat streaking along his forehead. "Just… just tell my wife I'm okay and that I love her." Jessie nodded and gripped his hand. "You can tell her yourself soon, but I'll make sure she gets your message."

"OR ready?" Tim called.

The medical assistant was already dialing before he'd finished speaking. "They're ready," she answered. The team piled equipment onto the stretcher as the second nurse hooked Danny up to portable monitors for the quick trip to the OR. When Jessie pulled open the trauma room door, a sea of blue stood silently, eyes wide, mouths agape. And as the stretcher moved through the crowd to the elevator, there were countless hushed words:

"We're with you, Danny."

"You'll be alright. I called your wife. Leo's bringing her in."

"Boston strong, Danny. Don't let us down."

Each whispered word of encouragement was accompanied by a pat on Danny's shoulder or a quick grip of his hands. Danny's eyes filled with tears, but he quickly blinked them away, feigning a strength he likely didn't really feel. "Get out of here," he said. "Go to Foley's and have one for me." They laughed in unison, the collective angst that had filled the narrow hallway replaced by a hopeful optimism. And then there were hoots and slaps on the back as the stretcher passed through the doorway, silence returning again to the small space once Danny was out of sight.

"Will he really be alright?" one of them asked.

Jessie drew in a deep breath. If there was one question she always dreaded, this was it. She could never be certain who might survive their injuries. Sometimes, the ones with injuries that seemed almost insignificant were the ones who bled out in the OR as soon as their chest was opened up. But hope was everything, especially for these guys. "I…" But before she could continue, she saw a familiar face.

CHAPTER 2

"Hey, Jessie," Detective Sam Dallas said, the silver flecks in his eyes sparkling. "I'm glad you're on tonight. Can you tell us anything?" He ran a hand through his thick chestnut hair speckled with thin streaks of gray.

The knot in her neck eased, and she flashed him a quick smile of recognition. "Hey, Sam. Well, you know he has a gunshot wound to the chest—his lung was punctured, and he's lost blood, but you saw him—he was awake and alert and worried about his wife."

"Nothing else?"

She shook her head. The group grew quiet, and she turned to them. "I promise, we'll let you know as soon as we hear anything." Sam moved closer and gripped her hand tightly, the warmth of him seeping into Jessie's skin.

"Thanks, Jessie," he said softly. "I'm glad you're here. I hate to ask, but how long do you think?"

"Tim Merrick just brought him to the OR, so at least a couple of hours, maybe less."

"You'll be gone by then, right?"

She paused. Her shift had just ended and she was dead tired. Tomorrow, she was due to rotate back to the Medical Examiner's office and Homicide. She was still new to this position and she didn't want to be late. Dr. Dawson—Roger, he preferred to be called—had stuck his neck out to hire her and she wouldn't disappoint him. "I'll stay a while," she said. "I'll give them some time in the OR and then I'll check in. Okay?"

"You're the best," Sam said as he turned to the crowd of men and women in blue. "I don't know how many of you know Jessie Novak, but she isn't just an ER nurse, she's recently come on board to work with us in Homicide as a forensic nurse. She will be our medical liaison, between us, the Medical Examiner and the victim. Remember her name. She's one of us now." He squeezed her shoulder.

A swath of crimson spread across her cheeks. She and Sam had been through a lot these last months, from almost-lovers to adversaries, and now back to… what, exactly? She wasn't sure, but the sparkle in his eyes attracted her once again. She heaved a sigh. It was probably best that they both move on. Become co-workers only, and look for love somewhere else. "If you guys take a seat in the waiting area, I'll keep you posted."

"His wife's here," one of the officers said. "Can I bring her in? Will you speak with her?"

Jessie nodded, her fatigue all but forgotten. "She can wait in the family room. Follow me." She led the group to the small, sparsely furnished room which held a threadbare couch, two sagging chairs and a scratched-up old table, evidence of the countless families who'd sat there waiting for news. It was a place that most ER staff avoided, preferring to send in social workers who were better equipped to deliver bad news. As a result, the physical space was neglected. The floor was sticky with old soda, the walls dingy, and a sharp stench of perspiration and fear hung low in the room. Jessie reminded herself to ask about getting it cleaned and updated—a fresh coat of paint and new chairs at the very least.

But Mrs. Coyle never seemed to notice as she was guided to the room, a policeman on each side ready to support her if she should need it. But she stood tall, leaning on neither of the men. She was young, Jessie saw, probably no older than she was at twenty-seven. Her eyes were wide with fright, her blonde hair tousled from sleep, her skin the whitest shade of pale.

"I'm Nicole, Danny's wife," she said, her lips quivering as she spoke. "Is he okay?" A tear streaked along her cheek and she hurriedly wiped it away, before folding her arms as if to protect herself from bad news.

"He just went to the OR. He was awake and worried about you." Jessie locked her gaze onto Nicole's bloodshot eyes. "He asked me to tell you he's okay and that he loves you."

A hush came over the group. A silent flood of tears spilled from Nicole's eyes, and Jessie felt a sudden burst of longing, and even envy, for everything this woman had: that special bond with a man who loved her and this family of police officers who surrounded her. But if she lost her husband, those things would feel very far away.

"Have a seat." Jessie swallowed the lump in her throat and passed her a box of tissues. "We can get you some coffee."

Nicole nodded, but continued to stand. "Please," she said softly, "tell me if he'll be okay. Please. I need to know everything. Where was he shot?"

Jessie hesitated. A chest wound often carried the worst prognosis, but Danny had looked good even though the bullet had pierced his lung. "In the chest…" she began.

Nicole gasped and covered her mouth with her hand. One of the officers reached to steady her, but she pulled away. "I'm sorry," she said, her voice cracking. "Please, go on."

Jessie explained his chest injury as Nicole dabbed at her eyes with the tissue and sank onto the couch, her head down, a sob escaping her lips.

Jessie knelt in front of her and took her hand. "Listen to me," she said. "It sounds worse than it is. Believe me. The surgeons had to take him to the OR to check for other injuries, but the lung wound may be all there is, and though a chest tube draining blood sounds frightening, it's a pretty common treatment and works well. Don't overthink this. Danny's in good hands." She glanced at the officers hovering over Nicole. "It looks as though you are, too. I'm going to give Dr. Merrick and his residents enough time in the OR, and then I'll take a run up there and see how he's doing. Okay?"

Nicole sniffled and nodded. "What's your name?"

"I'm Jessie. Jessie Novak."

"She's a forensic nurse, a detective," Sam added. "You can trust her."

Jessie swiveled and shot him an appreciative glance before standing and smoothing the front of her scrubs. "Dunkin's in the lobby is open. Maybe someone can get coffee."

"I'll go," a voice in the crowd said.

"The mayor and commissioner are on their way in," another said. "We'll *need* coffee." A smattering of nervous laughter erupted, and Nicole smiled. "Thank you, Jessie."

"I'm going to leave, but I'll be back as soon as I have news. I promise." She slipped through the crowd and back into the hallway, leaning against the wall to gather her composure. This had always been the hardest part of her ER job—reassuring family that things would be okay even when she knew that sometimes they wouldn't be. The best that she could offer was the gift of time—allowing loved ones time to adjust, to absorb the possibilities, to hope, or to pray—whatever worked. She'd always known a cop's job was dangerous, but to face death during a traffic stop… She couldn't even imagine facing that degree of danger every single day.

Jessie rubbed away the chill in her arms, took a deep breath and headed back through the hallway to restock the trauma room. She ran right into Kate Wagner, the travel nurse, one of those countrywide assignment nurses who worked wherever they were needed and, as an added bonus, traveled and saw parts of the country they'd likely never visit. Kate had been hired to help cover Jessie's hours. She was standing by Sheila Logan's office, her hand on the doorknob.

"You're still here?" Jessie asked.

Kate looked up, surprised. "I…" She paused. "I think I'm lost."

"Can I help?" Jessie asked, moving closer. Though Kate had only been here just over a week or so, she was taking longer than expected to catch on to the job. She'd explained it away, saying she was a recent grad and new to the ER. Donna had been confused. She'd thought the agency was sending a seasoned nurse, but by the time they'd discovered that Kate needed a longer orientation than usual, it was too late to send her back. They'd decided to make the most of it, and simply learn to work with her inexperience and bring her up to par. That seemed the best option for her and for the ER.

With her shoulder-length, honey-colored hair, Kate was one of those average-looking women who might have passed unnoticed but for her eyes—an unusual shade of blue with traces of violet. When she smiled, the soft sweep of her lids framed her eyes perfectly, the lilac specks glinting just so in the light. "Just finishing my charts. I won't be paid if they're not all signed off." She rolled her eyes dramatically as if to emphasize her frustration. "I thought maybe I could find a quiet place to sit and finish up."

Jessie shook her head. "That office was our old manager's. It's not being used right now. But it will probably be assigned to Donna. Best to just use the nurses' lounge."

"Okay," she answered, shoving her hands in her pockets and moving slowly away.

Jessie felt a wave of sympathy for this nurse who was new to Boston, new to the hospital, new to her whole situation here. "How are you managing with everything else? I know that winter is the worst time to come to Boston."

Kate offered a half-smile in reply. "I don't really have much time to do anything else. There's so much to learn."

"We want you to succeed, Kate. If you need anything, and I can help, I will," Jessie said, hoping she hadn't offered what she couldn't really deliver. She had enough on her plate these days; she was just trying to be kind, an effort that usually backfired on her. She changed the subject quickly. "Have you gotten out at all to see the city and meet people? You can't be all work."

Kate just shrugged.

This is downright painful, Jessie thought. Kate was reluctant, as always, to offer information about herself. She was quiet, keeping mostly to herself, and when asked where she was from, or if she had family, her answers were vague. She kept conversation superficial, revealing little.

But the truth was, Jessie wasn't forthcoming about her own life either. She'd always been a bit of a loner, keeping her own history to herself—she could count on one hand the number of people who knew that her mother had simply up and left when she was a baby. Jessie had been so ashamed that her mother had abandoned her that instead she'd created a story that her mother had died. That always elicited a decent amount of sympathy, and then—silence. People didn't want to dredge up old hurts. Jessie had hit on gold with that little lie, but, true to character, she was quick to judge everyone else. Maybe it was time to offer a little sympathy of her own.

Jessie began walking back toward the trauma room, hoping to move Kate along. "Do you feel as though you'll be able to master everything here?" Jessie scrunched her forehead, her concern evident, or so she hoped.

The sparkle left Kate's eyes, her features unremarkable once again. She puckered her lips and sighed. "I don't know, but I'm still trying. Your computer system has me baffled. It takes me longer than it should, which is why I'm here late every day, and why I thought maybe working in there," she said, nodding over her shoulder toward Sheila Logan's office, "might help me to finish up."

"You'll get used to it. Every hospital's EMR, electronic medical record, is different. Did you use EPIC, the one we use, in Wisconsin?"

Kate's brow furrowed. "What?"

"Our EMR, did you use it, or one like it?"

"Oh that, no," she said slowly, her eyes almost glazing over. "My hospital used a different one."

"Do you want some help? I'm sticking around for a bit."

"No. I have to figure this stuff out for myself, but thanks for asking. I may take you up on it, just… not yet."

Jessie sighed. She wished Kate would be more assertive about needing help with their computer system, and everything else. "Talk to Donna about taking the EPIC class again. You have to be able to navigate through it, but once you get the hang of it, it's easy."

"Thanks, Jessie. Maybe I will. Are you back tomorrow?"

"No. I'll be rotating to the ME's office."

Her eyes grew wide. "I'd love to follow you around, see what you actually do and how you solve crimes. It sounds fascinating. Real-life *CSI*." She sounded more excited about that than about learning how to do her own job.

Jessie forced a smile. "I'm still feeling my way around there. I have a lot to learn, and there's still some pushback from some of the detectives. They seem to think I'll slow them down, but I'm gonna stick it out. They'll come around. I hope. So, in that way, I'm working things through the same as you are. Just trying to learn everything and fit in."

Kate smiled, her eyes bringing her features to life once again, her nose crinkling, her lips parting to reveal perfectly straight white teeth. Once you really looked at her, she was pretty—not beautiful, but she had that ordinary, pleasing face that seemed to announce a kindness that people wanted to settle into. She was sweet, and everyone liked her. Including Jessie.

"One of these nights," Jessie said, "I'll bring you to Foley's. It's a great place to meet people—well, police and reporters, and the usual nurses and emergency medical technicians—EMTs."

"I'd like that. Have a good night." Kate turned and headed down the hall.

Jessie lingered in the hallway. She could tell that Kate was one of those quiet ones who'd never come out to Foley's; she'd find an excuse to avoid it. And that was okay, too. Jessie might have done the same in a new place. They were probably more alike than she cared to admit.

Jessie looked at her watch. Danny Coyle had been in the OR for almost an hour. There was bound to be some news. She sought out Elena, the night nurse in charge. "I'm just going to the OR to see if I can learn anything about the policeman who was shot, and then I'm going to head home. Are you all set?"

"I am. I just restocked the trauma room and paged housekeeping. Go home and get some sleep."

"I will," Jessie called as she took the stairs to the second floor and swiped her way into the recovery room to see if there'd been any news. One patient, surrounded by tubes, wires, IV pumps and the steady whoosh of a ventilator, lay in the farthest cubicle. A nurse was by his side, adjusting medication pumps and monitors. "Hey," Jessie said to a nurse sitting at the desk. "I'm from the ER. Just checking on the policeman who was shot. His wife's downstairs with us. Any word?"

"Yeah. The OR just called. He's on his way out." And almost as soon as the words had slipped from her mouth, the door banged open and an anesthesiologist and Tim Merrick arrived, pushing the bed along. The nurse sprang into life and grabbed hold of the portable bed, guiding it into the first cubicle where a slew of monitors, pumps and a ventilator awaited. Jessie followed but kept at a discreet distance, hoping only to get a quick look and a word or two from Tim.

Danny lay motionless, a tube snaking from his mouth to an ambu bag, the anesthesiologist manually inflating his lungs until the respiratory therapist appeared and set up the ventilator which breathed for him until Danny could do it on his own. He had the same two IV lines that she'd inserted in the ER, a heavy dressing on the right of his chest, the chest tube poking through to the drainage system which bubbled softly, the sound gentle and reassuring.

Danny stirred and lifted one arm, reaching for his breathing tube. Tim grabbed his hand and held it down. "Danny, you're in recovery. What you need now is rest. We're going to give you something to help you sleep. Squeeze my hand if you understand."

Jessie watched as Danny's fingers gripped Tim's hand, his eyelids fluttering as if he was trying to pry them open. Tim nodded to the nurse. "Propofol," the anesthesiologist said as the nurse hustled off to collect the drugs. Jessie stepped closer to the bed and into Tim's line of sight. "His wife's downstairs," she said in a whisper. "Can she come up, or can you come down to speak with her? It sounds as though things look good, right?"

"Yes," he said. "On both counts. Bring her up. We'll let her see him, but only for a minute."

"Thanks, Tim," Jessie said, backing away and slipping quickly down to the ER and through the hallways toward the family room. A hum of noise, of conversation and laughter rose up; a crowd had gathered. The mayor and his entourage filled the narrow hall by the family area. Jessie took a deep breath and steeled herself to deliver the news.

CHAPTER 3

Jessie straightened herself up to her full five foot three. "Excuse me," she said loudly, using her shoulders and elbows to move through the throng that had gathered. She wondered, only for a moment, what it must be like to be surrounded by such love and support, to know that no matter what, you were never alone.

The crowd parted, and she could see Nicole, her shoulders sagging, dabbing at her eyes with a tissue. A hush settled over the room as Jessie stepped inside. "Nicole," she said softly. "Do you want to see Danny?"

Nicole's head darted up, and she sprang to her feet, her cup of coffee splashing to the floor, everything forgotten except for her husband. "Oh, God, is he okay? Oh, please, tell me he's okay." She reached toward Jessie, her hands trembling.

"He's okay." Jessie took her hand and held it tightly. "I'm going to bring you up to see him."

Nicole's face crumpled, her shoulders heaved, and a line of tears slid along her cheeks. "Oh, Jessie. Thank you," she said.

Jessie shook her head. "Thank the surgeon when you see him. Come on." They slipped through the crowd until a hand pressed Jessie's shoulder. "Will you come back to update us?" the man said. Jessie nodded. "I'll be back in a few minutes." As she and Nicole turned the corner into the main hallway, she heard the hum of a hundred relieved sighs fill the small space behind her, and she smiled. These were the moments that she treasured. *Was there any better job in the world?*

In the elevator, Jessie explained that Danny was still connected to a ventilator and a chest tube. "It may look frightening, but it's only temporary, and it's helping him to heal. It can look overwhelming. Will you be okay?"

"Yes." Nicole's lip quivered when she spoke as though she were trying to convince herself.

"Stay here for a second while I make sure it's okay for us to go in." Jessie swiped her ID and stepped into recovery. Tim Merrick was at the nurses' station, his chair tilted back, his feet resting on the desk, his eyes closed. Jessie felt a surge of affection. He could be a royal pain, but he was a darn good surgeon. She nudged his shoulder softly. "Tim," she whispered.

His eyes flew open and he dropped forward, his feet hitting the floor with a thud. "Jessie, sorry, I just dozed off for a minute." He ran his fingers through his hair and sat straight.

"I brought his wife up," she said. "Okay for her to come in?" He cleared his throat and caught her gaze in his. She hadn't noticed how blue his eyes were, or how pale his skin, as though he'd never seen the sun.

He smiled weakly. "Ever think about how much time we spend together in the most intense of moments, when everything is on the line?"

Jessie shook her head. "To tell you the truth, I haven't. It's my job—trying to fix people who are broken. Yours, too."

"Jessie, you are one of a kind. Don't get too comfortable over in the ME's office. I'd like to keep seeing you around here."

Jessie smiled. "Well, I think I'll be with the ME for a while, unless Sheila Logan comes back and forces me to give it up."

"Sheila Logan?" he asked, his brow wrinkling.

"My old boss—never mind." She shook her head to clear away the last traces of Sheila.

"Anyway, I just wanted to say that we're a good team, you and I." He winked.

What is going on with Tim Merrick tonight, and what am I supposed to say to that? She'd learned long ago that it was best to keep her mouth shut, although more often than not, she struggled with just that. So instead, she offered a half-shrug. "I guess." She ran her fingers over the ID that hung from her neck. "Could I…?" But Tim was already speaking.

"How about some night, we go out for dinner, or a drink, whatever you like?"

She studied her fingernails and began to pick at the ragged edges. "Umm, sure," she said, stuffing her hands into her pockets before she managed to draw blood with her nervous picking. "But for now, will you speak to his wife?" She nodded to Danny who lay quietly, almost corpse-like on his bed, the machines around him whirring and beeping, his chest rising with every whoosh of the ventilator.

Tim stood, pulling himself to his full six feet, his scrubs wrinkled, his lips drawn in a straight line. He was all business again. "Bring her in. You and I can talk later?"

She flashed an easy smile and left to find Nicole, who stood in the same spot, her eyes wide and unblinking. "Is Danny awake?" she asked anxiously.

"He's sleeping, but the surgeon is there. So, you can speak with him and Danny's nurse."

Nicole chewed on her lip. Jessie took her hand. "Before we go in, I just want to be sure I have your permission to share Danny's condition with all those guys downstairs."

"Oh, of course. They're his family too."

"Whatever I tell them will probably be leaked to the press. That's okay?"

She nodded, and Jessie led her into recovery. Nicole's jaw went slack as she caught sight of Danny's inert form, tubes poking out, the ventilator forcing oxygen into his lungs. "Oh, no. I thought you said…" A cry burst from her lips.

Jessie gripped her hand. "He's okay. He's fine. He's just sleeping, that's all. Come on. See for yourself."

Nicole took a tentative step forward, her eyes scanning the machines and monitors that surrounded Danny. She hesitated, blinking away the tears that pooled in the corners of her eyes.

Tim stepped to her side before Jessie even registered her reaction. "I'm Dr. Merrick," he said without a touch of gruffness. "I'm his surgeon." He took her elbow and guided her to Danny's side. Nicole stood away from the bed, her back straight as a ruler, only her fluttering hands hinting at the worry she surely felt. Jessie stepped back as Tim spoke, explaining what had happened to Danny's lung, what the machines were doing and how long he might need all of those.

Nicole nodded and moved closer to the bed, reaching for Danny's hand as she bent to kiss his cheek. It was an intimate moment, so intense that Jessie felt as though she were trespassing on their privacy. She moved away and slipped out, heading back to the ER and through to the waiting room.

The crowd had thinned, but the police commissioner had joined the group. She could see Sam Dallas speaking to him. She cleared her throat and stepped into the room.

"Ahh, here she is," Sam said. All eyes turned toward her, and she felt a flush rise to her cheeks. He held out his hand and she moved to his side.

Jessie forced a weak smile. "Danny's wife gave me permission to speak with all of you and to let you know that things look good." She gave a quick summary of his injuries and expected outcome. "Dr. Merrick expects him to recover fully." She looked around. "That's it. I don't have anything else. Danny's asleep now, and looks good."

"Thank you," the crowd said all at once, and Jessie nodded. She hated to be the center of attention. "I'll pass your words on to Dr. Merrick and the team. Thank you all, and if there's nothing else,

I'm going to head out." She offered a quick smile and turned to go, the buzz of conversation starting up behind her.

"Jessie, wait," Sam called. "Hey," he said, drawing so close she could almost feel the heat of him. "They were really impressed with you. I just wanted you to know. "

Not sure if she was embarrassed or simply pleased, she smiled. "They shouldn't be. You should know that as well as anyone."

"Don't be so humble, Jessie. Take a little credit for what you do."

She wrinkled her mouth. "I have good reason to be humble. And, if Sheila were still here, I'd be in trouble for speaking to you guys. Old habits die hard, I guess."

"She was that nurse manager who disappeared, right?"

Jessie nodded. It was best not to speak her name, for that was sure to conjure up miserable memories. Sheila had been tough—too tough on Jessie—everyone agreed, but she'd disappeared months ago. Donna, the beloved day charge nurse, had been named manager and all was well with the world. Donna was the one who'd approved her new role rotating between the ME's office and the ER. Sheila would never have agreed to it.

"And no word? She's still just missing?"

"Nothing. Not a word."

"Strange, huh?"

Jessie shrugged. What could she say? The truth was she'd already forgotten Sheila.

"Hey," Sam said, his voice almost a whisper. "It's too late for Foley's, but want to catch a drink at the after-hours club? I think a lot of the guys will be there. It would be good for them to see you close up, get to know you as a nurse who's one of us, too. What do you say?"

*

And that was how she found herself at the club, the second-floor walk-up bar hidden in a nondescript building just blocks from the hospital. The place might have gone totally unnoticed but for the cluster of cars, both private and patrol, crowding the street. It was just one large open room with mismatched tables and chairs scattered about. A long Formica counter served as the bar and a single bartender took orders, though some patrons served themselves. It might have been just another seedy bar but for the police badges, emblems and awards that decorated the walls along with some classic neon signs advertising Budweiser or Miller Lite.

It was a lively crowd, and it was easy to get sucked into their celebration. But by two a.m., she knew it was time to go. She'd tossed back more shots of Scotch, or maybe it was vodka, than she'd intended or even wanted. She'd smiled, had her hands gripped, her back patted, her shoulders squeezed, and her cheek kissed, more times than she could remember. She was one of them, and they were letting her know that she belonged to this special, tight-knit group of men and women who risked it all every single day for one another and the city they so loved. She reveled in the attention, thinking this must be how it felt to be famous. In just hours she'd go back to being Jessie Novak, but for tonight, she was a star, and she was more than a little surprised by how much she liked it, though she knew she didn't deserve it and in no time, she'd be invisible once again.

She looked at her watch. If she didn't get moving soon, she'd be late to her real job: at eight a.m., she was expected at the ME's office. She slid from her stool at the bar, called an Uber and left before anyone noticed.

CHAPTER 4

Day 2—Monday

Jessie's alarm screeched at seven a.m., the blast jolting her awake
with a start. Her hand sprang for the snooze button, her fingers
fumbling aimlessly until she finally gave up, swinging her legs
over the side of the bed. And that was when the room began to
spin, and a wave of almost crippling nausea forced her back onto
the bed. She closed her eyes against the sudden pounding in her
head and prayed for relief. She was due at the ME's office in just
an hour. She could not afford to be late.

Dr. Roger Dawson, the state's Chief Medical Examiner, had only
returned the week before from vacation. His return had coincided
with a trauma room death that had especially interested Jessie. A
teenager with a gunshot wound to his forehead—he was essentially
dead on arrival, though the team made an effort to resuscitate him
because he was so young. While he was in the trauma room, his
friends were in the waiting room loudly swearing that he'd shot
himself, and they'd offered that information before they'd even been
queried. Jessie had always known to be suspicious when anyone
gave quick answers to questions before they'd been asked, and this
boisterous group definitely fit that bill. On the other side of the
waiting room the young man's heartbroken family were huddled,
insisting that he would never do something like that.

Jessie had called the Homicide Unit from the trauma hallway
and spoken to the team on call. She hadn't known this group, but

when they'd arrived they'd quickly taken a close look at everything, agreeing with Jessie. Though this wasn't her week working with the ME, she'd called and left a message for Roger asking if she could come by to watch the autopsy.

He'd called the next morning. "Jessie, good to hear from you. Please come by at eight and we'll get started. Sounds like an interesting case."

She'd arrived at seven, pulled on her PPE and waited in the hallway for Roger, who'd come in shortly thereafter with Tony, his assistant in tow.

"Hey, gorgeous, how are you?" Tony winked.

Roger shook his head. "Tony, you are incorrigible. Jessie, good to see you."

She quickly filled him in on the details and drama of the night before. "I don't think he killed himself. Homicide is pretty skeptical, too. I wanted to see for myself how you'd figure this out."

"Ahh, Jessie, this is precisely why I wanted you to work with me, to be a kind of liaison between the victim, myself and the police. I'm glad you're here.

"Tony, X-rays ready?" Tony nodded and pointed to the box reader on the wall. Roger approached, his arms folded. "Jessie, have a look."

Jessie stood behind him, peering over his shoulder. "What am I looking for?"

"See this," he said, his finger tracing the course of a bullet which lay in the area of the young man's cervical spine. "His entry wound is in his forehead, but the bullet took a downward trajectory." Roger shook his head. "Hard to shoot yourself in the forehead pointing the gun down at that kind of angle."

And she could almost hear the young men in the waiting room insisting he'd shot himself. The only reason, it seemed, to push that story was that they were covering for somebody. She'd leave a message for the lead detective about what she'd heard. If one of them hadn't shot this poor kid, she bet they knew who did.

Roger turned back. "Ready, Tony?" Tony nodded and Roger took his place at the side of the metal. A butcher's scale lay on a metal table off to the side holding what at first glance might have been carpenter's tools. A long scalpel, drill, bone saw, trauma scissors, and heavy-duty shears for cutting through ribs lay on another metal stand, much like the stands they used in the trauma rooms and operating rooms, but this was no OR. No anesthesia, no sterile field, no pumps or lines or monitors. There were no lives to be saved here, only causes of death to be determined and crimes to be solved.

Roger stepped on the remote which activated the overhead microphone and after a quick visual inspection of the body, he nodded. "Okay, no other injuries. I'm going to do internal organs first." Roger made the long incision from the shoulders to the young man's pelvis. He examined the organs in place and then on a side table once they were removed. "This all looks good," he said, declaring him healthy and disease-free except for the gunshot wound. "Poor kid."

He'd examined the skull and forehead closely then, directing Tony to take pictures at certain angles. He'd pointed out that the wound was clean, free of stippling and gunpowder residue. "Most suicides hold the gun directly on their skin. This wound seems to have been inflicted from a distance, maybe a foot, maybe more. His arms aren't long enough. Come and see this, Jessie."

She moved closer, her eyes tracking Roger's hand.

"No way you can shoot yourself at that angle. See there." He'd pointed to the bullet's route: the bullet had sliced right through the brain and landed close to the spinal column at C-1. He pointed to the wound. "Good call, Jessie. This young man did not kill himself. Someone else did that."

And Jessie remembered that moment clearly, the moment when she knew working with the ME and Homicide mattered, that what they did, grim as it might seem to the outsider, was vital to families and loved ones.

She'd left the morgue that morning feeling happy and fired up. She was going to be great at this new job. But that was before this colossal hangover. She sighed and cranked her eyelids open and stood up slowly, holding her head perfectly still to help ease the pain, but the dull thudding in her head continued. She stepped into the shower—the water, an icy-cold spray, sent shivers up her spine but somehow eased her vertigo and nausea. She swallowed a Motrin, chewed on some crackers, and pulled on jeans and a sweater. In the ME's office, she'd change into the scrubs she kept there.

After a quick stop at the corner store for coffee and a muffin, she was on her way, her headache already fading, but the neurons in her brain not quite connecting the way they should. She sipped her coffee and nibbled at her muffin en route to the morgue. She wasn't sure she'd ever adjust to eating there, and today was definitely not the day to try that. She headed across the street praying for a quiet day, but as she pushed open the main door and swiped her ID across the reader, a rush of activity and voices greeted her.

"There you are," a voice called. She spun around to see Roger standing in the hall, eyeglasses perched on his forehead, his thick graying hair wild as ever, but his skin, usually drawn and pale, was tanned and healthy-looking. He seemed to stand a little taller, too, an easy smile draping his lips as he walked toward her. "Good to see you, Jessie. We didn't get much of a chance to speak last week. You are settling in, I hope?"

She nodded and took his hand, his grip firm, his eyes clear. "I'm okay," she said. "I've spent a lot of time with Homicide, but mostly they had me reading procedures and protocols and following the forensics technicians."

"Anything exciting?"

She shook her head. "Some of it was, but memorizing every single word written on blood spatter and fingerprints and fibers left my brain numb."

He winced, and laughed. "Actually, I do find that stuff interesting. Soon, you will too, I think." His eyes swept the corridor behind her. "You can probably see that things are busier than usual here today. We have a Jane Doe who came in late yesterday, a presumed strangulation, or maybe a drowning. Homicide is coming in for a look. The body has been in the water for a while, I'd say. The cold and the ice protected it somewhat, but there's still quite a bit of decomposition." He cocked his head. "The body floated up once the ice shifted along the Neponset River. It's going to be a real mystery, this one. We'll have to try to work out what happened." He pulled his eyeglasses back down. "You ready to watch this one? It might be more gruesome than usual."

I'm an ER nurse, she thought, *I'm ready.* She offered Roger an enthusiastic smile. She was intrigued by this mystery: a Jane Doe— which she knew from the ER was an unidentified female—with an unknown cause of death and in water for who knew how long. She couldn't wait to start.

"Great," he said eagerly. "There's donuts in the break room if you want to eat first, otherwise, I'll see you inside."

She gulped in the familiar odor of formaldehyde and the coppery scent of old blood and decided she'd hold off on the donuts for now. She headed for the locker room, where she peered at her hazy reflection in the cracked and dingy old mirror that hung above the sink, a relic with rusty pipes poking out from the wall. She leaned in close and tried to rub away the red in her eyes, but to no avail. Once she'd donned her scrubs, tied back her unruly curls and made her way to the autopsy suite, her head was clear—well, almost, probably helped along by the fog of chemicals and misery in these halls. *Who knew? Maybe that was a cure for hangovers?*

As soon as she opened the door to the autopsy suite, a forensic technician, already wrapped in PPE, stood calmly by the body, which was laid out on a metal gurney with drains on either side and at the ends, to catch fluids and specimens.

"Ahh, now we can begin," Roger said. "Grab a lab coat and an apron over there, and then join me. The PPE is there too. Make sure you cover up well. These cases can get messy."

She quickly donned a face mask, eye goggles, gloves, a hair covering, and a heavy vinyl apron, all designed to protect her from any spray of fluids or tissue. She pulled on her final layer—the paper booties that covered her shoes—and moved closer to the table as Roger pulled his apron over his torso and slipped on two pairs of gloves. "Have you met Richard?" he asked, inclining his head to the technician.

"No," she said, turning to the man who'd donned his own mask. "I'm Jessie. I'm fairly new to this."

"Hi, Jessie. I'm going to help collect the physical evidence we need today. Last night, we had to remove a scarf that was wrapped tightly around her neck. It was caught on rocks along the shore and we wanted it to be intact."

"Is that how she died?" Jessie asked. "Strangled?" She glanced at the body, still covered in a heavy plastic shroud, and then toward Roger, who was busily arranging his instruments and seemed not to have heard her question.

"That's ultimately for Dr. Dawson here to decide," the technician said. "You'll see the deep furrows there on her neck—ligature marks—when Dr. Dawson begins. The body still had clothes stuck to the skin that we didn't want to disrupt and possibly destroy any evidence, so today, I'm going to get whatever I can. I'll help take photos, too, if Tony doesn't show up."

"This is going to be a tough one," Roger said. "I usually say that an autopsy won't just tell us how the victim died but how she lived, but with this degree of decomposition, I'm not so sure." He caught her gaze behind the goggles she wore. "Are you okay?"

Jessie nodded.

He stood a little taller. "Shall we get started?" His brow furrowed as he slipped his goggles and mask onto his face. Even through his mask, she could see the determined focus in his eyes as he began to speak into the overhead dictaphone. "Jane Doe, age unknown…" He motioned to the tech to uncover the body. "A white female—"

The tech uncovered the body, leaving Jane Doe exposed under the glaring overhead lights.

CHAPTER 5

Jessie moved to her place at the side of the gurney. The victim's clothes were almost intact. Spandex leggings and a sweater, though torn and threadbare and slick with mud and debris from the river's edge, were still identifiable, unlike the poor woman who'd donned them before she was killed. And though the woman's features were distorted beyond recognition, her fingernail and toenail polish—a bright iridescent pink—had somehow survived.

"Ready?" Roger asked.

She nodded.

"I'm not going to use our standard instruments just now. This skin is too damaged, too friable, so I'm going to use the ultraviolet light to find small bits of evidence that I might not see otherwise. Richard," he turned and motioned for him to move closer, "is going to collect everything in individually labeled plastic bags." Roger started with the victim's hands, removing the plastic bags that covered them and taking scrapings from underneath her nails before snipping off pieces of the nails themselves. Everything went into the evidence bags. Once he'd finished with that task, he turned his attention to her clothes. "I'll place the clothes that I can get in that basin there, and Richard will label them and transfer them to an evidence bag. This is the painstakingly and deliberately tedious part of my exam. And sometimes the part that garners the most evidence." He looked up suddenly. "Are the detectives coming? I thought they'd be here by now."

Richard shrugged. He was busy collecting the mud and small stones that clung to the body. "They were probably out late last night. That cop was shot."

"Ahh, I forgot. Were you working, Jessie?"

"Yes," she said just as the door opened, letting in a slight breeze and a wafting scent of welcome formaldehyde.

Jessie turned. Sam and another man, another detective, maybe, stood silhouetted in the doorway. "Come in, come in," Roger called. "Grab some masks and gloves over there and a vinyl apron if you plan to get close."

Sam blinked. "Well, one of us will have to." He looked at his companion questioningly. The second man, his skin a deep ebony, a silver wristwatch gleaming under the room's fluorescent lighting, straightened his tie and his suit coat, and backed away. "I'll be outside," he said, "going over notes."

Sam shrugged and pulled on the apron, mask and goggles and stood next to Roger, almost towering over him. "Sorry to be late. What do we have so far?" He winked at Jessie, who was glad that the mask hid her pleasure at his arrival.

Roger activated the microphone with a tap of his foot and repeated what he knew. "We have an unknown female found in the Neponset River. The water temperature and surrounding ice probably kept the body from decomposing entirely. That will help us to determine how long she's been in there, but not with any certainty. The face is bloated, the features quite distorted, making identification difficult.

"I think we'll be relying on dental records. And, you see this," he said, pointing to something, but already Jessie's mind was racing. She couldn't imagine how someone could do this to another person. Despite working in the ER and caring for victims of assault and even murder, she knew she'd never get used to the inhumanity of those acts, the utter cruelty involved.

She wondered why Jane Doe was killed, what was the story behind this terrible act. Had she known her killer? Had she fought back? Jessie shivered at the thought. Roger, still speaking, hadn't noticed that Jessie wasn't paying attention, that her eyes had that blank stare, but Sam had noticed. His forehead was creased, one eyebrow raised, his eyes laser-focused on her. She snapped to attention and nodded, hoping she hadn't missed too much.

"Interesting, huh?" Roger asked.

"It is," Sam said, his voice stiff. Jessie wondered if he were pushing through a hangover too.

"There was a scarf wound tightly around her neck, and you can see for yourself the deep grooves in the skin there. I have that scarf that the techs removed last night. I'll compare it to the wound later. But for now, it certainly appears that she was murdered by strangulation. I'm not sure I'll be able to zero in on the time or date of death—the best I can do will be to make an estimate, a pretty broad estimate at that." He cleared his throat and took a step back as if to observe the body from a different perspective, his eyes intent and unwavering. Roger was a man who seemed to come alive over the body of this woman, and the questions that she'd brought with her.

"Forensics," Sam announced, "took small samples of soil from the riverbank and water from the river itself, and, of course, you have the scarf, but other than that, there was no evidence at the scene to indicate a struggle right there, though any indication of that may have disintegrated, with the winter we've had. And she may have floated to that area, or she may have been killed and deposited there."

"Ahh," Roger said, bobbing his head. "A mystery to solve."

She watched intently as Roger continued to examine Jane Doe. Now that it was clear the woman had been murdered, Jessie was eager to get on to the next stage of the investigation—to help identify her and to find the person who did this. Whoever this woman had been, she was someone with a story, someone who was loved, someone who mattered to someone, somewhere, and Jessie knew there had to be clues. Sam had told her early on that murderers always left something of themselves behind, that they were never quite as clever as they thought they were.

Roger cleared his throat and continued. "Aside from the ligature marks, I haven't seen any other obvious injuries, and if she was out of the water for any significant length of time before she arrived here, that could cause further deterioration of the remains. Do we know how long she was out of the water, Detective?"

Sam nodded. "She wasn't removed from the water for several hours after she was found. Forensics was there, getting photos, and the whole crime scene was set up. Once she was removed, she was transported pretty quickly and placed in your refrig—" He seemed to catch himself. "Cooling unit, and that was about ten hours ago now."

Roger nodded and continued to gently remove the clothes and examine her skin. "I'm removing the bits of evidence that have clung to the body," he continued just as the door banged open again and Tony stood in the circle of dim light from the hallway.

"Need me, Doc?" he asked, smiling widely.

"Tony, yes," Roger said moving back from the dictaphone. "Get your things on and come help me. Richard already did the X-rays, but I'd like you to get moving, get measurements on everything." Tony hustled, pulling on PPE and rushing to Roger's side. The only sound was Roger's voice and the clang of the evidence and organ bowls as Tony rearranged them. Richard, a camera strung from his neck, positioned himself at the head of the bed and began to take pictures, the whir of the camera barely audible.

"Have you seen the X-rays?" Sam asked.

Roger nodded. "A quick look. She has a fractured hyoid bone consistent with strangulation, but no bullets, no foreign objects, no other bone injuries. I'll have a closer look later, but…"

"I'll be heading out then," Sam announced, moving away from the table and removing his mask, the fresh stubble on his jaw suddenly visible. He smiled, his full lips pulled wide in relief. "Jessie here is our liaison for this stuff now." He turned toward her, ignoring her heated glare. He winked in reply. "I'll catch up with you later, Jessie. Thanks, Roger." And then he was gone, pulling off his PPE as he turned the corner. Jessie was sure she could hear him whistling as he left. She adjusted her mask and turned her attention back to the body.

"Jessie," Roger said softly, "are you staying?"

She nodded. "Yes. I want to see this through, and besides, Sam will be expecting me to give him a report. I'm going to hang in." ·

He smiled. "Good. This body is the only evidence we have so far in this case, and that will often happen. This woman has a story to tell and she's counting on us to get it right. You know that old saying—a picture tells a thousand stories? Well, for us, it's the body that does that."

Once they were all in position in the room, Roger spoke up. "I'm about to start recording. No comments unless absolutely necessary." He looked around and began again. "I have a white female of unknown age found in the shallow water of the Neponset River just under the bridge, late yesterday. She measures five feet six, and weighed 143 pounds, though some of that is likely fluid and gases that formed after death. We have already taken appropriate blood samples including toxic screen, and I have removed vitreous fluid from the eyes as well as stomach contents and urine. Core body temperature was measured on arrival to the morgue and was found to be thirty-eight degrees, which is consistent with the ambient temperature of the river in which the victim was found." He motioned to Tony, who wordlessly handed him a small tool.

Jessie realized she'd been standing stiffly while she watched the post-mortem unfold. She wanted to stretch and wipe away the beads of sweat that had gathered on her forehead, but she knew the rules—don't touch your own skin when you're in protective gear.

"We're almost done, Jessie," Roger said. "Ahh, see here. The blood vessels and trachea are compressed, constricted even. That, along with the petechiae in her eyes and the absence of water in her lungs, confirms strangulation as the cause of death."

"What a terrible way to die."

"It is, and I know this has been a tough one for you, and since this is the end of the formal post-mortem, there's no need for you to stay for the remainder. I think you've seen enough for one day. I'm sure Sam is waiting for you."

She wanted to kiss him. Instead, she smiled through her mask. "Do you want me to wait for you? Maybe go over your findings?"

He shook his head. "No, Jessie, I'll see you tomorrow. We can talk then. You've earned a break today."

"I'll see you tomorrow, then. Thank you." Despite the awkward gait the PPE imposed on her, she moved more swiftly than she would have imagined. In the locker room, she tore off the PPE, the scrubs, and pulled on her own clothes. A burst of texts from Sam filled her screen. *Call me when you get out*, was the most recent. She slipped her jacket on and headed for the door, tapping his number to call. He answered on the first ring.

"Hey," he said. "How'd it go?"

"First, tell me why you left," she asked, hoping he heard the sarcasm in her voice.

"We don't usually stay for the entire autopsy, but this one is a real mystery, so I thought we'd make an appearance, see what we could get from an initial assessment. How about you? Got anything for me?"

"Actually, I do, but since you left, you're gonna have to pay for it. How about lunch?"

"You're on. What time?"

She checked her watch. "Wow, it's almost twelve now. I can't believe it's so late."

"The day is young, my friend. I can meet you at L Street Tavern in an hour."

God, last night seemed like a hundred years ago already. Her hangover had faded to a vague drumming at her temples. Even her appetite was back. *Who knew?* Maybe the scent of formaldehyde and old blood really was the cure. "I'll see you there."

CHAPTER 6

At one o'clock, Jessie was standing outside of the tavern, her face angled toward the faint winter sun, when she spied Sam and the other detective she'd seen this morning, walking toward her. She swallowed her disappointment. Ridiculous as it sounded, even to herself, she'd wanted Sam to herself. They'd been almost lovers once, and then adversaries and, if last night proved anything, it was that they'd become friends, maybe more than that, and she'd wanted him to herself, to share the details of the autopsy with just him and to get started on the investigation.

She took a deep breath and smiled as they drew close, and she could have sworn that his companion gave Sam a side glance and a shrug.

"Hey, Jess," Sam said. "You don't look any the worse for wear." He smiled impishly, the sunlight dancing in the silver flecks in his eyes.

"About that, thanks for bugging out."

"I told you, we don't usually stay. We trust the ME, but now that we have you, we won't even have to make an appearance."

Jessie smirked and was about to make a smart remark when she remembered they weren't alone. "Are you going to introduce me?" She turned to the other man.

"This is Ralph Thompson," he said. "I thought maybe you'd met, but he reminded me he was rotated off nights and came onto our team late last week."

"Hi Ralph," she said.

"You're a nurse, Sam tells me."

She offered a shy smile. "I am," Jessie said.

"My mom was a nurse, so I'm kind of partial to nurses," he said, smiling, the corners of his deep brown eyes crinkling, his head tilting toward her. His smile revealed a row of sparkling white teeth and dimples creasing his cheeks. They softened the sharp angle of his clean-shaven jaw and gave him an open, almost boyish look.

She couldn't help herself and she smiled in turn. "Nice to meet you, Ralph," she said, holding out her hand.

He gripped it tightly. "Likewise," he said.

"Since you're still busy getting to know each other, I'm just gonna run over to Sal's and order a pizza," Sam said. "I'll see you inside."

She'd almost forgotten he was standing there. *Oh, God,* she thought, *please don't let me have been looking like a pathetic idiot.* Ralph pulled the door open, the sun spilling in and splashing onto the gleaming mahogany bar. "Shall we?" he asked.

Once inside, they chose the bar stools closest to the exit. Most patrons gathered at the rear of the bar where privacy was limited, and eavesdropping was practically required. She might have been sitting back there, too, but for the need for discretion and privacy, at least in this instance. "Ready?" the bartender called to them.

"Diet Coke for me," Jessie answered, turning to Ralph, who nodded.

"The same." He turned back to her, his gaze locked on hers a beat too long, as though he was sizing her up, deciding where she fit in. "So, you and Sam are dating?"

"Huh?" Jessie asked, caught off guard by the question. "Where'd you hear that?"

"Oh, sorry," he said. "The way Sam speaks about you, I just assumed…"

A little ripple of pleasure surged at the thought of Sam speaking about her. "We're friends," she stammered. "Good friends."

Ralph smiled warily. "Sorry, again. I just thought, well… never mind. Hey, let's change the subject. Where do you work?" he asked.

Jessie ran her hands along the smooth mahogany of the bar. "The ER at BCH, conveniently right across the street from the morgue."

The corners of his lips turned up, showing off those dimples again, and she felt herself relax. "How about you? You're a detective?"

"I am. Recently assigned to Homicide, the job I've been working toward my whole career. Been a patrolman for five years, then a stint in narcotics, but those were interrupted by my deployments."

"You're a soldier, too?"

He smiled. "*Was.* Four years active duty in the army, and just retired from the Reserves. I was assigned to the Intelligence and Security Command, pretty interesting, but I decided to get serious and concentrate on my civilian career. I started law school at Suffolk University last year." He ran his hand over the fuzzy growth of hair on his scalp as if slicking it back.

Jessie's eyes grew wide. "Ralph, that's so impressive."

He laughed, an easy, natural laugh. "I like to be busy, I guess. It makes my wife crazy, but…" He shrugged.

"Hey, did you order for me?" Sam asked as he slid onto a stool. The bartender delivered their Diet Cokes. Sam looked questioningly at Jessie. "Is there rum in there?"

"No," she laughed. "I had enough last night. I'm all set." She watched him with renewed interest. *Maybe, just maybe.*

Sam turned to the bartender. "Same for me," he said. "So, Jess, what have you got for us?"

"Well, you saw the body's decomposition. Lab reports and Roger's microscopic and other exams are pending, but the cause of death was strangulation. No evidence of sexual assault that he could find, but the decomposition likely buried any sign of that. She had scrapes and abrasions, but Roger can't say for sure if they were caused by the riverbed or an assault."

"Definitely strangulation?" Ralph asked.

"Yes," Sam answered. "The ME has the ligature, a scarf. Forensics will pick it up later today."

Jessie nodded in agreement. "Yes. The deep furrows in her neck, the hyoid fracture, the blood vessel compression—all point to strangulation. So, we're definitely looking at murder."

Sam smiled. "This is why we have Jessie on board," he said. "She'll help us make sense of things. Could she have been alive when she went into the water?"

"Probably not. Not enough water in her lungs or chest to support that. And a toxic screen is still pending." Jessie played with her straw, swirling it round and round. "So, what next? How do we identify her? And fingerprints—with her skin so macerated, could you get any?"

"We did, but if she's never been in trouble or worked for the government, that will be a dead end. We've already started looking through missing persons reports. We'll check for a female who fits the physical description the ME can provide—height, weight, hair color, any tattoos or distinctive marks, though with that much decomposition, we might have to rely on dental records, if we can match up a few characteristics. I'll check to see if Forensics picked up any jewelry from the body—that can be a big help. Sounds impossible, but we'll get there."

Ralph whistled. "She's my first Jane Doe. Sounds daunting, and a bit like finding a needle in a haystack."

"For an unknown, it is. It can be tedious going through old missing persons reports, and as you know, some people are never reported missing. Either no one cared enough to report a disappearance, or worse—no one even noticed. Those are the cases that will get to you."

Their pizza arrived, the aroma especially welcome to Jessie, who wanted to get rid of the lingering smell of formaldehyde. She leaned in, took a large slice and angled it toward her mouth.

Sam laughed. "You should know that Jessie can eat through anything. If you're feeling squeamish, don't admit it to her." He passed around napkins and began to eat.

Ralph picked at a slice before pushing it away. "Not squeamish," he said quickly, pulling on the cuffs of his crisply starched white shirt.

Jessie couldn't help but smile. He didn't want to get the oil or sauce on his clothes. "Will we go back and start looking at reports, talk to the forensics techs?" she asked through a mouthful of cheese.

"We will," Sam said. "You're eager to get started?"

"Yes," she said and turned to Ralph, who was wiping the grease from his fingers. She took another bite, and felt an unexpected shiver run along her back. She looked up. Sam and Ralph were deep in conversation. Her gaze swept the far end of the bar where an older woman was watching her intently. She seemed not to notice that Jessie was looking back at her until Jessie caught her eye. The woman looked away quickly. "What the…?" Jessie muttered.

"What?" Sam asked.

"Nothing, just wishing we had fries."

"Where do you put it?"

"I run it off," she said, pulling off a piece of crust. "Might run later. Want to join me?"

Sam shook his head. "Not me, thanks." He turned back to Ralph, and they chatted again about forensics and identification. Jessie listened intently. This was her first Jane Doe, too, and she wanted to be sure she knew every step of the identification process.

"How do you even know which dentists to request records from?" Jessie asked.

"We have to have some idea of who the person is first," Sam answered. "The dental records will confirm an ID, but we can't do a blanket request. We'll start with what we found at the scene—the scarf, jewelry. Sometimes that's all we need."

Jessie nodded. Out of the corner of her eye, she saw the woman at the end of the bar leaning back, once again casting quick glances her way. Not so long ago, she might have walked to the end of the bar and asked the woman what was up, but she was trying hard to let things go, to be less confrontational.

Today she had to fight the urge, so instead, she stared back. The woman looked away again but not before Jessie had had a good long look. The woman was older, the far side of fifty, Jessie guessed, with dark hair, too dark for a woman of a certain age, with deep crimson lips and searing dark eyes. In that moment, the woman flipped her hair back over her shoulder and Jessie froze. There was something so familiar, so personal, in that faint movement. The woman glanced her way again, and this time it was Jessie who darted out of sight, disappearing behind Sam and falling right back into the conversation at hand.

"So, yeah," Sam was saying, "I have one sister, and we're pretty close. Her kids are great. My mom lives with her now, out beyond Worcester. I see them as often as I can."

Jessie sighed. Sam was one of a kind, that was for sure.

"Well," Ralph said, "as long as we're sharing personal stuff—I'm married, two kids, just out of the Reserves and still living by those stiff rules—no time for disorder or mistakes. Fair warning, I'm a little obsessive when it comes to my job. And, I'm in law school."

"That'll all help in Homicide," Sam said, and their eyes turned to Jessie, who felt her stomach drop. She was fascinated by other people's histories so long as she didn't have to share her own. She took a deep breath. "Not much to tell," she said. "My mother died when I was little." She paused, pleased with how easily that practiced lie slipped from her lips these days. "And my dad died a few years ago. No sisters, no brothers, no cousins. Just me." She took a long sip of her Diet Coke, hoping the conversation would move on to other topics, but it was not to be.

She watched as Sam gave her a questioning glance. Then she remembered—she'd told him only recently that her mother had abandoned her. That was the thing about lying. It was easy to get tripped up.

Ralph covered her hand with his. "Must be tough, huh?" His voice oozed with genuine concern.

The sad and sympathetic glances her admission elicited were almost as bad as having no family. She pulled her hand away. "No. It's what I'm used to. We all have something. And my dad was great. And, anyway, I hate talking about this stuff. It sounds worse than it is. Let's move on, hey?" They nodded in agreement, but she could see the pity in Ralph's eyes, the lingering question in Sam's. That was exactly what she didn't want.

She huffed out a sigh. "Remember, there are bigger things to worry about, like maybe this poor woman who died, and we don't even know who she is or what happened. I'm just saying." She stuffed another slice of pizza into her mouth before she said anything she regretted.

Sam shrugged. "You're right, Jess. So, shall we head back to headquarters, start looking through the missing persons files?"

Ralph nodded and slid from his stool. "Heading to the men's room first. Be right back."

When he was out of earshot, Sam leaned close. "You heard Ralph, Jesse—fair warning, okay?" he said. "Ralph's a nice guy, but he's an absolute stickler for rules, and he expects everyone to follow them. He has his eyes set on the commissioner's job and he's smart enough, he'll probably get there someday."

Jessie grinned. "And that should worry me why, exactly?"

Sam raised an eyebrow and spoke quickly as Ralph walked toward them. "He was all over one of the guys whose search warrant was too broad. He was right, but… he's new. Just keep it in mind."

"We ready?" Ralph asked.

"I am," Sam said, slipping his coat on. "You coming?" he asked Jessie.

"Give me a half an hour," she answered, planning to run home and have a quick shower to wash away the last traces of formaldehyde from her hair and skin. "And if no one wants the rest of this," she pointed to the remaining slices of pizza, "I'll take it for Rufus."

"Give him my best," Sam said, peeling off a couple of bills and leaving them on the bar.

"Thanks, Sam," Jessie said. "One of these days, I swear, my treat."

"Holding you to that. See you later?"

She nodded and blinked as they pulled open the door, letting a burst of sunlight slice through the darkness. The older woman, still at the far end of the bar, seemed to be watching her again. "Why...?" Jessie said softly. Suddenly, inexplicably anxious that this strange woman might decide to approach her, Jessie secured the pizza box, grabbed her bag and jacket and left, hurrying along to the safety of her apartment on K Street.

CHAPTER 7

"There you are, Jessie," Rufus, her beloved downstairs neighbor and friend, called as she pulled open the front door. He eyed the pizza box in her hands. "Smells good," he said.

"It was," she said, smiling. "I brought the leftovers for you." She was glad to have something to offer him.

He reached out, his knobby hands gripping the box. "You are the dearest girl. Will you come in and share it with me?" He opened his front door wide, the baseball bat that had saved her life still tucked there in the entryway corner.

She stepped inside, her eyes sweeping along the hallway clear through to the kitchen. "You've been cleaning," she said. "It looks great."

He nodded. "It does look good without all that clutter, doesn't it? My Mary would have been proud, but you put the bug in me. I just dragged another bag out to the barrel. I'm feeling pretty good, and thanks to you, now I can celebrate with pizza. Come on in and I'll brew us some tea."

Jessie followed him to the kitchen, which still held a pile of newspapers, a box of old knickknacks and another of magazines stacked against the far wall, but it was a long way from the hoarding she'd found when she'd first set foot inside, months ago. Every corner, every available space, had been crammed full of things—old clothes, newspapers, magazines, books, empty jars, and boxes that held old treasures and junk. It had taken some convincing, but she'd helped him out and they'd made a dent in the clutter, until her days and nights got off track with the crazy schedules her job demanded.

The radiator hissed with a fresh stream of heat while Rufus's cat watched warily as she took a seat. There was something inexplicably comforting about this room, even the clutter—it all revealed a life well lived, and more importantly, a life well loved. She leaned back against the chair and listened as the teakettle screeched out its readiness.

"Sugar?" Rufus asked. "I can never remember. I must be getting old."

She chuckled. "No sugar, no milk. I'm easy, Rufus, and you're not getting old. Any man who can swing a bat the way you did and bring another man down is ageless. I owe you my life. Don't forget that."

He smiled as he poured tea into a chipped porcelain cup. "Don't know what I'd ever do without you, Jessie."

"Likewise, Rufus. Likewise." And it was true. Rufus Buchanan was the closest thing she'd had to family since her dad had died. She worried about him, he worried about her, and her life was better with him in it. He'd softened her too-sharp edges, and gave her a reason to think about someone other than herself. She sighed and shifted in her seat, watching as he finished the last four slices of pizza, barely taking time between bites. He was hungry—there was no denying that. She'd promised to take him shopping on a regular basis, but she could count on only one hand the number of times she'd actually done that. "I haven't been around much," she said, pulling at her sleeves. "Have you been getting groceries?"

"At the corner store, yes, but the supermarket, only a little. I know it's close by, but it's too hard to manage with more than one bag on these snowy streets. I'll have to get one of those old lady shopping carts. But I've been making do. Don't you worry."

"Of course I worry. I said I'd take you, and I haven't."

"You've been busy." He blew the steam from his cup of tea and took a long swallow.

Jessie's shoulders sagged. "No excuse. Make a list and we'll go when I get back from work."

"Hospital?" he asked.

She shook her head. "I'm with the Medical Examiner again, but I'm going to head to police headquarters to check in on an investigation."

"Listen to you, my friend—a real detective."

She smiled. "Nurse first, and not-quite-a-detective second." She carried her cup to the sink and washed it out before placing it on the dish towel to dry. "I'll see you at four. I promise."

"I'll be ready," he said, relief etched into his gentle smile.

Jessie climbed the stairs to her own small second-floor apartment which included a living room, galley kitchen, one tiny closet and a postage-stamp-sized bedroom. It was all she could afford if she wanted to live by herself here in Southie, and she didn't regret it for one minute.

She peeled off her clothes as she turned on the shower, stepping under the stream of water whisking away the smells she'd carried with her since the autopsy. She pulled on a change of clothes, grabbed a bottle of water, swiped a fresh swath of color along her lips, ran her fingers through her curls, and headed back out. She was excited to learn how Sam and his team would identify Jane Doe.

At headquarters, she headed up to the Homicide Unit on the second floor and to the detectives' area. The office which housed the four detectives who worked with Sam was bordered by six-foot-tall gray file cabinets, creating makeshift cubicles, and at this hour, it was humming with activity. Four desks were pushed together, a whiteboard on the wall displayed progress on active cases, and a printer vibrated as it spit out reports.

"Hey," Jessie called in greeting. It seemed that everyone looked her way, heads popping out of nearby cubicles. She held her breath.

They hadn't always been welcoming; when she'd started there was more than a little griping about "who the hell she thought she was." Jessie had felt each of their barbs, but she'd stuck it out.

"She's a nurse, not a damn detective," one of them had murmured loud enough for her to catch. They'd each earned their gold shields the hard way—by working their way up, and they resented her sudden appointment. But she wasn't trying to be a detective; she was only trying to add her ER expertise to their investigations, and enough people thought she could do just that, that she'd been hired to work investigations with the ME and Homicide. She'd been determined to keep at it, to prove that she belonged, but it had been a struggle. She'd felt like she had to don a suit of armor each time she stepped into Homicide's hallowed halls.

"Hey, Jess," one of the guys called. "Heard about your work last night. You're a rock star. Thank you!" Another added his thanks, and then another, until everyone was smiling and congratulating her.

"Thanks, guys, but I'm a nurse. I was just doing my job."

"Last night you earned your gold shield. Heard that Danny's already awake. Believe me, we're happy to call you one of us."

Her jaw went slack. "I... I..." But she was at a loss for words, a strange sensation for Jessie Novak.

"Sam and Ralph are waiting for you. Go on in, give a shout if you need anything."

Jessie nodded and pushed through to Sam's office, relieved to be away from the sudden words of praise. Last night, at the after-hours club, she'd only hoped for a bit of respect for her new role, not this adulation. Talk about going from one extreme to the other. She shook her head and stepped into the office. Sam and Ralph were huddled over the desk, several plastic evidence bags in front of them.

They didn't seem to notice that she was standing there. "Hey," she said, "hope I haven't missed anything."

"Come on over," Sam said. "Have a look. We have some evidence from the scene—the scarf and some jewelry. Take a look."

She leaned over Sam's shoulder and peered closely at the clear plastic evidence bags and the contents they held—a multicolored silk scarf, the colors faded but still easily identified. She ran her hand across the bag. She'd seen that scarf before, but where? She was still mulling over that curious question when Sam moved the other bag closer. It held a black pearl necklace, bits of mud dulling the gloss, but Jessie could still picture them on the owner's neck. She'd worn them every day, always looking for compliments. "Don't you just love them?" she'd asked once. Jessie could almost hear her voice. *Is it possible?* A pressure deep in Jessie's chest threatened to cut off her breath and she slid into a nearby seat, her hands dropping to her sides.

"What is it?" Sam asked.

She pulled her gaze from the pearls and toward Sam. "I've seen those before. I know who they belong to."

Sam moved closer. "Who?' he asked. "Who is it, Jessie?"

"Sheila Logan, the nurse who disappeared," she whispered.

CHAPTER 8

He touched her shoulder. "You're sure?" he asked gently, his voice soothing.

She nodded. "I don't know why it didn't occur to me at the morgue. The height, the weight. Oh, God." She covered her face with her hands.

Ralph touched her back. "I'm sorry, Jessie. Was she a friend?"

She shook her head. "My old boss. We didn't get along very well."

And though she couldn't see his face, she could almost feel his grimace. The room began to spin, or maybe it was her head that was spinning. She shook her head. "She disappeared months ago," she said, though it had somehow seemed longer than that. Jessie, and everyone else in the ER, had adjusted quite happily to her unexplained disappearance. They'd never really questioned it—the outcome had been a happier workplace, but that thought now struck her as shocking, that they'd simply accepted it without question. "Months," she said again. "She's been gone for about three months. And I…"

Sam nodded. "That time frame is consistent with Roger's assessment."

Her heart pounded in her chest. *Sheila? Murdered?* It didn't seem real, and maybe it wasn't. "Could it be someone else?"

Sam nodded. "Could be, but we're going to work on chasing down some DNA and dental records to identify her."

Jessie exhaled slowly. "What can I do to help?"

"Nothing yet, and since we haven't confirmed anything, I want your word that you'll keep this information to yourself. Tell no one until we have a positive ID and a chance to notify her family."

She nodded and leaned forward, her hands rubbing the tension from her forehead, her eyes closed. This wasn't happening. *Sheila?* She stood slowly, her legs wobbly, her hands shaking as she glanced at her watch. It was almost four. Her workday was blessedly over. "I guess I'll get going then. I promised Rufus I'd take him shopping."

Sam smiled broadly. "Hey, tell him I said hello." He turned to Ralph. "Her neighbor, a great old guy."

Ralph offered one of those polite half-smiles and held out his hand. "It was nice to meet you, Jessie."

Jessie remained silent, her brain still trying to connect the image of the body in the morgue with Sheila Logan, but her synapses wouldn't, or perhaps couldn't, connect on this one. She had to leave it alone until they knew for sure who it was, and spending time with Rufus was a perfect diversion.

Day 3—Tuesday

Jessie slept fitfully and rose early the next day, a full hour before her alarm went off. She'd taken Rufus out for dinner and then shopping and when she'd arrived home, she'd collapsed into bed praying that sleep would come, but sleep was elusive. Images of Sheila fingering her pearls or wrapping her favorite scarf around her neck spun in her mind, and by five a.m. she gave up and slipped out of bed. By the time she'd brewed coffee and watched the news, it was still too early to go into the morgue or the Homicide Unit. They wouldn't be in until after eight. She decided to go out for a run, and head to the corner store where she could say hi to Patrick, get a muffin, a newspaper and a cup of his coffee which always tasted better than her own. She pulled on her spandex leggings, a shirt and sweatshirt, pocketed her keys and a twenty-dollar bill, and headed out along K Street before crossing Day Boulevard and beginning her loop to Castle Island, a route she could do with her eyes closed.

The morning sky was as gray as her mood. Winter still had a tight grip on the city in these last days of February, and an icy spray gusted in from the beach, the cold propelling her onward with the aim of finishing sooner. She ran two loops around the island, and by the time she stopped at the corner store and checked her time, she smiled. About four miles, she figured, in just thirty-nine minutes. Feeling pretty pleased with her time, she pulled open the door, the tiny overhead bell announcing her arrival.

Patrick, the owner, looked up and smiled. "You've made the newspapers once again, Jessie. I'll be asking for your autograph if this keeps up." His brogue was heavier today.

Jessie's jaw dropped open. What was it now, and why was *she* mentioned? Oh, God, it wasn't about Sheila, was it? She spun around and reached for the *Boston Herald. Cop Shot, ER Staff to the Rescue.* She released a long, slow sigh of relief and smiled. "That wasn't just me," she said. "It was the whole team."

Patrick shook his head. "Well, ya can see it right there in black and white. The police commissioner himself said that the ER staff saved this cop's life."

Jessie chuckled softly. "Don't be too impressed." She slapped the paper gently on the counter and fished through her pocket for money.

"No charge, Jessie. You remember what I said—I don't take money from heroes."

"And you remember what I said? I want to pay my own way." She placed her money by the register.

Patrick slid the money back. "If it'll make you happy, you can go back to paying tomorrow. Today's on me."

She tapped her fingers on the counter and folded the money into her hand. "Last time. Promise?"

He raised a questioning brow and smiled as he handed her her usual order—black coffee and a muffin. Today's muffin was blueberry.

"See ya, Patrick," she called as she gripped the newspaper, coffee and muffin and turned to go. As long as no one else made a big deal of the headlines, today might turn out okay after all.

Once at home, coffee and muffin in hand, she read the newspaper. The cover story recounted the shooting of Boston police officer Danny Coyle.

> *Officer Coyle,* she read, *had been shot during a routine traffic stop, underscoring the everyday dangers policemen and women face. The shooter, well known to law enforcement, had been apprehended shortly after the incident. His arraignment is scheduled for tomorrow and he is being held without bail until a dangerousness hearing is arranged.* It was hard to believe only thirty-six hours had passed since the shooting. It already seemed a lifetime ago. A photo of Danny's wife, Nicole, standing with the police commissioner at her side, quoted her as saying that "…*the staff at BCH saved my husband's life. We are forever grateful to this dedicated team.*"

She flipped past page one and on to the stories inside and there, buried on page eighteen between a tongue-in-cheek police blotter and a story about an adorable puppy, lay a small story, just four sentences long.

> *The body of a woman was found submerged along the Neponset River in Dorchester Sunday evening. There was no identification. The death is under investigation and police report they are investigating and checking all missing persons reports. They ask that anyone who has information call or text them at 1-800-888-CRIME.*

Danny's shooting took the whole of the front page, as it should, but poor dead Jane Doe, who was likely Sheila Logan, was only a footnote to the news that mattered. Jessie swallowed the lump in her throat. She needed to see Sam, learn if there was a positive ID. Roger would understand. She called the morgue and left a message saying that she'd be in later, that she had to help Sam ID the body.

That wasn't quite true, but she was sure she could somehow help to make a difference in this investigation. Sam and the rest of the team would need her on this. She was the only one who'd known Sheila Logan, and though their relationship had been rocky at best, at least it gave Jessie insight into who she really was. But she was getting ahead of herself. Maybe Jane Doe wasn't Sheila after all. Maybe Jane Doe was someone else entirely. Either way, she would do all she could to find her killer.

She took a quick shower, towel-dried her hair and pulled on jeans, a sweater and boots and made her way to her car, navigating through early-morning traffic and onto Melnea Cass Boulevard, past scores of homeless people huddled in makeshift tents, or pushing shopping carts overflowing with green garbage bags filled with all their worldly belongings. Her eyes scanned the group searching for Eddie Wilson, her homeless friend who spent much of his time in the ER. But there was no sign of him. She reminded herself to check up on him later.

She strode into Sam's office, where he sat alone. No Ralph, no other detectives, just Sam stooped over his desk, his eyes on his computer, so intent he didn't hear Jessie come in. She cleared her throat. He glanced up, his look of surprise making the silver flecks in his eyes sparkle. He forced a weak smile. "Hey, Jessie, I wasn't expecting you today."

"Ahh, gee, good morning to you too," she said, a generous hint of sarcasm in her voice. "And why weren't you expecting me?" She was more than a little puzzled.

"I thought you were with the ME for a few weeks."

"That usually includes Homicide. Anyway, I left a message for Roger. The truth is, I needed to see you, to find out if you've made a positive ID on Jane Doe. Have you?" She slid into the chair in front of his desk.

He didn't answer. Instead, he huffed out a long sigh.

A bubble of dread settled in her stomach. "Is it Sheila?"

"It is. Just got the confirmation. I'll be calling the state police in Ohio to make the official notification to her family."

Jessie fidgeted in her seat. "So, what's next? Where do we start?"

"We?" Sam asked, his brow wrinkled.

"Well, I'm a part of this unit, right?"

He shook his head. "You are, Jessie, but not on this one."

"What do you mean? I knew her. You need me on this."

He ran his fingers through his hair and leaned back. Instinctively, Jessie leaned forward. "What is it?" she asked.

"Until we've exhausted all possibilities and persons of interest, you can't be involved," he said. The wall clock ticked loudly, the rhythm of a heartbeat on a cardiac monitor, each second passing more slowly than it seemed possible. "And there's something else, something we found in the national database. There was another nurse murdered last year. She was found in the Blackwater River in West Virginia with a scarf around her neck. I just read the report. Strangled and thrown into a river…"

Jessie's jaw dropped. "Who was she? Why wasn't it on the news?"

"It probably was, locally, but this happened last year. Mary Stewart—she was young, only twenty-four, and a nurse in a nursing home. Worked hard by all accounts, to support her family. She'd grown up in a hardscrabble mining town, and when those old mines and the local businesses that supported them closed, she went home after graduation and took the nursing home job to be close to her family. State police there ran the investigation and came up empty. No suspects, nothing. It's still open, still unsolved."

"So, do you think they might be related?"

"Right now, it doesn't look like it. About three thousand women are killed each year, and ten percent of those die by strangulation. These deaths might just be a coincidence, but we'll see if there are any common threads. The West Virginia investigation focused on Mary Stewart's old boyfriend, but they couldn't prove anything."

Mary Stewart. Jessie filed her name in the recesses of her brain. She'd google her, see what she could find. "But if this is related, isn't that proof that you need me?"

A vein throbbed in his forehead. "Sorry, Jessie," he finally added. "Not until we know more, connect the dots, see what fits and what doesn't."

"But if this is a serial killer…"

"No buts. You need to be careful, though."

"So, do you think someone might be going after nurses?"

He shook his head. "No. These killings were miles apart, big difference in ages and in lives, so I don't think so, but they are similar—both nurses, strangled, thrown into rivers. A very long shot, but the fact is you knew Sheila Logan, and we don't know yet why she was killed."

Jessie felt her throat tighten. "Will you be going public with the news that Sheila Logan was the body that was found?"

"Yes, but not just yet. We'll be speaking to everyone in the ER and looking for anyone else at the hospital who knew Sheila or interacted with her. We'd like her ID quiet for now to see how people react to the news. So, please don't say a word. It's important. We'll want to speak with you as well."

Jessie suddenly realized what he was trying to say without actually saying it. "I'm a person of interest?"

And he only nodded in reply.

CHAPTER 9

"You can't possibly think I was involved," she said, her voice thin as a whisper.

"It doesn't matter what I think. Sticking to protocol and policies matters, especially in this case. You knew Sheila Logan. You actively disliked her. Sorry, but those are the facts. I can't let you in on the investigation. Maybe later, but not yet."

"But I can help. I know I can." She stopped herself. She was begging. She'd never begged for anything in her life, and she wasn't about to start now. She sat a little straighter.

Sam leaned across his desk, his eyes flickering before he dropped his gaze.

Jessie squeezed her own eyes shut and willed herself to be quiet. Speaking up—no matter how justified and noble her argument— had too often turned sour for her. She stood up and grabbed her bag. "I guess I'll go then." She turned for the door.

"Jessie?" Sam called as she was about to leave.

She spun around. He'd changed his mind. She could hear it in his voice.

He was standing, his hands stuffed deep into his pockets. "I'm sorry, Jessie. I'll try to bring you in for questioning as soon as I can, and we'll see if we can get you back here, maybe even to help out on this one. I promise." He offered a weak smile.

She sighed. "Thanks, Sam. I'll see you around, I guess." There was no point in arguing. He was convinced he was right, and she was equally convinced that she was. Her shoulders slumped as she headed out, passing Ralph along the way.

"Morning," he said. "From the look of you, I'm guessing you heard, huh?"

She stopped and sucked in her cheeks. "Has everyone heard?"

He shrugged. "That Jane Doe *was* your boss after all? Yeah, probably. It's not personal, Jessie. Rules are rules." A flicker of sympathy flashed in his eyes.

She blanched. She didn't want anyone feeling sorry for her, and her irritation reared its ugly head. "Yeah, whatever. I'm going. See you later."

As soon as she'd heard herself, she wanted to apologize, but Ralph was staring at his phone, preoccupied with whatever he was reading. He probably hadn't even heard the tone in her words. She wanted to shout to get his attention, and Sam's, to remind them that she should be involved in this investigation, but she bit her lip instead and strode quickly through the door, the snap of cold air forcing her head down into her collar.

She wasn't sure if she was pissed off or sad, or maybe both. Some days it was hard to tell one from the other, almost as if she were pushing a heavy load uphill. She wondered if this forensics assignment was worth the trouble. Maybe she should just go back to the ER, to the place that felt like home, where she knew her job, and everyone else's, and no one questioned her loyalty or integrity. And where she could start looking into Sheila's murder herself without needing permission from anyone else.

She called Roger from her car. "Turns out that Jane Doe is Sheila Logan. She was my manager, until she disappeared right around Thanksgiving."

He paused, maybe a beat too long. "Ahh," he finally said, "so, our Jane Doe was a nurse with you in the ER?"

"She was a manager. She didn't actually work in the ER, but she was no fan of mine. Sam said I can't be involved, and I wanted you to know because I think it means I can't be involved in her case at the morgue with you either. At least for now," she added hopefully.

"Well, of course. That makes sense, doesn't it?"

"No," she said softly. She wanted to say, *someone who knew her should be involved, she deserves that.* But she kept her mouth shut and nodded agreement, though she knew he couldn't see her. "But you sound just like Sam. I didn't get along with her, but I didn't have anything to do with her disappearance, or her death."

"I don't imagine anyone thinks that," Roger said. "But an investigation has to be pristine, no hint of self-interest or influence. Someday, hopefully, this case will come before a judge and jury and when it does, it must be perfectly clean. I've testified, and I know how the defense will nitpick at every aspect of an investigation. You see that, don't you?"

Her cheeks flushed. Not everything was about her. "Yes," she said softly. "I guess I do. I don't much like it, but when you put it that way, I understand it."

"Jessie, you're still in the learning stages. Give yourself a break, and some space. Even if you didn't get along with her, it's still a sad time."

She wondered if that was what she was feeling—a kind of sadness for Sheila and the way she died. No one deserved that. No one.

"What are you going to do?"

"Go back to the ER, I guess, until this is sorted out." And though she didn't tell him, she'd already decided she was done with waiting for other people to tell her what to do, and when to do it. She was an ER nurse and, in this case, the ER was the best place to start looking into things.

Sam and his team had no idea what went on in ERs—how long-held grudges could explode, or how patients and visitors could turn on the staff when things didn't go their way. And then there was Mary Stewart, the young nurse in West Virginia who'd suffered a similar fate to Sheila. Maybe she'd worked in an ER before the nursing home, and maybe there was a connection that

Sam had missed. And Mary Stewart was only a Google search away. That could be her first step in finding out exactly what had happened to Sheila Logan.

"Good thinking, Jessie. You'll be back with us in no time."

She turned her attention back to the road just in time to slam on her brakes at the red light on the corner of Mass. Ave., the ER entrance visible just to her right. And suddenly an image of Sheila, arguing in that entryway with a man, flashed across her brain. "I'll get to it, buddy," Sheila had said loudly. "Now, get out of here…" She'd paused when she caught sight of Jessie, the man turning for a split second before whispering something to Sheila and hurrying away. It had been one of those seemingly inconsequential moments, and Jessie wasn't even sure why she'd remembered it, but perhaps the clear view of the ER entrance had jogged her memory.

Beyond saying that he was average, she couldn't even conjure up a proper description, or a name. Sheila had called him "buddy" in that condescending way she had of insulting people. Jessie sighed. She was looking for suspects where they didn't exist.

An insistent car horn wrenched her from her thoughts, and she caught sight of her homeless friend, Eddie. Since spending time with the ME and the detectives, she hadn't seen much of him. She'd always worried about him alone on the street, in the bitter cold days and even colder nights of winter.

But it wasn't just the cold that worried her: it was the violence that stalked these men and women. Eddie, wearing the scarf, hat and gloves she'd given him not so long ago, was in the street, his hand held out to drivers who didn't seem to notice him. She searched her pockets and pulled out a ten-dollar bill, passing it to him just as the light changed and cars honked, eager to get through. In her rearview mirror, she could see him waving to her as he dodged through traffic to the relative safety of the pedestrian island.

Distracted, she swung into the hospital garage so swiftly her tires squeaked and the security guard wagged his finger at her. "Sorry," she shouted, pulling into the first space and racing to the ER. She arrived as the day was in full swing. Kate greeted her with a wide smile. "Where's Donna?" Jessie asked.

"The old manager's office, I think."

Jessie followed the corridor to the all too familiar space and poked her head inside. Sheila's mahogany desk, her ornate Persian carpet, and a tiny desk lamp were pushed into a corner of the room. Donna was bent over a large box, rearranging books and papers. "Hey," Jessie called. "What's going on?"

"I thought you were with the ME for two weeks. No?"

"No. Things have changed, and I have to speak with you. In confidence."

Donna stood, pushing an errant strand of hair behind her ear. "What is it?"

Jessie turned to close the door. "First—you have to promise you'll never repeat what I'm about to tell you."

"Jeez, that's dramatic, but yes, I promise. What is it?"

Jessie sighed. "Sheila's been found."

"Darn. I knew this was too good to be true. Guess I'd better start putting her things back. Want to help?"

"No. Just listen to me. Her body's been found. She was murdered."

Shaking her head in disbelief, Donna sank into the closest chair. "Are you sure? How? Why?"

"She was strangled and thrown into the Neponset River."

"Why isn't it on the news? Where are the police?"

"They've just ID'd her. I don't know if her family has been informed yet."

"Why are you here, then? Shouldn't you be working on this, following up leads, filling them in on the ER's inner workings?"

"You would think, but I'm, well, all of us, are persons of interest."

"We're suspects?"

"No. I don't know. I don't think so, but I'm not allowed to be involved. I only know this much because I was at her autopsy before we knew who she was."

"You didn't recognize her?"

"No, she'd been in the river for a while, and she was bloated and pretty badly decomposed."

Donna held up her hands. "Say no more. Too graphic for me."

"Yeah, it was pretty awful to see. We weren't exactly friends, but I wouldn't wish that on anyone."

"So, are the police focusing on the ER?"

Jessie shook her head. "They just got the ID. I'm sure they will be in, but I don't know when."

"Hmm," Donna said, her hand on her hip, her eyes scanning the room. "When I came in here today, things were just as she'd left them, her desktop uncluttered until I started rearranging things." She shrugged. "I guess I'll just let the police worry about it."

"I should probably get going now," Jessie said. "I'll be back to work here in the ER until this investigation moves along, but I just wanted you to know about Sheila."

"I'll be glad to have you back, but I don't need you today. Take a day off, and I'll put you on the schedule starting tomorrow. Sound good?"

Jessie nodded.

"But first help me move her desk back, will you? I don't want it to look like I was getting rid of her stuff to move in here."

Jessie smiled as she gripped one end of the desk. "But that's what you were doing, right?"

"Exactly right. She's been gone for months." They both groaned as they slid the desk back in place, and Donna found the desk phone and set it on the top, the red message light blinking furiously.

"Have you checked her messages?"

"No. I figured she'd be back, and there was no way I wanted her to know I'd listened to them."

Jessie's gaze was fixed on the phone. "There might be something important in there."

Donna shook her head. "Maybe. I'm sure the police will take it, don't you think?"

Jessie nodded.

"Listen," Donna said, her hand on the doorknob, "I have to get back to work. You coming?"

"Not yet," Jessie said. "Do you mind if I take a few minutes?"

If Donna realized that Jessie meant to listen to those messages, she gave no indication. "Sure. Just lock up when you leave."

"Donna, not a word to anyone, okay? And not to the police either. When they show up—and they will—act surprised."

"That will be easy. Call me if you learn anything."

"I will, and I'll be back to work here tomorrow," Jessie said, sinking into a chair, her fingers tapping anxiously on the desk.

CHAPTER 10

Jessie picked up the handset and tapped the voicemail access button. *'Enter your ID,'* an automated voice directed her. "Darn," she thought as she pulled open the top drawer to see if it was taped in there. No luck. The drawer held a blank notepad, a few pens, perfume, a comb, lipstick, and change. Nothing to do with work. She blew out a long stream of air. "Where…?"

And just like that, she knew. Most staff wrote their voicemail code and taped it to the underside of their phone. She picked it up, held it upside down, and there it was. Smiling to herself, she entered the code and grabbed a pen and paper to record anything that might be important.

The first two calls were hang-ups, the long drone of the dial tone filling the two-minute message timer. The next three messages were from Administration, inquiring about her return-to-work date after the Thanksgiving break. Those messages were increasingly tense, the last one informing Sheila that her position would be terminated. Jessie realized with a jolt that she was already dead by then. But no one knew that she lay alone and rotting in a riverbed just a few miles from the hospital.

Jessie clicked into the next message. "Listen, you," a menacing male voice said, "I told you we'd never forget, and we never will. You'll pay for what you did to my sisters and me. You had no business doing what you did. I haven't forgotten, and I'll make sure you don't either."

The voice was chilling, and Jessie shivered as she hit repeat and listened again, before tapping information to learn the date of the call and the number from which the call had originated. She shook her head, astonished at her luck that the caller had been so careless, thinking they couldn't be traced. All phones in the hospital had that option—a callback number was just a tap away. A Western Massachusetts area code had her wondering if this was from a neighbor of Sheila's, but what could she have done to make someone angry enough to leave a message like that? There were two more calls from that same number—one of them threatening that Sheila's days were numbered. "This isn't over," he said. Jessie shuddered at the thought.

Three more messages were work-related. Two from billing, inquiring about some ER charges on patients, probably the most annoying part of any manager's job, and finally, three messages from a man about signing off on new charges. "Let's get this done right away," he said angrily, more tension in his voice than she'd expected a business caller would have. Jessie wrote down the dates and phone numbers and quick summaries of the calls, though she thought the only ones that really mattered were the frightening calls that seemed to indicate something bad was about to happen to Sheila. Had she heard them? Had she realized that she was in danger? Or had her killer struck out of nowhere?

Jessie ran her fingers through her hair. Whatever had happened, she knew that the clues would ultimately lead to the killer of the woman who'd once sat behind this desk. And though she and Sheila hadn't been friends, Jessie knew that no one else would be as committed to this case as she was.

Suddenly aware that she'd been here for over an hour, she folded the notepaper and stuffed it into her pocket. She'd have a closer look at home. She marked each voicemail as *new* and smiled as the red message light began to blink once again. She opened the door slowly, peering around to be sure the hall was empty before slipping out through the rear entrance. Maybe she should have avoided the ER today, but it was her work home, and it was too late to worry about that now. She just needed to get home, fire up her iPad, check these numbers out, and google the other murdered nurse, Mary Stewart.

Jessie turned onto her street and stopped cold. There, in front of her house, stood the strange, dark-haired woman who'd been watching her at the L Street Tavern just yesterday. She was talking animatedly to Rufus. Jessie had held her frustration in all day, but who was this woman, and what was she doing here? She took a deep breath and stayed out of sight, darting behind a parked car to watch.

The woman was smiling and talking as Rufus listened before turning and pointing to Jessie's second-floor apartment windows. The woman looked up, nodded and took Rufus's hand. When Rufus stepped back inside, Jessie sprinted toward the woman, who'd begun to walk away. "Hey," Jessie shouted. The woman turned, a surprised smile on her lips. Jessie, her heart pounding, stopped in front of her. "Why are you following me?" she said, her voice raw.

"You don't remember me?" the woman said.

"Just tell me who you are, or I'll call the police. Maybe I'll call them anyway."

The woman stepped back, her eyes wide. "You really don't know me?"

Jessie shook her head.

"I'm your mother, Jessie."

Her mind reeling, Jessie paused to take a long look at the woman—the dark hair, the crimson lips, the deep lines that wove their way around her eyes and mouth. There was something familiar… but she caught herself and shook her head. If there was one enduring lesson she'd learned in the ER it was that everyone had an angle, and though she wasn't sure what this woman wanted, she was certain of one thing—she didn't have, or need, a mother. This strange woman didn't even deserve a response. Jessie pushed past her and started up her front steps.

"Look at me," the woman pleaded. "You must remember me. Don't you see yourself when you look at me?"

Jessie turned. The woman's hazel eyes, dark hair and bright red lips mirrored Jessie's own, but that was the extent of any resemblance, and how many other women shared those same characteristics? Jessie shook her head and pushed on the front door.

"You were born at two a.m. on October 6, 1993 in the Emerson Hospital in Concord."

Everything suddenly stopped—the hum of traffic, of people, of everything. Jessie turned back. "That's public information. I don't know why you're stalking me. Wouldn't a real mother just call me or write a note, or ask to speak with me? Keep it up and I'll call the cops."

The woman moved a step closer. "I've tried, Jessie. I have. Please, just listen. We weren't living in Concord, that town was too rich for us, but I worked not far from that hospital. I was a waitress and bartender, and when my labor started, I had to go to the nearest hospital. And you were born only six hours after I was admitted. It took your dad a full day to get there. He was a trucker and was still on the road." She stopped to take a deep breath. "We didn't have cell phones then. Some people had car phones in those days, but not us. Too pricey," she said, her gaze fixed on Jessie. She offered a tentative smile, her dimples flashing.

But Jessie had stopped listening; the only sound she heard was the pounding of her own heartbeat as it hammered in her chest, the echo pulsing in her ears. "My mother's dead," she shouted.

The woman's jaw fell open, her hand flying to her mouth. "Did your father tell you that?"

"No. I decided that for myself. A mother who abandons her baby is no mother. If that's who you're saying you are, you're dead to me." She slammed her front door behind her after she stepped inside, her heart still racing, her breathing shallow, her brain on fire. She stood there a minute, trying to slow her thoughts, catch her breath and get her bearings. Her phone buzzed with a message. She pulled it from her pocket, half expecting it would be from that crazy woman, but it was Donna. She exhaled a noisy sigh of relief.

Can you work a double tomorrow?

Jessie hesitated. What she really wanted to do was curl up on her couch with a glass of wine and a bucketful of self-pity and plan to sleep till noon. What a freaking miserable day this had been. Sheila's strange death, and now the woman on the street. She climbed the stairs to her apartment and fished for her keys before fumbling with the lock. Once inside, she slipped the deadbolt into place and looked warily around before dropping her bag and keys onto the table.

She sank onto her couch, her phone still in her hand. She glanced down, glad to focus on something other than that bizarre run-in with the woman from the bar. She'd had experience in the ER with delusional and schizophrenic people, and that stranger seemed to fit the bill perfectly. But on the other hand, the woman knew details that only Jessie and her father knew. She shook her head to clear her own swirling thoughts.

It couldn't be. Her mother had abandoned her when she was still a baby; maybe she'd shared that personal information with someone else, someone who'd decided to use it for her own gains—money, or God knew what. She ran her fingers through her mess of curls. She had to get back to her real life, get away from her own head. She bent to her phone.

Yes, she typed. *I'll be there at seven!*

She showered, pulled her hair into a knot, slipped into a pair of sweats, and when she peered into the mirror she saw, not her own image, but instead that woman on the street. She blinked the vision away and stepped back into her room, before heading down for a quick chat with Rufus. Maybe he could fill her in on what that woman had really wanted.

But Rufus had little to offer. "Yes, I met that lady. Very nice, but I didn't get her name. She said she was looking for you, said she knew your father, and she'd come back later. So, she found you?" His smile smoothed out the deep lines on his face.

"She did," Jessie said, trying to keep her tone calm. "But I don't know her, Rufus, and I don't think my father did either. I don't know what she's looking for, but please don't speak to her if she comes by again. Just let me know. Okay?"

His face and shoulders sagged. "I'm sorry, Jessie. I didn't mean to…"

"Oh Rufus, I'm so sorry. I'm sounding like an idiot. I don't know her, but of course you can speak to anyone. You know how I feel about you. It's just been a bad day, and I'm taking it out on you. I'm so sorry." She threw her arms around him, the jutting bones of his back reminding her how frail he was.

"Oh, Jessie, don't you worry. An old man like me can be taken in too easily. And if she comes around again, I won't talk to her. I promise." He offered a small smile.

She picked at her fingernails, stopping only when she drew blood. She needed to work on herself, to control her emotions, and put an end to her habit of speaking first and thinking later.

Once upstairs, Donna texted her again. *Call me,* she wrote. "Your friend Sam's here," she said in a whisper once Jessie had called back. "He's asking questions. He asked me if I'd seen you today. I told him I hadn't. He's tough, though. He had Sheila's office locked and he has the key, but I have another I didn't tell him about."

"Oh, thank you. It's not as if either of us has done anything wrong, but being on this side of an investigation kind of sucks. I feel as though I'm being looked at suspiciously."

"Me too. I'm the one who benefited from her disappearance, which that other detective pointed out, by the way."

"Who?"

"Ralph. All business, that one."

"Oh, no. He's a good guy, just a stickler for rules."

"He told me the same as Sam told you, that I can't tell anyone until they have confirmation that her family has been notified, and then he asked me for a list of people who knew her. He seems to think her murder wasn't random, that she was targeted. And if he's looking at the staff here, I can't think of anyone who liked her, well, except for Tim Merrick."

"Tim Merrick?"

"Yeah. They were dating. I'm not sure if they still were, but they were definitely an item not so long ago."

"Tim Merrick? How did I miss that? He asked me out a few days ago. Wait, isn't he married?"

"Divorced, or maybe separated, I think, but he's always had a roving eye."

"And you're sure he and Sheila were dating? When I mentioned her name to him, he seemed not to even remember who she was."

Donna laughed. "Typical man, huh? Anyway, I gotta go. I'll talk to you later."

CHAPTER 11

Day 4—Wednesday

It was the screech of the alarm that woke Jessie at six. She sat up and stretched. It had been days since she'd had a full and restful night's sleep. There was just too much going on—between Sheila, her job, and that crazy woman claiming to be her mother—she couldn't seem to get a grip on anything. She hadn't even looked up those numbers she'd taken from Sheila's messages, or even googled Mary Stewart yet. She whined to herself and to Donna, when she arrived to work at seven a.m., that *this* would never be over.

"It will be over, but I have other problems today. I've had two sick calls, and I've had to put our travel nurse, Kate, out in triage. The only other option was the acute side, and she's just not ready for that. She's not even ready for triage, but I had to put her somewhere. I was hoping that you could work with her, help her along. She's a nice girl, just inexperienced. I think maybe she just needs a little more time."

Jessie grunted, and strode into the crowded waiting room where patients gathered to be triaged, the homeless came to wash up in the bathroom and still others came just to sit. Kate was standing by the small triage office, her eyes on the patient sign-in list. She was scanning the list, her back rigid, seeming almost afraid to call the next patient. "Hey, Kate," Jessie said. "I'm here to help out. I'll call the next one, okay?"

Kate smiled, her relief almost palpable. "I need the help. I'm just no good at this."

"Well, watch me for a bit. Sometimes, newer nurses just need to see how we do things."

Kate nodded as Jessie called in the first patient, who complained of chronic foot pain. The next was an elderly woman with a fractured wrist, followed by a young woman with tears in her eyes and a large leaking cyst on her face. None of them critical, all of them easy to triage. She caught Kate reaching for bandage material, her eyes riveted to the patient's cyst. *Good,* she thought. *She's paying attention and knows what to do.*

It was then that an older man came running in. "Help me!" he shouted. "My wife isn't breathing!"

Kate stared blankly at the man. Jessie grabbed a pair of gloves and an ambu bag and raced to follow the man. "Kate, get a stretcher," she called over her shoulder, hoping she knew where to find one. Outside, a small group had gathered around an open car door, a woman slumped over.

"Get out of the way," Jessie shouted as she moved toward the woman, quickly determining that she was in cardiac arrest. "Help me pull her out," she called, and hands reached out and hauled her from the car, placing her on the ground. Jessie leaned in, checked again for a pulse and respirations and began CPR. "Go inside," she directed a young woman. "Tell someone I need a stretcher and the automatic defibrillator, the AED. Hurry!"

The young woman ran inside just as Kate appeared with a stretcher. "Help me with the CPR," Jessie directed her. "Take over compressions." But Kate stood perfectly still, seeming to be frozen in place. Before she could react, a security guard arrived with an AED. Still leaning over her patient, Jessie applied the AED pads, ordered the onlookers to move away and delivered the first shock to the woman's heart. Almost immediately, the woman had a pulse.

They lifted her onto the stretcher and ran inside, Jessie calling for the trauma team as they raced to the trauma room. Once she'd given report to the team and asked the social worker to look for the man who'd brought the woman in, Jessie went in search of Kate, who'd disappeared. She found her outside in the ambulance bay, cigarette in hand. "Jeez, Kate," she said. "You can't smoke here."

Kate stubbed out her cigarette. "I'm sorry. I just... I know I screwed up with that patient. I just froze. If you weren't there, I don't know what would have happened." She fixed her gaze on Jessie, her blue eyes as flat and icy as a winter sky. "I'm sorry," she repeated. "I'll do better next time."

"Listen," Jessie said, trying to keep her voice even, "you just have to pay attention. You have to at least try. I'm sure you know this stuff, and we're always here to help. Okay?"

Kate nodded, her eyes shimmering with tears. "I do know it. It's just that things are so different here. Please be patient with me."

"We will, Kate. Why don't you go into the trauma room and just watch? Okay? I'll head back to triage. Come out when the case is over."

Kate nodded and headed in and along the trauma hallway. Jessie shook her head and followed her inside. Donna was standing by the break room, watching. "What happened?" she asked.

"She's just nervous. You were right. She needs time. Where did she work before?"

"The company that sent her said she was an ER nurse, but a fairly new grad, so it makes sense that she's struggling. I wish they'd sent a more seasoned nurse, but..." She shrugged. "Believe it or not, she said she'd like to work nights, but no way I want her working without supervision. I thought maybe she could do some evenings with you. We have to give her a chance."

"I agree. I'll keep working with her. I just sent her to the trauma room to watch that resuscitation, and then I'll keep her in triage with me. Before I forget, any word from Sam?"

Donna's smile faded. "He's on his way in to meet with me. Said again he'd like a list of everyone Sheila came in contact with here. I told him he should see someone in Administration for that, since she wasn't actually in the ER much."

"What did he say?"

"Just that he wanted to speak with me. He asked if you'd be working, too."

Jessie groaned and shook her head in exasperation. "Let me know when he gets here," she said. "I'll be in triage."

"Thanks, Jess."

Jessie triaged the remaining patients, some to Urgent Care, some to X-ray, the rest waiting to be called inside the ER. With so many patients triaged to other areas, the waiting room had cleared enough for Jessie to have a good look at the hangers-on, the people just sitting there, not waiting to be seen. Most were homeless, like her friend Eddie, who was curled onto his side sleeping, a soft snore, a hum almost, slipping from his mouth. Jessie smiled and took the seat next to him. "Eddie," she whispered.

He turned and stretched, a look of recognition in his eyes. "Hey, Jess, got a sandwich?" He pulled himself upright, scratching his head as he did.

She shook her head. "Too early for the kitchen to drop them off. I'll save one for you, though."

He smiled. "Thank you. For the money you slipped me at the light, too. Someday I'll pay you back."

"Don't worry about that."

"Is it okay if I sit here for a while?"

She couldn't help but notice that he needed a shave and a haircut, not to mention some fresh clothes. The scarf she'd given him was wrapped around his neck, the gloves and cap hanging from a pocket. "You don't have to ask."

She sat forward and patted his shoulder just as the intercom flickered to life. "Jessie to Trauma Two."

"Oh, no," she muttered. "Don't go anywhere. I'll be right back." She hurried to the trauma room, where the staff were getting the resuscitated cardiac arrest patient ready to move to the ICU.

"We're going to send Kate up with the patient," Susan Peters, who was assigned to the trauma room, said. "We just wanted to make sure it's okay with you."

"Sure, that's a good idea," Jessie said, turning to Kate. "You okay with that?"

Kate, her eyes wide, barely nodded. "I guess so, if you think it's alright."

"It'll give you a chance to see the ICU, where so many of our patients wind up. I'll see you when you get back."

Jessie helped to set up the portable monitors and slip the IV drips to the poles, and watched as they wheeled the patient to the elevator. Kate turned back and gave her a slight wave. Jessie turned and made her way back to the trauma room, where Susan was busy restocking. "How'd she do?" Jessie asked.

Susan shrugged. "Same as always. She's timid."

"Well, I'm going to see if I can get her up to speed. This can be a pretty intimidating place, especially for a fairly new nurse."

"Good luck," Susan called as Jessie headed back to the triage area.

The waiting room was almost empty except for a heavily pregnant woman, a screaming child, a man holding his bleeding hand, but no Eddie. She craned her neck to see if he'd stepped around the corner, but he was nowhere to be seen. She huffed out a sigh. He was gone once again.

She called the man with the bleeding hand into the triage office, bandaged his hand and sent him off to X-ray to see if there was any glass or metal embedded in his wound. She was sitting there mulling over how to help Kate out when a shadow crossed her desk. "Hey," she said, looking up, fully expecting to see Kate.

Instead, Sam and Ralph were standing over her, their expressions serious.

CHAPTER 12

"Morning, Jess," Sam said. "Can you swipe us in?" Jessie breathed out a sigh of relief.

She nodded and walked to them to the ER entrance, swiping her card and watching as the door swung open.

"Thanks," Sam said with a wave. Ralph, his face unreadable, only nodded.

Once they'd passed through, Jessie went back to work and with no names on the sign-in list, she approached the pregnant woman. "Do you need to be seen?" she asked, leaning close.

The woman ran her hand over her bulging belly. "They sent me home," she answered softly, a heavy accent evident in her voice. "But I'm afraid the baby will come, and I'll have no time to get back. Please let me stay. That security guard said I had to leave if I'm not signed in." Her eyes, black as coal, sparkled with the tears that gathered there. "He said none of us could just stay here unless we're going to be seen. He said I should leave, but I'm afraid to."

Jessie touched her hand. "Of course you can stay. Do you want something to drink? Some juice?"

The woman nodded, a smile parting her lips. "Please."

"I'll get some, see if we have crackers, too. I'll be right back." She started for the staff lounge to retrieve the juice and crackers they kept there and stopped. Donna was in the main hallway, hemmed in by Sam and Ralph. She was shaking her head, but she was too far away for Jessie to hear what was being said. Anxious to avoid them, she retreated and went through the back way to the pediatric ER, where she grabbed a sleeve of crackers and a couple of juice boxes. Juggling it all, she stepped back into the hallway.

"Jessie, I've been looking for you. Got a minute?"

She turned to see Tim Merrick, his hands stuffed into the pockets of his white coat, a stethoscope dangling around his neck.

"Sure, just let me drop these off. I'll be right back." She headed to the waiting room, aware that Tim was following her with his eyes. *Please,* she thought, *now that I know he's a skirt-chaser, don't let him ask me out again.*

Once she'd delivered the items, she started for the hallway just as Tim appeared in the doorway. "I have to ask you something," he said. "But I'd like to be sure you'll keep this confidential." His eyes darted, as if checking that there was no one around to overhear.

Tim Merrick, the god of all surgeons, was nervous. "I guess so," she answered, though she wanted to tell him she'd had enough trouble of her own these last months, and she sure didn't need to be burdened with his.

"Can we go somewhere?" he asked.

"I can't go anywhere, but you can come into the triage office and we can shut the door." She immediately regretted that invitation until she remembered the panic button installed there to summon help when a nurse was being attacked, a sad fact of life in hospitals everywhere. Not that she thought for a minute that he'd attack her, but something wasn't quite right with him today. And with Sheila's murder… well, it paid to be on her toes.

Once inside, Tim shut the door behind him and took a seat. "This is really serious, Jessie. I need advice." He looked down and picked a stray piece of lint from his scrubs.

"Advice?" she asked, not bothering to hide the impatience in her voice.

"It's about Sheila Logan," he answered. "Is it true that she's dead?"

"It is true, but I thought you barely knew her," she said, deciding to echo what he'd told her. "At least, that's how it seemed a few days ago when I mentioned her."

He nodded. "I didn't want anyone to know that I knew her outside of work. I—"

Jessie held up her hands. "Whoa. Stop right there. I don't think you should tell me anything. The detectives are here. Talk to them."

Tim shook his head. "The detectives are exactly why I need to speak with you first. You work with them. You know how these things go now."

She sank into one of the seats. "Not really, Tim. I just started with the ME and Homicide, and I'm back in the ER precisely because of Sheila Logan. Believe me, I'm the last one to ask for advice. I didn't like Sheila, and I don't think she liked me, so technically, I'm a person of interest as far as the police are concerned."

Tim slumped back in his chair. "I had no idea that you didn't get along."

"It wasn't a matter of not getting along. She just didn't like me. I couldn't do anything right. She always had an axe to grind with me. Remember, months ago, after that tragic Hart shooting, when I was in the ICU?"

He nodded. "Yes. You were there for a change of pace, right?"

Jessie shook her head. "No, not at all. I hated being there. I was assigned to work there as punishment. Sheila had banished me to the ICU after a story leaked to the press about a patient. I was blamed, though I hadn't leaked anything. It was a set-up."

He raised a brow. "A set-up? That sounds sinister."

"It was, and it's a long, complicated story for another time. I have to get back to work shortly, so…"

"I know. I just have to tell someone, and I thought you'd be the best person to advise me."

Jessie groaned inwardly but offered a slight nod of her head. "Tell me what's going on then, and if I can help, I will, but I have to warn you, if it involves keeping information from the police, please don't tell me. I'd rather not be involved."

"No, no, it's nothing like that. It's just that Sheila and I dated for a short time. She thought it was more than it was, and she took my breaking it off pretty badly. She threatened to go to Administration and file a harassment complaint against me. I don't know if she ever did, I never heard anything, but I hadn't done anything wrong either, and I suppose that's my problem. It sounds as though you know firsthand that Sheila was the type to make someone look bad."

Jessie nodded in sympathy.

Tim cleared his throat. "This is kind of embarrassing for me." He shook his head sadly. "I just can't believe this is happening."

"You and me both," Jessie said.

"So, I guess I should just tell you the rest." His shoulders hunched down, he seemed to be sinking into himself. He'd always been larger than life, and this new Tim Merrick was a little disconcerting.

"It's the police you have to talk to. Just tell them the truth. If you hide anything, or even tell a little lie, it casts a shadow over everything else you say. Whatever you have to say, they've heard worse. You don't want to lie or stretch the truth." Jessie sat forward, hoping he'd hurry this along. She couldn't waste her whole day on this, and Kate would be back soon.

He crossed his arms and sighed. "She'd told me she thought that maybe she was pregnant. I told her that was nonsense, that she was too old to be pregnant. I shouldn't have said that, at least not in that way. She was so angry. She said if I abandoned her, she'd make sure that everyone knew." A trickle of sweat ran along his forehead. "The last thing she ever said to me was that she'd report me to the Board of Medicine, and effectively end my career."

"Oh, no. When did you last speak with her?"

"She threatened me in November. I blocked her on my phone after that, and avoided the ER. I heard a few weeks later that she'd left. I was relieved but afraid that she was planning something—that maybe she'd show up here with a baby or something and try to get back at me." A tic erupted in his right eyelid and he tried to rub it away.

"I probably shouldn't tell you this," Jessie said softly, "but at the autopsy, before we knew who she was, the ME didn't make a note of a pregnancy, and I'm sure he would have. So, a pregnancy seems very unlikely, but please don't tell anyone I told you."

He breathed a noisy sigh of relief. "Oh, Jessie, thank you for letting me know. That's one weight off my mind."

"You still have to speak to the police. And if you call them, instead of waiting for them to call you, it will look good. Just tell them you dated her, and it ended badly."

He stood up and wrapped her in a warm hug. "I will. I'm so—"

The door opened with a loud whoosh.

"Well, what do we have here?" Ralph asked, the corners of his mouth turned down.

Jessie and Tim quickly untangled themselves from their awkward embrace.

CHAPTER 13

"Sorry to interrupt," Ralph said, forcing a smile, his dimples flashing. He glanced quickly at Sam.

Tim stepped back nervously, his arms dangling at his sides, before he thought to adjust his stethoscope and shove his hands into his pockets, as if to remind them that he was somebody important.

"Ralph, we were discussing the policeman who was shot the other night. Danny Coyle. Remember him?" Jessie couldn't help herself. She didn't want Ralph, or more importantly Sam, thinking that she and Tim were a thing. She turned to Tim, hoping he might speak up, or at least ask to speak with Sam later. But he was silent.

Sam stepped into the small space. "Dr. Merrick," he said. "Good to see you. And Danny?" he asked. "We heard he's going home tomorrow, is that right?"

Tim nodded, and with a glance at his watch, excused himself and said he had to get back to the OR. "I'll see you later, Jessie," he said as he squeezed by Ralph, who didn't budge an inch to let him pass.

Sam turned to Jessie. "We wanted to arrange to speak with you."

But before she could answer, Kate suddenly appeared, all wide-eyed and shy, and looked from the police to Jessie. "Should I come back?" she asked.

"No, no, come in," Jessie replied, turning to Sam. "I'm working till eleven thirty tonight. You can call me tomorrow morning. Okay?"

Sam nodded. "Okay. Have a good night."

"Let's go," Ralph called, a nervous edge to his voice.

Sam gave him a side-eye. "Coming," he said, smiling.

"What's going on?" Kate asked. "Is it about that nurse manager, the one they say was found dead?"

"I thought it was supposed to be kept under wraps. Does everyone know?"

"I heard people talking about it in the elevator. I didn't know it was a secret."

"I guess it's not a secret now," Jessie said.

"Did she kill herself?"

"Where did you get that idea?"

"Someone on the elevator said that, I think."

Jessie rolled her eyes. "She didn't kill herself."

"So, they know how she died?"

"Why all these questions?"

Kate shrugged. "It's kind of interesting, I guess. A real-life mystery."

Jessie didn't want to feed any of this gossip. "Discussion over. Let's get back to work."

"Y'all aren't angry, are you?"

And for the first time, Jessie caught the faintest hint of a southern accent, that pleasant, lilting manner of speech. "Where are you from?" she asked, her interest suddenly piqued. Maybe getting Kate to talk about home would help to make her more comfortable here in the ER.

"What do you mean?" Kate replied, her brow furrowed.

"Your accent. Southern? Louisiana? Mississippi, maybe?"

Kate smiled nervously, her blue eyes glittering. "No," she said, "Wisconsin." She spoke slowly, enunciating each syllable. "The Midwest."

"Ahh, yeah," Jessie answered. "I know where Wisconsin is. It's just that your accent sounds a little southern. I never noticed that before."

"What can I say?" Kate shrugged. "I've never been to the south. Maybe someday."

The soft roundness of her shoulders told Jessie more about her than her words ever would. Here was a woman who didn't want trouble or confrontation, or even to be noticed, or at least she made herself seem that way. But, Jessie reminded herself, her job was to see if Kate could be whipped into shape as a nurse. It didn't matter where she was from, or that she was a shy, doe-eyed young thing, or just pretending to be. She wouldn't get by on that. Not in this ER.

"Let's get back to triage," Jessie said. "Will you call in the next patient?"

The day dragged. Kate was hopeless, or perhaps just nervous. The only thing she could really manage was blood pressures and pulses, and all she had to do for those was hit a button on the machine.

As the day wore on and Jessie listened to Kate speak, she was certain that she had a slight southern accent, not a Midwestern accent as she'd insisted. But why in the world would she lie about that? And why did Jessie even care? She was too suspicious. She could blame it on a hundred things, but the truth was she'd been born a skeptic. She took nothing at face value; instead, she was always looking for the angle just underneath the surface. And Kate, she was beginning to think, had an angle… or maybe she didn't. She had to stop overthinking things.

"If something sounds too good to be true, it probably is," her father had always said.

Words to live by.

A late run to the cafeteria had meant getting the day's leftovers—cold fries, lukewarm soup and stale bread that was advertised as "crusty." But she didn't care. She was starving. She'd thought she could grab a sandwich earlier, but patients and ambulances just kept coming, and at three o'clock, once Kate's shift was over and

Jessie had taken report from Donna, it was still too busy. Now, at almost seven, the lull seemed to have set in. She wondered again about where Eddie had disappeared to.

She took a seat in Donna's makeshift office, the former EMTs' room, set her food down and logged into the computer. She planned to look up the phone numbers she'd jotted down from Sheila's messages. Just as she typed in the number and shoved a handful of soggy fries into her mouth, the overhead speaker crackled to life.

"Jessie Novak to the front desk."

Her shoulders tensed as her fingers hovered over the keyboard, trying to decide if this search could wait. But she'd waited long enough. She needed to find out just who it was that hated Sheila Logan as much as those messages had seemed to indicate. She googled the sites that did reverse phone number searches, clicked on one and typed out the number. She leaned back and hit enter, watching as the little timer spun, and there it was. *Information not available, but a private search is available here.* She knew that the other search sites would have the same information.

Jessie clicked on the link which immediately asked for her credit card information. She wouldn't mind paying for it, but she was wary of leaving behind virtual fingerprints that Sam would likely find later. She pushed away from the desk, brushed the crumbs from her lap, and stood. Maybe she'd check on Mary Stewart instead. But for now, she might as well head to the front desk and see why she'd been paged.

The waiting room was quiet as she passed through, a few stragglers sitting, another sleeping in a corner. But the night was young, and if she'd learned anything, it was to expect the unexpected. At the front desk, she was directed to an older lady who stood alone by the glass-fronted entrance, her gaze fixed on the night sky, a black wool coat hugged tight around her thin body, a slight droop in her shoulders, a pair of gloves held in trembling hands. A wisp of a woman, she seemed to be deep in thought.

"Excuse me," Jessie said, almost afraid to interrupt. "You were looking for me?"

The woman turned, her eyes red, her wrinkled skin thin as parchment, her hair a silvery bit of fluff framing her face. "Are you Jessie Novak?" she asked, forcing a half-smile through bright pink lips.

"I am," Jessie said. "What can I do for you?"

She reached a thin, frail hand toward Jessie. "I'm Sheila Logan's mother," the woman said, her voice faltering.

CHAPTER 14

Jessie's throat constricted. "Mrs. Logan?" she asked.

The woman nodded, her puffy eyelids almost hiding the filmy brown of her eyes. "I know this is a busy place, and I'm sorry to come without any notice, but I just had to see it for myself, the place where my Sheila worked, the place she so loved."

"I…" Jessie was too stunned to speak.

"I know, dear," she said, gripping Jessie's hand with an unexpected firmness. "It's a terrible shock for all of us. If you have some time, will you let me see where she worked, and tell me a little about her time here?"

"Of course," she answered, wishing Donna were here to do this instead. "Have you spoken to the police already?"

"I have." Her eyes filled with tears and she dabbed at them with a tissue, her knobby fingers trembling as she slipped it into her pocket. "They tried to soften the news, but I understood." She dropped her gaze to the floor.

Jessie's eyes scanned the area, but it was empty except for a young man waiting by the taxi pickup. "You're not here alone, are you?"

"I'm afraid I am," she replied. "My other daughter couldn't leave her children, and well… my husband died four years ago. Bless him, this news would have just broken his heart. Sheila was his favorite. I know that's a terrible thing to say—that a parent has a favorite—but it was true. She had him wrapped around her finger." She sighed. "I'm sorry. I don't mean to prattle on."

"Please don't apologize," Jessie said. "You obviously loved her very much." And she felt that old familiar ache in the center of her chest. Her thoughts drifted to the woman in the street claiming to be her mother. She seemed to have little in common with this devastated woman standing before her. "Would you like to see her office?" she asked, hoping she could find the key in Donna's desk.

"I'd love that," she said softly.

Jessie led her through the ER and into Donna's tiny office, her dinner congealing on the desk.

"Oh, no, is that yours?" Mrs. Logan asked. "I've interrupted your meal, haven't I? I'll come back another time." She backed away.

"No, no," she said hurriedly, "that was Donna's lunch. She forgot to throw it out." She swept the tray into a nearby wastebasket.

"Just let me see if I can find the key." She rifled through Donna's top drawer, her fingers curling gratefully around the small silver key. "Got it," she said, holding it up. She closed her eyes briefly, steeling herself for what would come next. She turned back. "We're just heading down this back hallway."

Mrs. Logan followed her along the narrow hallway to Sheila's office. Jessie slipped the key into the lock, praying that Sam and the detectives wouldn't have turned it upside down in a search for clues. She swung the door open, flipped the overhead light switch and breathed a sigh of relief as the room came into view. It was just as it had been yesterday, the desk, the chairs, the fancy rug, even the little red message light still blinking. *Thank God she'd marked all those voicemails as "new."* The room was untouched. Maybe Sam hadn't had a look yet after all.

"Ohh," she exclaimed. "It's lovely, isn't it? It's just as Sheila described it. May I?" she asked, lingering at the doorway.

"Please," Jessie said, holding the door open as Mrs. Logan walked through, stopping to run her fingers along the polished mahogany desktop.

"She ordered this special, the rug, too." She bent to the floor, her knees cracking loudly as she straightened back up. "Is it alright to sit? Could you take a few minutes to tell me about her, what she was like here at work?"

Jessie's chest tightened. She couldn't describe Sheila as she'd known her—demanding, intimidating. But she'd known her only as a boss, never as a friend. She'd just have to make something up.

Mrs. Logan sensed her hesitation. "I'll start," she said, sinking into the leather-upholstered chair behind the desk. "I'd love to talk about her to someone who knew her. We can fill in each other's blanks. How does that sound?" She crossed her hands on the desk, and Jessie noticed the same iridescent pink polish that Sheila had worn till her death.

"Please," Jessie said. "Go on." And for the first time in her life, she understood that this was how mothers who loved their children, whatever their age, behaved. She felt more than a twinge of envy that Sheila had been so adored.

Mrs. Logan sank further into Sheila's chair, a smile playing at the corners of her lips as she remembered her daughter. "She'd always wanted to be a nurse. From the very beginning, she wanted to take care of others, to make a difference, she used to say. She even came here to Boston for school because she said Boston had the best hospitals, the best places to learn. It broke our hearts when she left us. I think we knew she wouldn't be back, but…"

Jessie's thoughts strayed again to the woman on the street claiming to be her mother, and she felt a flush rise to her cheeks.

Mrs. Logan cleared her throat and continued. "We were worried about her, of course," she said, "when she didn't turn up for Thanksgiving. But we knew that she was busy at work, that her role here was important. I left phone messages for her at home and finally called the superintendent at her building, and he checked her apartment and said it looked fine. Nothing was out of place. So, her sister and I thought maybe we'd missed a message, that she was away, maybe at a conference." She paused, her eyes glazing over as though the memory was too much.

"You don't have to…" Jessie began.

"Oh, but I do. It will keep her closer if I can speak about her."

Jessie nodded, afraid to interrupt the woman's memories once again.

"I finally called the police in December. As bad as Sheila had always been about calling, she would have been in touch a few weeks before Christmas to find out what everyone wanted. The police there said exactly what the superintendent had said—that they'd checked, and nothing was out of place, that perhaps she went away without telling anyone. They weren't interested in hearing an old lady say that her adult daughter had simply disappeared, but they agreed to put her on the missing persons list and mention her in their weekly briefs. And that was all. I waited every day for news, and I had a feeling that when it came, it would be bad, but this…" She bowed her head, her shoulders quivered, and a soft cry escaped her lips. "Forgive me," she said softly.

Jessie stood and moved closer, patting her back. "I'm so sorry, Mrs. Logan. Sheila was so lucky to have had you."

She sniffled and raised her head, her eyes puffy and red, locking onto Jessie's. "Thank you for saying that. I loved her, but she was headstrong, and we often butted heads. I'm not even sure she knew how much I loved her."

"I'm sure she did. She was a strong woman because she came from a foundation of love." But as Jessie said it, she wondered why a woman who was so loved, and seemed to live such a charmed life, was so angry. Jessie, at least, had a reason to be angry. She'd inherited it, or maybe just absorbed it, from her dad.

"What a kind thing to say, Jessie. I know she tried hard to be a good nurse and a good leader. She loved the nurses who worked with her and she often talked about them. In fact, she mentioned you by name."

"Well, we didn't always…" she began, hoping to explain their relationship. But Mrs. Logan hadn't seemed to hear, and she continued on.

"She said that you seemed as headstrong as she once was. She thought that she could mentor you, and that perhaps one day you would be the nurse leader here. She said you were just the type of assertive person that was needed in the ER."

Jessie's reply momentarily caught in her throat. "I… I'm surprised to hear that."

"You shouldn't be. All of you here were family to her. She'd always wanted the white picket fence, the perfect husband and a houseful of children, but she invariably chose the wrong man, and she'd finally just given up on that dream." She fidgeted, linking and unlinking her fingers, and then running them along the smooth leather of the chair.

Interesting, Jessie thought, that they'd had that in common—the knack for choosing the wrong man—but she would never let herself wind up like Sheila: angry, impatient. And then it hit her—in many ways, that described her already. She folded and then unfolded her hands. "I'm so sorry, Mrs. Logan," she said softly. It was a trite comment, she knew, but there was nothing else she could think of to add that wouldn't sound insincere.

"The detectives told me that you work with them sometimes. One of them said that you were in the morgue with Sheila before anyone knew who she was. Is that true?"

Jesse could only nod, afraid that her thin veil of composure might crack.

"Well, I can't tell you how much that means to me. To know that she wasn't entirely alone," she said, shifting in her seat. "The police have suggested it would be best that I not see her, that it would be too much, so I'm very grateful that she wasn't alone, and hopeful that perhaps you might be able to find the person responsible. You're still so young, but for a mother, the worst thing possible is to lose a child, even if she's all grown. I'm sure your own mother feels that way about you."

The stirrings of a headache pulsed just behind Jessie's eyes. *Her own mother hadn't lost her, she'd willingly left her.* Jessie could only nod.

Sensing her discomfort, Mrs. Logan gripped Jessie's hand. "You've been such a dear girl to speak with me. I want you to know how much I appreciate it. I know you'll help to figure out who did this terrible thing to my Sheila."

Jessie locked her gaze onto Mrs. Logan's. "I will, and I hate to ask this, and I'm sure the detectives already have," she said, leaning forward, placing her hand over the frail hand of the older woman. "But do you know of anyone who might have wanted to hurt her?"

"The detectives did ask me that, and I couldn't really think at the time, I was still processing everything they had told me. But now that I've had some time, I remember that years ago, when Sheila was a staff nurse at another hospital here in Boston, a young drug-addicted mother had overdosed and was brought by ambulance to the ER. She had three terrified and obviously neglected, malnourished children with her. Sheila called social services, who took the children away. Sheila tried to follow their trail to see what happened, but all she knew was that the mother died later after another overdose, and the children were separated and placed into miserable foster homes."

Jessie nodded encouragingly.

Mrs. Logan continued. "A year or so ago, Sheila started to get threatening calls from the oldest. He'd been just a small child at the time, but so many years later, he was all grown up and he blamed her for everything. He said that she'd ruined their lives, that his mom was doing her best at the time, but at least she loved them until Sheila got involved and ruined everything." She took a long, slow breath and began running her fingers along the desk again. "Sheila changed her phone number, and I don't know if he called her again, but, well, it's probably not even important. The police seemed to think that maybe she made enemies here at this hospital. At least, that was how it sounded to me."

Jessie bristled at the suggestion. "Maybe those threats are important, though," she said through gritted teeth. "Did she ever give you a name?"

Mrs. Logan wrinkled her brow. "No, I don't think so." She looked at the desk. "But maybe there's something in this office that will help." Her hands on the desk, she pushed herself slowly to a standing position. "I've taken enough of your time. I have to make arrangements. They said I could take my Sheila home tomorrow, and there's still so much to do."

Jessie stood. "I can walk you out."

"No, dear," she said, taking Jessie's hand. "But thank you for your kindness. Your mother raised you well. She's a lucky woman to have you."

Tears welled at the corners of her eyes. "I…"

"No need to say anything, dear. Please keep in touch with me. The police have my information." She leaned in and kissed Jessie on the cheek, running her knobby fingers along the smoothness there.

When she left, Jessie sat back down. She had seen a totally different side to Sheila tonight. The blinking red lights on the phone caught her eye. She wouldn't risk being caught by listening again, but she would, somehow, trace those calls. Maybe one of them had come from Sheila's killer.

CHAPTER 15

Day 5—Thursday

A shrill, insistent buzz pierced the silence. Jessie's hand darted out, fumbling for her phone before finally raising it to her ear. "What?" she shouted, closing her eyes to blot out the rays of sun that leaked through her blinds.

"Good morning to you too," Sam said drily.

"Oh, no, sorry. What time is it?" Jessie sat up, running her fingers through her hair.

"It's ten thirty. Late night?"

"No. I worked, remember?" Her mind wandered. When was the last time she'd had a late night with someone special—someone who'd touched her in that way that made every inch of her tingle, someone who'd kissed her with such intensity that she'd almost felt faint, someone who'd held her tight as she drifted off to sleep? It had been months ago, and while she didn't miss that man, she missed that connection, that bond, that... She realized that Sam had been speaking while she was lost in her thoughts. "What?" she asked.

"Jeez, you really are asleep, huh?"

"No, sorry. Go on."

"We have to speak. Today, Jessie."

"I know. I have to work at three. How long will this take?"

He sighed, a long, noisy sigh that meant he was wondering how to answer. "Well, Jess, it's hard to say."

"Oh, for heaven's sake. It's not that hard. Should I just bring my scrubs? I'll have to leave by two for work."

"Then bring everything you'll need. If it takes less time, I'll treat you to lunch."

"You should treat me to lunch anyway. I met Mrs. Logan, by the way."

"Nice lady, huh?" he said. "Sad for her."

"She was nice, the way I imagine most mothers are, and she got me to thinking, so I have a favor to ask." And that favor involved the woman who'd suddenly appeared saying she was her mother. She wanted Sam to look into this woman, and though she didn't get a name, if the woman really was her mother, her name was Angela Novak, a name she only knew from her birth certificate.

"Okay. You have a deal. See you shortly."

And just like that, he disconnected the call. *Jerk.* He didn't even ask what the favor was. *What did I ever see in him anyway?* She climbed out of bed, showered, pulled her curls into a knot, applied some lipstick and a swipe of eyeliner over her hazel eyes, pulled on jeans and a sweater, grabbed her scrubs and work clogs and headed out. She made it to headquarters at eleven thirty. Her red ID allowing quick entry, she was happy to note that the place was buzzing with activity and no one gave her a second glance.

"Hey," Sam said when she appeared in his doorway. "We're going to have to film this in the interview room."

Jessie dropped her bag on the floor. "Are you kidding?" A swath of heat rose to her cheeks. "Mrs. Logan said you were looking at suspects at the hospital, but me?" She remembered the telephone messages on Sheila's phone. He hadn't heard them yet. It was best that she learn to just keep her mouth shut and let the investigation continue. He'd get to them eventually, though she was beginning to think she'd probably get to them first.

"Jessie, relax. Technically speaking, everyone is a person of interest, and you might know something you don't even realize you know."

If you only knew, she thought, her mind still on that little winking red light.

"Please don't take this personally," he continued.

"Oh, God, why does everyone say that? Some things are personal."

"I'm not going to argue with you. Come on. Let's get this over with." He held his arm out as if to guide her along.

"Will Ralph be in there? I don't know what's up with him, but yesterday..." She was still bothered by Ralph's reaction to her hug with Tim. He clearly seemed to think it was more than it was, and she didn't feel like trying to explain it again.

Sam smiled meekly. "Nothing's up with him. He believes in rules and policies and that's a good thing, but one of us had to go check Sheila's apartment. Natick PD called to say that since they'd last been there—when she was first reported missing—it's been ransacked. Somebody was looking for something." He scratched his chin. "Ralph volunteered to go."

"Any idea what they were looking for, or if they found it?"

"Not yet. I told Ralph to see what he can come up with. He'll have to work with the Natick police and the state police detectives, the CPAC—the crime prevention and control unit. He'll probably be gone for hours."

For the first time that day, Jessie smiled. "Okay, let's do this." She followed Sam to the video room, the small room where she'd watched a trembling suspect questioned in another murder case. The same round wooden table and three straight-backed chairs were pushed into the far corner. Sam turned on the cameras and audio equipment. "Have a seat, Jessie. Should have asked before—can I get you anything?"

"Coffee," she answered.

"I can send out for one of those double mocha soy espresso latte things, if you want."

She curled her lips. "I'd rather drink sewer water," she said, wondering why he was being so solicitous. "Just coffee—real coffee. A large one, black, no sugar."

He nodded. "I should have remembered that."

Once Jessie was alone, she was tempted to wander around the small space, see where cameras and mics might be hidden, but she was already on tape; she didn't want to look suspicious.

Sam reappeared with coffee and a napkin that held two donuts—one chocolate and one cinnamon. "Thought you might be hungry." He placed the coffee and food in front of her. "Thank you," she said, reaching for the coffee. "Do you want one of these?" She pointed politely to the donuts.

"Jessie, you know me better than that. I'll never stand between you and food." He winked and sat down across from her.

Jessie took a long sip of the bitter coffee before reaching for the donuts. "I didn't have a chance to eat," she said, chocolate glaze rimming her mouth.

"Okay, let's get started. First—the usual, please state your name."

"Jessie Novak," she replied through a mouthful of sweet dough.

"And you're aware that we are here to question you regarding the disappearance and subsequent murder of Sheila Logan?"

Jessie rolled her eyes. "Yes."

And so it went—the verbal sparring, the back and forth, the endless questions, and the recitation of the little she knew.

Finally, Sam read over his notes, flicking his pen cap up and down before tossing it back onto the table. "I think you know something. I think you're holding something back."

A quick burst of heat rose to Jessie's cheeks and her heart pounded against her ribs. She inhaled deeply to calm herself. But it was no good. There was nothing easy about this situation. "Why do you think that, and what do you think I know?"

"I'm not accusing you of anything. I don't think for a minute that you harmed Sheila Logan, but I'm pretty sure you're holding out on me." His lips parted in one of those phony *I'm really your friend* smiles.

Jessie tried not to squirm in her seat. She shook her head. "How am I holding out?"

"For starters, what were you discussing with Dr. Merrick yesterday?"

Jessie looked away. *Darn.* What could she say? She didn't want to lie, but she didn't want to be involved in Tim Merrick's troubles either. "Can't you just ask him?"

"I intend to, but right now, I'm asking you."

Jessie blew out a long, exasperated sigh. "This is what being interrogated feels like, huh?"

"I'm not interrogating you, Jessie. I want this investigation to be over with as much as you do. Just help me out here. Please."

The silver specks in his eyes sparkled in the glow of the fluorescent lights that bathed his face. She remembered how she'd been so attracted to his eyes when she'd first met him, the way the charcoal gray shimmered in the right light, or when he was happy. She tapped her fingers on her knee to distract herself. "I want this to be over with, too," she said. "Tim pulled me aside yesterday and told me he'd gone out with Sheila for a short time, and it had ended badly. I told him he had to speak with you guys, not me."

"And?"

"That's it. He said he would, but judging by your expression, he didn't. That's all I know."

"Anything else?"

To really come clean, she had to tell him about the phone messages, but he'd find them on his own. If she mentioned listening to them, she'd be in trouble with him or the hospital. She had to improvise, and she repeated Mrs. Logan's story about the angry foster kids and the threatening calls. "She didn't know if there were any recent calls, but that should be easy enough for you to find."

Sam raised a brow. "Why didn't she tell us that?"

"She said she only remembered it at the hospital. And, this is probably not even connected, but yesterday I recalled seeing Sheila a few months before she disappeared, arguing in the hallway with a man. Maybe it was one of those kids, all grown up and out for revenge."

"Did you catch a name?"

She shook her head. "She called him buddy, the way you call a stranger *buddy.*"

"Description?"

"No. His back was to me and he turned for only a split second. Average and youngish, is all I remember. Sorry, it just never struck me as important at the time."

Sam nodded. "Alright, we'll look into it. I'll call Mrs. Logan, see if she can tell us a little more." He sat forward, his elbows on the table. "What about that favor you were going to ask?"

Jessie shook her head. She'd changed her mind; she wasn't quite ready to tell him about the woman claiming to be her mother just yet. "I'm all set," she said, smoothing a loose strand of hair to calm her jittery hands.

"Are you sure? It seemed important just a while ago."

Jessie shrugged. "Maybe another time. It doesn't matter right now." And it didn't. She'd told the woman in no uncertain terms to stay away, and she probably would. And that would be the end of that story. "I'm going to get moving," she said, picking up her bag and turning for the door.

"What about lunch?" Sam asked.

"Another time. I want to get to work." And she did. But, more than that, she wanted to avoid discussing her mother, the crazy woman on the street. After the way Sam had just treated her, she didn't feel like trusting him. It was best to simply forget some things.

CHAPTER 16

Day 6—Friday

The next morning Jessie rose early, slipped into her running clothes and headed out along her usual route to Castle Island, and though there were plenty of cars and pedestrians about, she felt that familiar rush of endorphins which made her feel light as air, her feet barely touching the ground as though she were floating on the morning wind. The early fog hovered just along the shoreline, making it difficult to see beyond the edge of sand, and aside from the breeze and the sounds that swept in from the ocean, she might have been alone.

It was only when she passed Sullivan's, the scent of their fried clams and burgers in the air, that she slowed just long enough to inhale the sweet smell, and then she was off, flying over the road, her arms pumping, her lungs grabbing the air greedily as she made her second pass over the island. By the time she turned for home, she was free of the worries that had plagued her—the strange woman who claimed to be her mother, and Sheila Logan and her murder, though she was sure she was missing something in that investigation. She could just feel it. When she slowed to a walk, the wind in her face eased to a comforting sigh. Nothing much mattered after a good run. She'd just stepped into her apartment building when Rufus's door swung open.

"Oh, Jessie, I was about to knock on your door."

"Are you okay?" she asked, her eyes scanning him for any sign of sickness or injury.

"Fit as a fiddle," he answered with a smile. "But I have something for you." He pulled a scrap of paper from his pocket.

Jessie leaned forward, her hand out. "Oh?"

He held it back. "Now, don't be angry with me."

"Rufus," Jessie said. "I won't be. What is it?"

He smoothed the paper in his hand and held it out. "That lady stopped by again. She was very nice, and asked me to give you this. I couldn't tell her to go away. I... well, I just couldn't."

Jessie took the paper and unfolded it, a tiny well of discomfort causing her stomach to churn. She quickly glanced at the paper before slipping it into her own pocket. "Thanks, Rufus. I'm sorry I was such a jerk about this before. No excuses. I need to work on myself."

Upstairs, she peeled off her leggings and shirt, her fingers curling around the folded piece of scrap paper in her pocket. She smoothed it out and read the elegant handwriting—*Angela Novak*—and a number underneath. If she didn't do it now, she never would, so with trembling fingers she tapped the numbers into her phone and hit call.

She was almost glad that her call went to voicemail, and she decided against leaving a message. Maybe she'd call again, or maybe she'd ask Sam to help poke around into this woman's background, see if her story might be true. But that would mean peeling away yet another layer of lies she'd told him.

Jessie heaved a pent-up sigh of relief as she hurried through the hallways leading to the ER. Lost in her thoughts, she ran right into Sam as he rounded a corner by the ER entrance.

"Whoa there," he said. "Where's the fire?"

"I was just thinking about you," she said, an easy smile on her lips.

"Well then, I'm flattered. I was just about to call you." He held up his phone as if to prove his point.

"It's not more bad news, is it?" She felt her shoulders sag.

"No, I don't think so. I wanted to see if you could fill me in on Tim Merrick."

Out of the corner of her eye, Jessie saw a few workers slow down and turn her way. Hospitals were dedicated cesspools of gossip, where the truth was never allowed to get in the way of a good story. "Can we speak somewhere privately?" She swept her gaze past him, resting her eyes on the nearby lingerers. "To keep down the rumors?"

Sam turned and nodded. "I'm parked in the ambulance bay. Private enough?"

She laughed. "Perfect. It will spark gossip about you and me."

"I'm all for that then," he said with a sly wink.

And she wondered all over again. *What if?*

Once they were in his car, with the heater blasting cool air, Jessie shivered. "This is the winter that will never end, isn't it?"

"It's only March first. We're still due another storm or two."

"Don't even think that. I'm ready for spring. These cold, gray days just make everyone miserable."

"True enough. So, tell me what you know about Tim Merrick."

"Not much. Nothing more than I told you yesterday. You probably know more about him than I do. I work with him. That's it."

He raised a brow. "The embrace I saw the other day looked a little more than a hug between work friends."

She wondered if he was asking for himself or the investigation. "You've never worked in an ER. The intensity of it brings people close, but only on the surface. As soon as the drama is over, so is the closeness. Haven't you spoken with him yet?"

"We have. Well, we've started. He's not the most cooperative man I've ever questioned."

"He's a trauma surgeon. Arrogance is his middle name, but he really is a good guy. He's nervous about this getting out."

"Did you know he's still married?"

Jessie's jaw fell open. "Are you sure? The gossip is that he's divorced."

"They're in the process of divorcing but still living in the same house while they hash things out."

"Jeez, you just never know, do you? And… he asked me out recently." She shook her head. "I thought I was becoming an old man magnet."

Sam's gaze caught hers and held it tight, his gray eyes sparking until he blinked and looked away. "That's no surprise, is it, Jess?"

"That old men like me? Yes, it's a surprise. I'm still hoping— Never mind."

"You're right. Never mind. But surely you know it's not only old men."

A sudden flush heated her neck. "If you don't need anything else, I have to go," she stammered, reaching for the door handle. "You'll keep me posted?"

"I will, and if you hear anything, any gossip at all, call me."

She nodded. "Thanks, Sam," she said, and headed back towards the ER. Then she stopped, remembering that she'd decided to ask if he'd look into Angela Novak. She turned, but he was already pulling into traffic. She sighed and stepped inside.

"I see you caught up with Sam," Donna said. "Did he say anything?"

"No. He just wanted to know what I knew about Merrick, so it was a quick conversation."

Donna stuffed her hands into her pockets. "I was hoping we'd hear something."

"Well, I do have something. Seems our Dr. Merrick is still married."

Donna's eyes grew wide. "Tell me everything," she whispered.

"That's all Sam said. Merrick's married, in the process of divorce but still living together. That would explain why he was so nervous when he told me about his relationship with Sheila."

"Didn't he just ask you out?"

"He did. The dog."

Donna laughed. "We better keep quiet about this latest revelation. I don't want to be involved in this. Hey, you don't think Merrick… No, never mind, that's too wild."

"That he killed her? No. I can't imagine him killing anything more than a few junior surgeons' egos. Besides, he's always here. When would he find the time?"

"But the ME doesn't know exactly when she was killed."

"Not exactly, but probably right around the time she disappeared. She was here on Tuesday two days before Thanksgiving, right? That was when she let me come back to the ER, and asked if I'd work a double the day before and the day of Thanksgiving."

Donna nodded.

"If she was driving to Ohio, she likely planned to leave on Wednesday or even late Tuesday, but she never left, so that's got to be the time frame for the murder."

"Jeez, you're good at this stuff already. Did you tell Sam?"

"He never gave me a chance, said I couldn't be involved in the investigation, but I guess I should call him, make sure he knows."

"Was Merrick around the day before Thanksgiving?" Donna asked.

Jessie ran through the images in her mind. "I don't think so. It was my first day back, so I remember it pretty well. That was the day that truck driver lost his arm and vascular surgery managed that. The gang of midgets, those teenagers who shot one another in the legs as a kind of gang initiation, were at it again, but the surgical chief resident took care of those minor gunshot wounds. And later I went to the surgical ICU to see the charge nurse, and Merrick definitely wasn't there."

"That reminds me," Donna said, her voice dropping to a whisper. "You won't believe this. I don't know how I forgot, but I have Sheila's stuff—her ledgers, notebooks, schedules, emails, all of it. I got everything when I was named manager. I never looked at anything. I was just too busy." A satisfied smile on her lips, she raised her arms as if in surrender. "I can't believe I have it."

"Holy you-know-what! And you never looked, never went through anything?"

"I've been covering the floor almost every day. I thought getting a travel nurse would ease things, but it just hasn't happened."

"Wow, the answer might be somewhere in there. What about the emails?"

"I asked IT to transfer only her work emails to me so I could catch up on any loose ends and administrative stuff, but they sent me everything, even her personal emails. And once they closed her email account, they had all of her current emails automatically forwarded to me as the new manager."

"And you never…" Jessie paused, considering the possibilities.

"I started to, but there were just too many to go through, so I created a folder on my computer and dumped them all there. I forgot all about them. I just might have whatever it is Sam's looking for." She whistled. "I don't know what to do."

"Two choices," Jessie said. "Call Sam, or have a look at them first. See what's in there."

Donna shoved her hands into her pockets. "What do you think? Have a look with me before we call Sam?"

Jessie smiled in reply. She and Donna settled into the small space she'd been using as her office. It had been a charting room for EMTs and medics, but since space was tight, Donna had taken the room for herself, leaving a few disgruntled medics in her wake until she invited them to use the staff lounge instead, reminding them that there was always coffee and usually food available there.

Donna retrieved a large box from under her desk. "This is what I have." She peeled back the edges and peered inside before pulling out an armful of ledgers, notebooks and loose papers. "This isn't even half of what's in there. Want to have a look?"

"I do, but I can go through this stuff anytime as long as you leave me your key. I can't get into the emails by myself. How about we start there?"

"I can just forward that whole folder to you."

Jessie shook her head. "No way. If there's one thing I've already learned, it's that we'll leave virtual fingerprints if we move her emails. Forensics can follow emails and internet activity. If we look at them here, I don't think they'll ever know. It's work stuff, right?"

"As far as we know." Donna booted up her computer and logged into her email.

Jessie dragged a chair over and studied the screen as it came to life. Donna's inbox exploded and included one hundred and twenty-eight new and unread emails. "No wonder you can't keep up with this."

"No kidding, and half of these new ones were forwarded from Sheila's old account which they've only just closed down. I've had to sift through them every day, and most were junk." She clicked on one and pointed to it. "See, this one's an invitation to some online medical group. *Send in your articles. We'll publish them for you*," she read aloud in a mocking tone. She clicked on another. "This one's from Macy's. A fifteen percent off coupon."

Jessie frowned. "That's it?"

"That's what she gets these days. The automatic accounts that spit these out don't know that she's died. The older ones that I saved to the folder might be a different story."

"What are we waiting for?" Jessie scooted her chair closer and watched as Donna clicked on the folder labeled *Logan, S.* It was a bit like opening Pandora's box. Hundreds of emails filled the screen.

"When are these from?"

"I asked for October and November. I'm responsible for the department budget now, so I figured I'd need to see any emails that had that information. I was thinking maybe I should have asked them to go back earlier, but…" She knit her brow and shrugged. "Probably too late now."

Jessie exhaled noisily. "There are so many."

"Which is why I haven't tackled them yet. Where should we start?" Donna asked.

"The beginning," Jessie said. "Definitely the beginning."

CHAPTER 17

"Hey," Donna said as she scrolled through the emails. "I'm not going to stay. You have a look. We can't both be in here. What if Sam or someone else comes looking for us? I'll stay in the ER and keep an eye out. You have a better feel for what's important to this investigation."

"Agreed," Jessie said.

Donna giggled as she pulled open the door. "I feel a little like a detective myself."

Once Donna had left, Jessie turned the lock on the door and settled into her seat and began to scan the emails—subject line, sender and date. She wasn't sure what she was looking for. She just hoped she'd know it when she saw it. Most were from Administration—ER census numbers, patient complaints, staffing issues, equipment changes, the daily minutiae that drives management.

More were from outside agencies seeking to do business with the ER—offering supplemental staffing, documentation services, ER follow-up services. The list seemed endless. Jessie shook her head. *Why did Sheila hold onto junk emails? Why not just hit delete?* She leaned back. Maybe they weren't junk. Maybe there was something there.

She chose several at random and hit print. She could look at them later, maybe google the senders and see what came up. It was probably all a waste; maybe there wouldn't be anything in there after all.

She studied the screen and filtered the emails by sender, and suddenly a flurry of messages between Tim Merrick and Sheila appeared. Though Donna had requested emails from October and November, this conversation went back to September. The IT department must have been busy when Donna had made her request because they sure hadn't been careful.

The subject line on each was *message* or *re: message.* She clicked on the first one:

September 17:

From: Timothy Merrick, MD

Dinner? I can come to your place. I'll bring dessert. Let me know. T

From: Sheila Logan, RN, MSN

Oh, Tim, I'd love to see you. Do we really need dinner? Bring wine! ♥

September 18:

From: Sheila Logan, RN, MSN

Last night was the best… S

The messages continued along that same line until October, when Sheila's messages began to be more strident.

October 10:

From: Sheila Logan, RN, MSN

I have to see you, xoxo, S

October 14:

From: Sheila Logan, RN, MSN

Where are you? I've been paging you? S

October 18:
From: Sheila Logan, RN, MSN
Tim—call me! S

His replies grew more distant and then angry as October wove itself into November.

November 2:
From: Timothy Merrick, MD
Please stop. I'll call you when I can. T

November 4:
From: Timothy Merrick, MD
Do not page me again. I mean it. T

November 8
From: Timothy Merrick, MD
You know how I feel about you. The timing right now just isn't good. Please bear with me. Don't worry. Sending love. T

And then she stumbled into the last emails they'd shared in November, right after the Hart shooting.

November 12:
From: Sheila Logan, RN, MSN
It was wonderful to see you in our debriefing today. Wish you could have stayed a bit longer. I miss you, Tim. I need to see you. S

Tim seemed to be having none of it.

November 16:
From Timothy Merrick, MD

Please stop emailing, calling and paging me! You know that I have to deal with things at home. I hope that we can pick back up, but not if you keep this harassment up. T

That was Tim's last email to Sheila, but she wasn't giving up so easily.

November 17:

From: Sheila Logan, RN, MSN

Do NOT ignore me. Remember, I am pregnant, and I just want to be with you, but I won't hesitate to ruin you if you fail to respond. I don't want to go to Administration or the medical board and say you've forced yourself on me, but I will if I have to. Just call me.

He must have called her and smoothed things over, because her next emails were conciliatory.

November 19:

I love you—this will be fine. S

Sheila sent her final email two days before Thanksgiving, the last Tuesday in November.

November: 23

I'll see you tonight and we can talk. I'm leaving tomorrow morning and can be back by Saturday. Wish you could come with me. Next Thanksgiving, we'll be together. I love you! xoxo S

Jessie read the email again. Sheila planned to see Tim right before she left for Ohio. If she had, Tim Merrick just might have been the last person to see her alive. Which made him a prime suspect. Jessie let her breath out in a long, slow arc.

Lost in the emails and her own thoughts, Jessie missed the first soft raps on the door, but a succession of hard knocks and an insistent jiggle on the doorknob snapped her to attention. She turned the computer screen toward the wall, smoothed her hair and opened the door.

"I've been looking everywhere for you," Kate said, her face drawn into a scowl.

"I was busy," Jessie answered. "Your class is over?"

"Yup, same old stuff. I just have to practice documenting."

"Good. Why don't you find something to do? I'll be done shortly."

Kate eyed the computer and extra chair. "Can I just wait here?"

"No," Jessie said a little too quickly, beads of sweat collecting on her forehead. She didn't want anyone seeing what she'd been looking at. "Have a cup of coffee in the lounge, and then go to the non-acute side and let me know if you need help."

Kate's hand rested on the doorknob. "Okay," she said, her eyes scanning the room.

As soon as she was gone, Jessie took one last look at the emails and logged out. She reached for the emails she'd printed and stood, ready to head back out, when the box of notebooks and ledgers caught her eye. She pulled out a wad of the papers, before pushing the box back under Donna's desk with her foot. She took the time to lock the door before stopping to store the documents in her locker for safekeeping. She'd have a look later.

She found Donna to return the key, explained what papers she'd taken and took the change-of-shift report. Before she could even start her rounds, the intercom blasted. "Jessie Novak to the front desk." She mumbled to herself and headed through the waiting room to the ER entrance, expecting an angry patient or relative.

Instead, she saw a tall woman, her arms crossed tight across her chest, her high-heeled foot tapping angrily on the tile floor. She turned and scowled as Jessie approached. "Are you the person in charge?"

Jessie crossed her own arms and raised a brow. "I'm the nurse in charge. Can I help you?" She spoke slowly, a hint of exasperation in her voice.

The woman dropped her arms and sighed noisily. "I'd like you to page someone for me."

Gimme a break! Jessie wanted to say, but she caught herself. "And who is that?"

"Dr. Merrick." She emphasized the word *doctor* as if Jessie might be impressed.

"I only page him for traumas. You can use one of the hospital phones and ask the operator to page him." Jessie turned away.

"I'm his wife," the woman added quickly.

Jessie turned back and noticed that Mrs. Merrick looked a little like Sheila—blonde, though not as brassy a shade, tall, thin, perfectly colored lips set in a hard line. A cashmere coat was belted, showing off her slim waist. She was one of those women whose age you never really know—somewhere between forty and sixty—a recipient of pricey procedures designed to keep her skin taut, her age a secret.

She wondered if Sam had been in touch with her and that was the reason for this visit. But Jessie didn't care. She wasn't paging Tim, or getting involved in his drama. She nodded toward the clerk in reception. "They can page him for you. You can tell them I said it's okay."

"And who are you?" she replied, her voice shrill. It was no wonder that Tim Merrick cheated.

"Jessie Novak," she said. "The nurse in charge." She turned and swiped her ID against the reader as the woman called after her.

"But…"

CHAPTER 18

Jessie considered, for only a millisecond, sending a text to Tim to warn him that he had a visitor. But, considering that she'd just read an email indicating Sheila had planned to see him right before she disappeared, Jessie knew she needed to steer clear of him. Instead, she went in search of Kate, who seemed to have vanished. She wasn't on the non-acute side, or in any of the patient areas, and when Jessie cut through the back hallway to have her paged, she saw her standing there looking a little lost.

"What are you doing back here?" Jessie called, trying to remember her pledge to be kind.

Kate seemed to jump. "I… I wanted to go over my notes from that last class. I thought I could use a computer in one of these offices and practice."

"You can use a computer in the lounge. Please don't wander into offices. And this one," she pointed to Sheila's office door, "has been locked by the police. None of us are allowed in. Understand?" She hoped no one had noticed that she'd used Donna's key to let Mrs. Logan in.

Kate's eyes blinked and she puffed out her lips. "I'm sorry. I just want to do a good job, and I know that, right now at least, I'm more hindrance than help. I didn't know the police had it locked. I guess I didn't realize that it was part of their investigation. I thought if I could practice in a quiet place…" She clicked her pen nervously. "I wanted to make a private call, too," she added suddenly. "A friend. Seems I never get the time to call him."

"Try the lounge," Jessie said. "That's as quiet a place as you're going to find here."

"Okay," she said softly, hanging her head limply, clearly looking for sympathy.

"It's almost four. Your shift is over. Just go home, and we'll start fresh on Monday. Okay?"

Kate nodded and walked away, her back stooped, her shoulders hunched. Jessie rolled her eyes and headed back to her locker to retrieve the emails and documents she'd secured there. She slipped into Donna's office, leaving the door open this time so that she could hear the loudspeaker. She was just sinking into Donna's chair when Sam appeared in the doorway.

"There you are," he said. "I've been looking for you."

Jessie slid the emails and documents under Donna's blotter and swiveled the chair toward Sam. "What is it?" she asked.

"Looking for Tim Merrick. Thought you might know where he is."

Jessie couldn't help herself. She started to laugh, a low but impossible-to-hide-with-a-cough kind of chuckle. "Sorry, it's just that everyone's looking for Tim this evening."

"Everyone?"

"Well, you and his wife. I'm glad you told me he's married. She was spitting fire."

"Did she find him?" Sam pulled over a chair with his foot and plunked down with a sigh.

"I have no idea. She wanted me to page him. I told her to ask the clerk out front."

"I'm still trying to catch up with him. He is one elusive guy. I think we're just going to have to bring him in."

He's more elusive than you know. "Is he a suspect?"

"He's definitely a person of interest. Ralph had a look at Sheila's apartment, and it's been ransacked alright. Computer's gone, IDs. Her desk drawers were pulled out and papers were scattered everywhere. Quite a mess. Someone was in a hurry."

"So, it was a robbery?" If it was, that would likely exclude Tim. He was no robber. He was no killer either, she thought, despite that email.

"Don't think so. They left her jewelry, a fifty-inch flat-screen TV, credit cards, and a roll of bills in plain sight. They were looking for something else."

"Any ideas?"

"Some. We've got our warrants, but Verizon and her banks will take their time getting information to us. But we have possession of her work computer, and luckily, she left lots of personal stuff there. Her emails might be the key." He rubbed the back of his neck as if working out a kink. "Anyway, it seems Miss Logan and Dr. Merrick were deep into a relationship. In the emails at least, she seemed to be threatening him. He was making promises he probably couldn't keep."

Jessie tried to act surprised, to pretend that she hadn't just read those same emails. "Really?"

Sam leaned back in the chair. "Really. So, we need to speak with him."

"You checked his office?"

"I did. I left a message with the secretary there. I also checked the OR, the ICU and now, here I am. Still coming up empty. Have you seen him?"

She shook her head. "No. Come to think of it, I last saw him two days ago when you were here to speak with Donna."

Sam ran his hand across his forehead as if he could ease the lines that had settled there.

"I can see if he's on call tonight. That would mean that he's here somewhere." She turned back to the computer and searched for the surgical schedule. "Sorry, looks like he was last on call two days ago. He's probably gone home."

"You said his wife was looking for him. He's probably not there. Could we page him to the ER?"

Jessie wrinkled her mouth. "I don't want to do that. It's sneaky, and just for the record, it's hard to imagine him being involved in this. He's a royal pain, but he's not a killer. He's devoted his life to saving lives. You don't really think he had anything to do with this, do you?"

He shrugged. "The best of men have been known to commit the worst of crimes. I'm not saying he did this—I am saying I want to speak to him, and he seems to be avoiding me."

"Why don't you see if his wife is still here? She was out front not too long ago."

Sam stood. "What does she look like?"

Jessie laughed. "Like she doesn't belong here. You'll spot her right away if she's there."

Sam smiled. "Well, that's a description for the books, huh? Hey, before I forget, today is one of the older detectives' last day with the department. He's retired as of midnight. We're going to take him to Foley's tonight. You should come."

"I can socialize with you guys?" she asked in her most sarcastic tone.

"Yes, Jessie. And you'll be back to work with us soon. Maybe sooner than you think. We probably need help going through those emails, to be sure we don't miss anything. So, what do you say? I think everyone would like to see you there." He smiled slyly.

"I'm finally off tomorrow and Sunday, so I accept." She stood and walked him to the door. "See you later, Sam."

The evening was quiet: no traumas, no sign of Tim Merrick or his wife, no drama, nothing much going on in the ER, leaving Jessie time to scroll through Sheila's emails. They mostly seemed pretty benign except for those between her and Tim, and the puzzling emails about ER follow-up services and equipment requests which the ER didn't provide. This was likely one of those phishing scams to see if they could lure someone in, and not worth another minute of Jessie's time.

At eleven o'clock, she logged out of Donna's computer, gave report to the night charge nurse, and picked up the emails and documents she'd taken from the box of notebooks. She didn't want to leave them here over the weekend, and she didn't want anyone to catch sight of them at Foley's. She rolled them, secured them with an elastic, and slid them into a corner of her backpack. Satisfied that the papers were safe, she pulled on her coat and slipped the backpack over her shoulder.

By eleven thirty, armed with fresh lipstick, eyeliner and finger-combed hair, she was on her way. The streets were quiet for a Friday night, but once she pulled onto East Berkley, the street was packed, cars parked nose to fender, and people were huddled outside, feet shuffling while they smoked, their breath coming out in frosty plumes.

Jessie slipped through the group on the sidewalk and headed inside, trying to peer above the crowds. But at only five foot three, her view included shoulders and chests, and no people that she could identify. She passed into the back of the bar where, at this hour, the serious drinkers and partiers were gathered. Jessie squeezed in between the revelers and caught Sam's eye.

"Hey," he shouted, barely audible above the clamor, "I have a glass of wine for you." He raised the full glass high, the contents shimmering in the dim light. Jessie smiled and watched as he made his way toward her. Planting a chaste kiss on her cheek, he passed her the glass and tapped his bottle of beer against it. "To better days, Jessie."

She smiled, shrugging her backpack off before dropping it to the floor. "To better days indeed," she whispered, her foot sliding the backpack under a chair. She turned to get a better look, to see if she knew anyone here, and her eyes opened wide.

What was she *doing here?*

CHAPTER 19

Kate Wagner, in a tight black dress showing off curves that scrubs never would, stood by the bar. She shimmered, the dim overhead lights picking up on the violet flecks in her eyes. One hand held a drink, a shot glass filled with an amber-colored liquid. *Whiskey?* She hadn't seemed the type. She tossed back her honey-colored hair and turned, her gaze landing on Jessie.

Too late to look away, or try to ignore her, Jessie offered a half-smile and watched as Kate moved toward her. "I'm surprised to see you here," Jessie said.

"I decided if I want to fit in, I need to try harder, so here I am." She smiled, her eyes scanning the crowd behind Jessie.

"Did you reach your friend?" Jessie asked, trying to figure out if she meant to meet a boyfriend here. Not that it should matter, but…

"Yes, I did. Thanks." She smiled sweetly and tugged at her dress. "Ahh, there he is." She raised a hand and waved.

"Your friend?" Jessie turned and craned her neck.

"No. *Your* friend, Sam, the handsome one."

And suddenly his hand was on Jessie's shoulder, but his eyes were planted firmly on Kate. "I'm Sam Dallas," he said, his voice smooth as silk. He offered his hand and Kate took it, sweeping her gaze demurely down, a faint smile on her lips.

"It's nice to finally really meet you, Sam Dallas. I've heard so much about you, and of course I've seen you in the ER." Her voice was soft, the distinctive southern accent more obvious.

Sam leaned in closer and Jessie smirked. Kate was obviously playing him, but why did Jessie care? She reminded herself that she and Sam were just friends now, and if he wanted to fall for Kate, that was his business. But as she watched Sam guide Kate to a booth in the back, a sting of jealousy swept right through her.

She turned away, her eyes scanning the bar in search of anyone she might know, when she noticed that a man at the bar was looking right at her, almost through her. She looked back quickly to see if someone else had his gaze, but the crowd was absorbed in their own conversations and laughter. She turned back. His gaze was fixed firmly on her, almost as though he was studying her, his eyes narrowed and unblinking. Did she know him? He was ordinary-looking. Average height, average looks, a puffy jacket still zipped tight, nothing remarkable about him, and maybe she did know him—a policeman, maybe? But why was he looking at her so intently? She stood a little straighter and stared right back, sweeping away the chill that had run along her spine.

"Hey, Jessie, you okay?" a familiar patrolman asked, blocking her view of the man at the bar.

She smiled easily and tossed her hair back. "I am," she said, glad for the distraction. He draped his arm over her shoulder and that slight movement allowed her a full view of the bar once again. But the man had disappeared. Jessie twisted to see if he had moved, but he was nowhere to be seen. He was gone, and Jessie huffed out a sigh. She'd probably only imagined that he was watching *her.*

"Let's go find everyone, shall we?" the patrolman said, taking her hand as he led her through the maze to a smaller crowd of patrolmen and detectives, some of whom she recognized from the ER or headquarters. She took a deep, steadying breath and smiled.

"Good to see everyone," she said, raising her glass in a mock toast. And, without missing a beat, they smiled in turn; a few drew their arms around her, while others offered to buy her next drink. Things seemed to have moved on, and it was probably because of Danny Coyle's shooting. Her role in the ER that night had turned the tide. She slid into an empty spot in a booth, and the toasts and roasts began, with a smattering of "retired cop" jokes. One of them pulled out a mug for the retiree. *Retired cop. Time for arrest.*

The retiree laughed heartily, tapping his glass against everyone else's until finally, he stood, banging his fist on the table to get their attention. "I can't thank you all enough for the education and friendship you've provided me with these last many years. And now, I look forward to sleeping late, enjoying life, and forgetting all of your damn names." He raised his glass. "Which I probably will anyway after a few more of these." They all guffawed at that one, slapping his back, serving him more drinks than he could ever consume, and the hours flew.

As the crowd thinned, Jessie realized that Sam and Kate were nowhere to be seen, and the sting of jealousy she'd felt earlier blossomed into a full-fledged throbbing pain in the middle of her chest. She looked around. Couples were forming, men were planting kisses on girlfriends' lips, and people were heading out. A wave of envy filled Jessie. She still longed to have that for herself—a hand to hold, a mouth to kiss. She inhaled deeply. It wasn't going to happen tonight. Her eyes scanned the floor for her backpack. Darn. Where had she left it? A bead of sweat trickled along her forehead.

"Are you looking for this?" a familiar-looking man asked, holding up her backpack.

"Thank you," she said, reaching for it. "I thought I left it under this seat."

"Well, you've got it now," he said, backing away.

And as he moved further back, she realized that he'd been the one watching her earlier by the bar. She gripped her backpack. "Hey," she began, but before she could ask if she knew him, he was gone once again.

She slid through the group of hangers-on by the door and hurried to her car. As she pulled onto K Street, she saw that the houses were locked up tight, lights out and people likely long asleep. The streetlight by her house had been fixed, but the bulb was one of those new low-watt energy savers that did little to illuminate the night. And with fresh clouds and little moonlight, the street was eerie as ever. Jessie retrieved her backpack, locked her car and jogged to her front door, acutely aware of every shadow that hovered in the tiny spaces between the houses. At her own front door, she stopped, her fingers fumbling with her keys, and it was then she heard it.

Footsteps, the unmistakable sound of hurried footsteps breaking the night's silence, coming toward her.

CHAPTER 20

Her keys slipped from her fingers, landing with a clang on the stoop. She froze. The footsteps stopped. Jessie reached for the key ring, slid the key into the lock, and in one swift move, pulled the door shut behind her. She took the stairs two at a time, let herself into her own apartment, slid the lock into place, and let out a long, slow breath of relief. She peered through the blinds, and only when she was certain that the street was empty, did she drop her bag and turn on the lights.

A killer had stalked her not so long ago, and that had made her a paranoid sort, jumping at every noise, peering into the darkness, imagining a man at the bar watching her. But for now, the troubling coincidence, if that's what it was, of two nurses murdered in the same way, sent shivers along her skin. She rubbed the tension from her neck, peeled off her scrubs and crawled into bed, grateful for the quiet and the next two days off. She could catch up on sleep, have a look at Sheila's emails, google Mary Stewart, and maybe, just maybe call that woman who claimed to be her mother. With her weekend plans set, Jessie drifted easily into a blissful sleep.

Day 7—Saturday

It was the stark, bright glare of daylight pouring in through her window that nudged her awake. She pulled the sheets over her eyes. Why hadn't she closed the blinds in here? She chuckled to herself. Probably the same reason she hadn't washed her face or brushed her teeth. Too darn tired. She reached for her phone—ten thirty. She sat up and stretched. A run was the perfect way to start her weekend off.

She stood and peered outside, her shoulders and her spirit drooping at the sight. What she'd assumed was the sun lighting up her room was actually the bright, white dazzle of snow. Lots of it. The streets were quiet, not a plow or shovel in sight. It was Saturday. No one was in a hurry to clear the streets this morning. Darn. Not that she had any plans, but on a full weekend off from work, she liked to get outside. Even in the winter she craved escape from the tiny apartment she called home.

She clicked the TV on, set the coffee maker to brew, and stepped into the shower, the soapy water splashing over her, and by the time she stepped out, she was invigorated enough to appreciate the forced quiet the snow imposed. She tugged her wet hair into a knot at her neck, pulled on sweats, poured a cup of strong coffee, and curled up on the couch. The news anchor reported that the snow was expected to continue through most of the day. She sighed. She'd hoped that, by afternoon, the streets would be cleared, the sky would be bright, and she could get out. But it seemed that was not to be today. Undeterred, she reached for her backpack. She could at least start looking into the mystery of Sheila Logan's death.

She fished through the bag, her fingers searching for the emails she'd printed and the documents she'd taken to read, but they seemed to have disappeared. Finally, she stood and dumped the bag out, watching as her IDs, makeup case, stethoscope, sweater, gum wrappers, pens and work notebook fell to the floor. She bent to the mess. *Where were they?* She peered into the bag, scrutinizing every nook and cranny, but the papers were gone. The color drained from her face and she slumped back onto the couch, praying that Sam Dallas didn't have them.

It was the sudden jingle of her phone that suspended her fear that Sam had the papers. If he did, he'd be plenty angry. She'd defied his orders to stay out of Sheila's murder investigation, not to mention obstructing that same investigation by holding onto what she assumed were suspicious documents. She blew out a long stream of air and picked up her phone, the number only vaguely familiar. "Hello," she said, wondering who was on the other end, but there was only silence. "Hello," she said again, the irritation in her voice unmistakable.

"It's me," a woman said softly. "Angela Novak. I saw your number in my missed calls. Is this you, Jessie?"

There was an almost desperate pleading in her voice, not so different from the melancholy tone in Mrs. Logan's. Maybe she should give this woman a chance. She didn't have anything to lose.

"It's me," Jessie said, mirroring the other woman's words. "I... I called you yesterday. I didn't leave a message. I wasn't sure what to say."

"I'm so glad you called. Can we meet somewhere, maybe get lunch?"

Jessie's eyes were drawn to the window and the swirling snow just outside. "I don't know. Unless the snow stops, and they plow the streets, I don't think anything will be open."

Angela laughed nervously. "This is Boston. If my memory serves me, the streets and shops and bars will be open in an hour or two. What do you say? We could meet at L Street. They'll be open for sure, and from there, maybe we can find a place to eat."

Jessie hesitated a beat too long, trying to weigh her options. She knew that she should speak with Angela, to learn the truth, whatever it turned out to be. But today, she had so much on her mind. Sheila Logan—whom she'd not liked but had never wished dead, and this woman, whom she'd always assumed she'd despised, not caring if she was dead or alive. She smoothed the loose ends of her hair. Her feelings said far more about her than they did about either Sheila Logan or Angela Novak. She didn't want to be that girl—consumed with anger about things that were over and done. That kind of misery could ruin a life.

"Are you there?" Angela asked.

Jessie had somehow forgotten that she still held the phone tightly to her ear. "Sorry," she said hurriedly. "I was just thinking. And yes—I'll meet you at one. You're right. L Street will be open by then."

"Oh, Jessie," Angela said. "Thank you. I'll be there."

The soft click let Jessie know the call was over. She sat back and sipped her coffee, her mind on the papers again, trying to work out if she could have lost them. She shook her head and then it dawned on her. *Her car.* Of course. She always threw her backpack haphazardly onto the floor. The papers were there. She was suddenly sure of it. Satisfied that she'd at least solved that mystery, she headed down to check on Rufus. She'd rapped on his door only once when he pulled it open.

"My favorite neighbor," he said, pulling the door wide. "I guess you saw the snow?"

"I did." She grimaced. "I don't know about you, but I'm about ready for spring."

He smiled. "This means you have time for tea, I'm guessing."

She followed him to the kitchen, past the growing piles of newspapers and things he'd saved. She wanted to comment on how uncluttered they'd made it just months ago, but she held her tongue. As long as his home was safe, it was okay. These were his memories, not hers. She reached into his cabinet and took down two cups while he set the water to boil. "No muffins today, I'm afraid," she said.

"Not to worry. I have leftover donuts. Just from yesterday, so they're not stale yet."

Jessie laughed. She loved the rules he lived by—milk was still good beyond its expiration date as long as the smell wasn't too pungent; wilted lettuce and bruised apples were best because they were easier to chew, and bread, well, bread could last weeks. That mold was penicillin in the making. "Aged food," he called it, was like fine wine or good men—better with a little bit of time under the belt.

She slid into a chair while Rufus set out a plate of donuts, the glaze long melted into the dough, and poured the tea. He sat with a heavy sigh, his knees creaking. "My bones," he said, "aren't what they used to be. Wish they'd quiet down."

Jessie chose a chocolate donut and bit into it. It might be a little stale, but it was still a donut, and any day that started with donuts was bound to be good. "Delicious," she said, tapping her teacup against his.

Rufus smiled, his hand curling around a donut with congealed lemon stuck to the side. "I'm glad you didn't choose the lemon," he said, licking his fingers, "it's my personal favorite."

"No worries there, Rufus, I'll always leave the lemon for you."

"Ahh," he said. "I knew we'd be good friends, you and me. So, what are you up to today?" A tiny drop of lemon glaze clung to his lower lip.

"I'm going to meet that woman at L Street."

"The woman who said she knew your father? Well, that's good news, isn't it? I hope she has something happy to tell you."

Jessie licked the last of the chocolate from her fingers. "I hope so, too," she said, standing to clear the table. "And I should get going, get a start on my day." She rinsed her cup and placed it in the drainer to dry. "Are you all set? Need anything? I could stop by the supermarket on the way home if you do."

Rufus leaned back, his teacup in hand. "I'm all set. I knew the snow was coming, so I picked up a few essentials yesterday. The donuts were part of my storm prep."

Jessie laughed. "You are definitely my kind of man, Rufus Buchanan. You have a knack for knowing what matters."

*

Upstairs, she pulled on jeans, a heavy sweater, a jacket and snow boots. First order of business was to get to her car and make sure the papers were there. She grabbed the shovel from the front porch. The owner had hired someone to shovel but he was invariably late, probably on purpose because someone else usually gave in and shoveled first. And she'd noticed that someone was often Rufus. She was determined to beat him to it today.

Mercifully, the snow was light and fluffy, and with the houses packed so tightly together, it meant a short sidewalk to clear. Within minutes, hand on hip, Jessie surveyed her work. A sharp rap on the front window caught her attention and she looked up to see Rufus wagging his finger at her. His voice was muffled through the heavy glass, but she could read his lips enough to understand that he was telling her the shoveling was his job. She wagged her finger back and smiled. "Mine now," she called. "You rest."

She replaced the shovel on the front porch, shoved her mittened hands into her pockets, checking to be sure she had her car keys, and headed up the block to look in her car. She'd parked only a block away, and though she had to trudge over mostly unshoveled sidewalks, she made it to her car quickly. She cleared off the windows and slipped inside, scanning the front and then the back seats, but aside from candy wrappers, empty cans of Diet Coke, a hairbrush and a long-forgotten sweater, there was nothing there.

Undaunted, she slid her hands under the seats, but the only paper her fingers retrieved were a couple of old parking tickets. She checked her glove box, which held only her car registration, the owner's manual and a wad of paper napkins. She slammed her hand hard against the steering wheel and looked again, and then again, but the papers were nowhere to be found.

She was about to curse out loud when she remembered. *Foley's.* Of course! She'd dropped her bag onto the floor and under a chair.

It had been dark and crowded and noisy. The papers had likely slipped out and were still there, sitting in a sticky pool of old beer. She silently thanked God that there was no patient information in the papers. Even without Sheila, a second HIPAA violation would cost Jessie her job. She breathed a sigh of relief as she locked her car and trudged home, where she grabbed her cell phone and googled the number for Foley's.

A man answered on the first ring, and Jessie explained that she'd lost a bunch of papers. She asked him to have a look, and she heard the soft thud as he placed the phone down and the squeak of chairs being moved. It seemed forever before he picked up the phone, cleared his throat and announced that there was nothing there.

"Okay, will you let me know if someone finds them?"

He must have sensed the disappointment in her voice. "Don't worry," he said. "Give me your number. If you left them here, they'll turn up. I'll call you if they do."

"Thank you," Jessie said before reciting her number. "Call me anytime."

"I will."

And that was it. He'd hung up. Jessie stared at the phone. She could print out the emails again, and if anyone other than Sam's team found the other documents, they'd probably just throw them out. Without the background, those papers were meaningless. The more she thought about it, the more likely it seemed that someone had just tossed them into the trash. She had to stop worrying.

She had more to think about today. She'd been so consumed with Sheila Logan's murder, she'd lost sight of the woman who should have mattered most. She had to focus on her, on the woman who just might be her mother.

She checked her watch, slipped into a heavy jacket, pulled a woolen cap over her curls, wound a scarf around her neck, and headed out to L Street, wondering if her life was about to change.

CHAPTER 21

The snow had stopped by the time Jessie stepped outside, but the frigid air stung her skin as swiftly as an unexpected slap. She pulled her cap down and her scarf up, shoving her hands deep into her pockets and hunching her shoulders against the wind as she headed toward the bar. *Would this winter never end?*

At L Street, she stamped her feet against the mat to clear the snow from her boots and pulled the door open wide, squinting against the dark interior after the stark-white glare of snow. She brushed the snow from her coat, pulled off her cap and swung her head to loosen her knot of curls and looked around. Aside from two older men huddled at the end of the bar, the place was empty. She slid onto a stool at the other end of the bar and pulled out her phone to check for messages. But the screen was empty. The weather was likely holding Angela up. Her thoughts had drifted to the missing papers again when the bartender, a plump older man with a spray of thinning white hair, put a napkin in front of her.

"What can I get ya?" he asked.

She looked up. "Umm, this is probably a stupid question, but do you have hot chocolate?"

Thick white eyebrows went straight up, and he laughed. "Well, it's not the stupidest question I've ever heard, but the answer is no."

"Coffee?"

"That, I've got. No fancy brews, if that's what you're after."

"Nope. Strong and black for me."

He poured a cup and placed it in front of her. "Planning on starting a tab for your wild afternoon?"

Jessie laughed. "I do, and I might order a beer later. Depends on how things go."

"Ahh, a gentleman friend then?"

She shook her head. "A lady."

He raised a questioning brow.

"My mother," she said wryly, realizing that was the first time she'd said those two words out loud without a lie following them.

The bartender nodded as the door swung open, a gust of cold air announcing someone's arrival. Jessie turned to see Angela in the entrance. "Looks like she's here," he said, polishing the bar with a wet towel. His voice carried to Angela, who dipped her head and smiled, her dimples almost dancing at the corners of her mouth.

If the bartender noted the resemblance and assumed that Angela was her mother... well, maybe.

"Hey," Jessie said, scooting from her stool. "How about if we sit up there, away from the door? We'll have more privacy there," she added with a sideways glance toward the bartender.

"I'll just follow you," Angela replied, clutching a manila envelope tightly in her hand.

They found a table in the back and slid onto chairs facing each other. The bartender appeared, wiping his hands on the towel that hung from his belt. "What'll ya have?" he asked.

Angela glanced at Jessie's coffee cup. "I'll have what she's having."

"Another black coffee coming up." He shook his head. "Looks like this is gonna be a slow day," he mumbled as he walked away.

Jessie hid her laughter behind her hand. "We'll have to tip him well, I think." She focused her eyes on the woman across from her and had to admit, they looked enough alike to really be mother and daughter. "So, why...?" she started to ask, but paused to allow the bartender to set Angela's coffee down. "Why now?" she asked when they were alone. "Why now, after all these years?"

The woman laid the envelope on the table and folded her hands. "Does this mean you believe me?"

"No, it means that if you are my mother, why wait twenty-five years and then just show up?"

"That's a long story, Jessie."

"I've got all day." She forced a weak smile and took a sip of her coffee, wincing when it scorched her tongue.

"Are you okay?"

"Yes. Just tell me why I should believe you. And start at the beginning, please."

Angela shrugged out of her coat, leaned forward and rested her elbows on the table. "Well, the beginning is you." She slid the envelope across the table. "You can have a look if you'd like while I speak."

Jessie reached out and ran her fingers along the clasp before shaking her head. "Just tell me what you came to say. Then I'll decide if I'm interested in looking at this."

Angela inhaled deeply and began. "You were born at two a.m. on October 6, 1993 in the Emerson Hospital in Concord."

"I know that."

"Well, as I told you before, we didn't live in that upscale town. I was working there when I went into labor. Your dad was a trucker. He didn't get back for a full day after you were born, but to tell you the truth, I barely noticed that he wasn't there. I was in love with you from the moment you arrived, all wrinkly skin, full, pouty lips, clear, beautiful eyes. You were the most beautiful baby in the world, and I loved you more than I'd ever thought possible. You were mine, my perfect baby."

"If I was all that, why did you leave me?"

Angela ran her fingers through her thick hair. "It's complicated, but I didn't leave you, Jessie. You have to believe that. Your father threw me out."

Jessie crossed her arms. The tangled thread of sadness and confusion that she felt finally wound itself into a familiar knot of anger settling in her gut. "Really? He threw you out because he was so eager to raise a baby alone?" She shook her head in disbelief. "That's a little hard to swallow. Once you left us, I was raised by babysitters and neighbors while my father worked to keep a roof over our heads. What loving mother would do that?"

"Oh, God, Jessie, please listen to me. I loved you then. I love you now. And this is so hard to say, but when you were about two and a half, I got pregnant again. With another man's baby." Her eyes glistened with the tears that hovered there. "I made a mistake, a terrible mistake. Your father was gone so often, and this man was so good to you and me, fixing things, shoveling. I didn't mean for it to happen, but it just did. I thought of having an abortion, but I couldn't do it." She sighed.

"I couldn't pass the baby off as your father's either. We hadn't been together in that way for months. I had to tell him, but I'd been sure he'd forgive me, that he'd see I'd made a terrible mistake, and we'd just move past it." Tears began to track along her cheeks, and she used a napkin to wipe them away. "But instead, he threw me out, threw my clothes and everything into the street. It was the worst day of my life." She paused, her lip quivering, her eyes sweeping down, her lashes wet with tears.

Jessie cleared her throat. "Why not hire a lawyer? Try to get custody of me?"

"I saw a lawyer. But it was 1996. Infidelity was still a disgrace. Having another man's baby while married was a big deal then, the stuff of soap operas. I was painted as a bad mother, a whore who was sleeping around on her hard-working husband. The judge didn't even listen to my side. He granted the divorce, gave your father physical custody, refused to provide me with any alimony and advised us to work out visitation. But your father simply refused. He said I could take him back to court. By that time, I was six months pregnant, and broke." She stifled a sob. "What could I do?"

Jessie remembered her father's anger starting about that time. He'd swept away all memories of her mother—photos, clothes, jewelry, all of it, just as she said. He'd sold whatever was left, wiping the house clean of any hint of her. It was as though she'd never been there at all. She began to pick at her fingernails. "Even if I were to believe you, why wouldn't you have tried to see me all those years?"

"I did," Angela said. "I called and went to the house again and again. But your father refused to let me in. Finally, I went there one day when I knew you were both out, and I took what was left—my photo albums, your baby clothes and your birth certificate. And then I moved to Austin, Texas. My sister lived there, and she said I could stay with her until I was back on my feet."

Angela tapped her fingers nervously on the table and Jessie noticed her ragged, messy fingernails. She looked at her own and wondered if she'd inherited that habit. "So, you moved to Texas and forgot all about me. Is that what happened?"

"No, I sent you cards and letters that I'm sure your father never gave you. I called, too. I left telephone messages, and when you joined Facebook, I followed you there. I knew you were in nursing school and I came up for your graduation. I was about to approach you when your father caught sight of me. He shooed me away with his hand and an angry glare."

"Why didn't you say anything? Why didn't you just come up to me?" Jessie asked, her voice a whisper.

"Your father would have made a scene. He hadn't forgiven me. I was sure of that, and I had no idea what he'd told you, but I knew that a public event was not the place to find out. So, I left—in tears, but I left. My heart was broken once again."

Jessie felt a gnawing emptiness in the pit of her stomach, remembering Mrs. Logan and her palpable love for her daughter. Was Angela trying to create a relationship like that? *Too little, too late,* she thought; *she should have tried harder.* "What about the baby? Do I have a sister, a brother?"

Angela smiled wanly. "Yes," she said. "You have a sister, a half-sister."

Jessie's breath caught in her throat, her hands gripping the table. *A sister? I have a sister?*

CHAPTER 22

Jessie's heart pounded in her chest. "Were you at least a good mother to her?" she asked, her voice cracking.

"I did the best thing I could for her. I gave her up for adoption. I wanted her to have a better life than I could provide. She went to a family who'd badly wanted a baby, but they insisted on a closed adoption, which meant I had no access to her information, that I gave up all of my rights. But someday, if she chooses, she can find me. I'm still hoping she will…" She dropped her gaze and folded her hands on the table.

A sudden coldness gripped Jessie at her core, and she felt herself stiffen. So, Angela had abandoned not one, but two babies. Her lips tight, she inhaled through flared nostrils.

"I… I'm sorry, Jessie. For all of it. I wish I'd had more courage in those days, to stand up for myself and for you, to raise a baby alone, but I didn't. And I have tried to reach out to you. I know I should have come sooner, but over time, my courage waned. I'm trying to fix that now."

Jessie's stomach churned. Yesterday, she was all alone; today she had… what, exactly? Perhaps the beginnings of a family, if this woman was telling the truth. But she'd been alone so long, she wasn't sure if what Angela said even mattered anymore. She gripped her coffee cup, the heat seeping through to her fingers, chasing away the sudden chill she'd felt. "My father," she said, "died five years ago. Why not reach out then? Why come back now?"

"I didn't know about his death until recently. I never searched the obituaries. It always struck me as morbid, but those stories a few months ago in the *Boston Herald* about a killer coming after you, that had me worried, and I decided it was time. I had to try. I had to give you a chance to know me, to know that I always loved you, and I had to give myself a chance to explain." Her voice cracked. "That's when I finally discovered that your dad had died. I'm sorry about that, too, that you've been alone these last few years."

Jessie nodded. 'Why not approach me when you saw me here in this bar earlier in the week?"

"If you remember, you ran out. I never had a chance. That's why I checked at your house. I thought I'd see you there, but you were so angry, you wouldn't listen."

Jessie set her elbows on the table. "So, you read the *Herald*? You live here, in Boston now?"

She shook her head. "I'm still in Texas, but I read the Boston papers online and I google you too, just to see how you're doing."

"Google, the *Herald*, and Facebook, huh?"

Angela smiled, a full, bright smile, her dimples on display. "So, do you believe me?" she whispered hopefully.

"I don't know," Jessie said, smiling warily. "I'm just not sure. It's a lot to take in, you know?"

A swell of tears filled Angela's eyes and she dabbed at them with her napkin. "I'm sorry for everything, Jessie. No matter what you think, I've always loved you."

Jessie swallowed the heavy lump in her throat and nodded. It was then she noticed the buzz of conversation, the ripple of laughter and the clink of glasses, and she turned to look. The bar was packed, every stool taken. From the corner of her eye, she caught the bartender heading her way. "Okay to just stay here for a while?" she asked Angela. "I'm not sure what else is open."

Angela nodded as the bartender approached their table.

"Ladies," he said, "can I close out your tab?"

"No," Jessie said hurriedly. "I'll have a glass of white wine, and…" She nodded toward Angela. "The same," she added.

He raised a brow. "That's it?"

"For now, but do you know if Sal's is open?"

"It is," he said. "They're delivering today. If you're ordering, I have the number."

"Pizza okay?" Jessie asked.

"Anything is fine," her mother answered, and Jessie realized that was the first time the word *mother* had simply replaced *Angela* in her mind. She smiled warily. She wasn't at all sure she was ready for this. So many doors had closed in her life recently, and now a very unexpected door to family was wide open. If this woman was telling the truth. She called their order in and watched as Angela opened the envelope she'd brought, pulling out a cluster of glossy photos, papers and a handful of tiny trinkets. She spread them out on the table.

"These are some of your baby pictures, and this," she held up a tiny, beaded baby bracelet. "I bought this for you. The beads spell out your name."

Jessie wrapped her hand around the memento, her fingers running over the beads, imagining this wrapped around her wrist long ago. An unfamiliar surge of self-pity filled her chest, and she dropped the bracelet back onto the table. Too many years had passed. She couldn't just accept any of this at face value. Nothing, she'd learned the hard way, was as simple as it seemed at first.

She needed time to think about it all, to absorb everything. A familiar voice broke through her thoughts and her eyes darted through the crowd, half expecting to see Sam, eager to get his opinion. But the voice belonged to a stranger. Sam wasn't there, and wishful thinking wouldn't make him appear.

"Are you okay?" Angela asked, her eyes filled with concern.

But before Jessie could answer, the bartender appeared and slid their glasses onto the table.

Angela raised her glass and tapped it against Jessie's. "To you, Jessie, my daughter, and to more days like this," she said before taking a sip.

"What about those photos?" Jessie asked, suddenly interested in seeing some real proof of Angela's claim. Anyone could buy a bracelet.

Angela pulled her seat next to Jessie's and picked up the first photo. "This," she said laughing, "was your hospital photo. In those days, they took pictures when newborns were hours old. That's why your little face is so scrunched up and your eyes are closed against the flash of light. Even then, you were feisty."

"Was I a lot of trouble?" She'd always wondered if maybe she was an unlovable baby, if that was why her mother had left.

"No, you were the easiest baby. You smiled and cooed at everything. You were perfect. And I was over the moon with love for you. That's why…" She paused and cleared her throat. "That's why I wasn't allowed to see you again. Your father knew that you were my world, and to take that away would destroy me—and for a time, it did."

"This is a little hard to imagine," Jessie said. "I always believed what my father said, that you'd deserted us, that you'd run away because you didn't love us. Maybe I should have asked more questions, but I was a little girl. And you were the one who left."

Their pizza arrived, and over Angela's old photos and older memories, she painted a picture that Jessie hadn't even known she needed to see—a picture of a sweet and much-loved baby, not the image of the unwanted and troubled child that her father had described. She didn't blame him; she was too much like him—quick to anger, quick to judge and quick to strike back.

They nibbled pizza and ordered more wine and went through the photos, each one depicting a story—a day in the park, her baptism, her first Christmas, her first steps. Jessie ran her fingers lovingly over the glossy prints, a rush of hazy memories sweeping into her thoughts—the scent of a lilac perfume, an infectious laugh, a gentle voice, a soft touch.

"I still have that little dress and that blanket," Angela said, pointing to another photo. "I have a lot of your baby things, and more photos. I can bring them next time I come up."

"You're leaving?"

Angela nodded. "Tomorrow morning. I've been here almost a week. I have to get back to work."

"I guess I thought you'd be here longer, that I'd have more time to figure this out, to get to know you." Jessie bit back the unexpected trace of tears that pricked at the backs of her eyes.

Angela slipped from her chair and wrapped her arms tight around Jessie. "I know you still have questions. I'd half hoped you'd run into my arms, but I understand your reluctance. It's good to be careful." She tilted Jessie's chin up with her hand. "But I am your mother, and I do love you. You can't get rid of me now."

She forced a smile. Angela certainly had the photos, the stories and the mementos to back it all up, but Jessie was a born skeptic. She wasn't ready to just accept all of this. She needed reassurance, and she needed Sam to look into it. "It's going to take me some time to get used to you," she said. "To the whole possibility of a mother, and a half-sister out there somewhere."

"Take all the time you need, Jessie. I'll love you, no matter what."

They spent the afternoon at the far end of the bar, Angela sharing bits and pieces of memories and moments—some long forgotten, some hovering at the edges of Jessie's dreams. It was almost six when Angela looked at her watch. "I have an early flight. I should get back to the hotel and pack."

"Already?" Jessie whispered.

Angela tucked a stray hair behind Jessie's ear and slid the envelope with photos into Jessie's bag. "I'll call you tomorrow from the airport. I love you, Jessie. You've given me more this afternoon than I could ever have imagined. Just a few days ago, I thought today would never happen. I was sure I'd be going home broken-hearted, but you've given me back everything I've ever wanted." She gripped Jessie's hand before holding it close to her lips. "I love you, Jessie, and wherever your sister is, I love her too."

When the taxi pulled away from L Street, Jessie hooked her bag over her shoulder, shoved her hands deep into her pockets and dipped her chin into her scarf against the biting wind. There was so much she hadn't asked—was Angela remarried? Were there other children, other relatives?

She was distracted as she trudged through the snow toward her apartment, the streets dark but for the soft glare of the snow, and all quiet except for the crunch of icy slush under her feet and the soft hum of distant traffic. Lost in her thoughts, she was slapped back to reality when she felt a sharp tug on her bag. Instinctively, she pulled back, and turned to see the shadowy shape of a man, a ski mask covering his face, pulling at her bag.

"Let go or I'll shoot," he snarled.

CHAPTER 23

Jessie froze for a split second, the length of time it took for her to see that he had both hands placed firmly on her bag, and she knew that if he had a gun, or a weapon of any kind, he would have pulled it out already. She decided to call his bluff and held tight to her bag, determined not to give up her newly acquired memories without a fight. She screamed then, a loud, piercing shriek that split the silence of the night. Windows opened. A man shouted, "What's going on down there?" Footsteps pounded toward her. She yanked on her bag and held on tight as her assailant ran.

A group of teenagers suddenly surrounded her. One of them peeled off and chased after the would-be purse snatcher.

"Are you okay?" a young girl asked.

"Joey called nine-one-one," another said as they huddled around her.

The boy returned, breathing out rapid plumes of frosty air. "I couldn't catch him," he said, leaning over to catch his breath.

Suddenly, a siren sounded, a crowd forming to see what was going on. The group of teenagers filled them in, regaling them with their own heroic exploits. "Aww, come on," an older man said. "You kids saved her?" He didn't believe a word they said, and Jessie could see their shoulders slump, their heroics dismissed.

She stepped toward them, drawing them in with her arms. "These wonderful kids saved me tonight." She looked right at the man who'd belittled them. 'You should all be grateful that they live here."

The kids smiled and stood a little straighter as a young, fresh-faced patrolman stepped out of his car and took her story and then theirs. "I'll file this for you," he said, "but to tell you the truth, it's not likely we'll ever find him." He glanced again at her ID as he passed it back. "Hey, are you that Jessie Novak? ER nurse at BCH?"

Jessie nodded.

"Are you okay?"

And Jessie realized she *was* okay, that aside from being surprised at the suddenness of the attack, she hadn't been afraid at all. She'd sized up the situation and knew what she had to do. That creep never expected her to fight back, or to scream. He was probably more frightened that he might be caught. She smiled. "I'm fine. Thanks."

"Come on," he said, opening the door, "I'll drive you home."

She shivered and slid inside, the welcome heat of the car wrapping itself around her. She hadn't realized until just then how cold she'd been.

"Can I call anyone for you?" the policeman asked.

Jessie shook her head. "I'm fine. Really."

"I wasn't going to tell you this, but those kids had seen that guy lurking in a doorway by L Street. They thought maybe he was waiting for you."

"Those kids were great, but I think he was waiting for anyone with a bag. I was just in the wrong place at the wrong time." As he pulled up in front of her house, she opened the door and turned to him. "Thanks again," she said. "If I can ever help you, please come and find me in the ER."

He smiled. "My name's Dennis Feeney, and you, Jessie Novak, are everything they said you were."

"Oh, God," she moaned. "Don't believe a word of it." She waved goodbye as she climbed the steps to her house and let herself inside. Upstairs, she locked her door and pulled the photos from her bag, and watched as her cell phone—neglected all afternoon—fell to the floor. She picked it up and saw a flood of voicemails, the first one from Foley's. She sighed. She'd forgotten all about those darn papers and emails, and Sheila Logan's murder.

She slipped out of her coat and gloves and sank onto the couch, tapping the message from Foley's first. She held the phone to her ear and listened as the bartender reported that they hadn't found any of her lost papers, but they'd let her know if someone turned them in. *Fat chance of that happening.*

The next two messages were from Sam. "Please give me a call," he said each time. No information, no urgency in his voice. She'd call him tomorrow. The next message was from the ER, asking if she could work that night. She shook her head and hit delete.

The final message was from Angela Novak. "I love you, Jessie, and I'm so happy that you agreed to see me today. I have so much more to share with you. I just wanted to be sure you know that I've always loved you. Sleep tight, sweetheart." She'd waited her whole life to hear a message like that, and when it came, she wondered if was too good to be true. After all this time, a mother slipping into her life as though she belonged there. Jessie leaned back into the couch and remembered her father's advice—*"if it seems too good to be true, it probably is."*

She peeled off her jeans and sweater and turned the water on in her shower, but before she could step in, she heard someone knocking on her door just as her phone began to buzz. "Who is it?" she shouted as she turned the water off and pulled on sweatpants and a T-shirt.

"It's Sam, Jessie. Open up."

She reached for her phone as she unlocked her door. Sam rushed in, a burst of cold air following him. Jessie shivered. "What's the emergency?" she said icily.

"Dennis, that young patrolman, called me. Are you alright?"

"Of course, I'm alright. It was a purse snatcher, but he was scared off."

"That's not the way I heard it. Dennis said the kids thought he was waiting for you."

"They're kids. They have active imaginations. Trust me, it was a crime of opportunity. He was waiting for the first person who was walking alone. That person happened to be me. End of story." She heaved an exasperated sigh. "I appreciate your concern, I do, but I'm fine." She reached out and swept her photos into the envelope. She wasn't ready to share them just yet.

Sam sank onto the couch. "Okay. I'll leave that alone. For now. But I'm not convinced."

His eyes sparkled in that way Jessie had first noticed, and she forced herself to turn away.

"Did you get my messages?"

"I just got them. I figured I'd call you tomorrow. You didn't say it was an emergency."

"Have a seat," he said, patting the cushion next to him.

And suddenly, she knew. Sam had the papers she'd lost at Foley's. *Damn!* He began to speak, but her mind was on possible excuses, reasons why she had them. She worked in the ER; they were looking into some fuzzy discrepancies in the budget. Well, she was, wasn't she? It wouldn't be a lie. Not really.

"Are you even listening?" Sam asked. "This is important, Jessie."

"I know," she began, "and I probably shouldn't have had them, but—"

"What are you talking about? I'm talking about Sheila Logan."

Me too, she thought, but maybe he didn't know about the papers after all. "What about her? I thought I wasn't allowed to know what was going on?"

"Things change. Tim Merrick is coming in tomorrow to be questioned. With his lawyer."

"On a Sunday?"

"He finally agreed, so we'll take it. I'm betting he chose Sunday because there won't be any people at headquarters. No one to recognize him, and no press hanging around in search of a story on Sunday."

"So, you're focusing on him?"

"We don't have anyone else yet. We just want to speak with him, with his wife, too. But she's harder to get hold of."

"Why are you telling me this? I thought I was a person of interest."

"You *were* a person of interest, in that you're an insider. But you were right. We need you on this case, and I'd like you to be there tomorrow, behind the scenes, to watch. Let me know if we're missing anything."

Jessie sat a little straighter and remembered that last email from Sheila to Tim, indicating that she'd be seeing him right before she left for Ohio. Sam must have seen it by now. "I'll be there. What time?"

"I'll pick you up at eight."

"I can get there on my own."

"I'd rather bring you in the back way, make sure he doesn't see you." He planted a quick kiss on her forehead as he stood to go. "Lock this door behind me, Jessie," he said, making his way out. "Be careful." His intent was clear. She'd just been assaulted, and Sheila Logan and Mary Stewart, both nurses, were dead.

Once he left, she booted up her iPad and googled Mary Stewart, the young nurse from West Virginia who'd been strangled and thrown into a river. The information, including a grainy photo, was scant, and added little more than Sam had shared.

"Mary Stewart," she read, "age twenty-three, a well-respected nurse from Bluebell Creek, West Virginia, had been found floating in the Blackwater River, not far from the town of Thomas, a former coal town that reinvented itself as a tourist destination. Other than a scarf tied tightly around her neck, there'd been no clues, the investigators had announced. She'd worked at a nursing home not far from the river and was a case manager responsible for coordinating Medicare/Medicaid requirements and payments. The case, though open, was more than a year old, the chances of solving it diminishing with each day that passed."

Jessie sighed. The deaths of Mary Stewart and Sheila Logan seemed to be more than coincidence. What had Sam said once? *There are no coincidences in homicide investigations.*

CHAPTER 24

Day 8—Sunday

Jessie slept fitfully, her brain trying to reconcile the new facts of her life. She'd been a motherless child for most of her life, and she'd adjusted, grown a thick skin, learned to navigate life on her own. That hadn't always worked out. And now, at the age of twenty-seven, she had a mother. Or did she? Already, she was having second thoughts, wondering if she could really trust Angela Novak. She scrunched up her pillow once again and curled into herself, willing sleep to come.

At seven a.m., her alarm screeched her awake. She reached out to turn it off just as her phone rang. Wiping the sleep from her eyes, she sat up and grabbed her phone, tapping *accept* to take the call. "I'll be downstairs at eight," she said stonily. "You don't have to remind me."

"What?" a woman's voice said.

"Donna?"

"Yes, who were you expecting?"

"I thought it was Sam. Sorry. What's up? I can't work today, if that's why you're calling."

"No, that's not it. I guess you haven't seen the news or the headlines today."

"Oh, no. What now?"

"The *Globe* and the *Herald* and every television news report has announced that the body found last week is Sheila."

Jessie's jaw went slack. Tim Merrick's appearance at headquarters would be all over the news. She wondered if he'd heard, and if anything would change today. "Did the police release the news?"

"It was her family. They put out a statement late yesterday. They wanted Sheila to be mourned the way she should be, and they hoped someone would come forward now with information that will help catch the killer."

Jessie slipped out of bed and headed for the living room, clicking her TV on and searching for the news. "Have the police said anything?"

"Not yet, but there's a crowd of reporters outside police headquarters. It makes me nervous that we have her emails and papers. I think we have to tell Sam. Thank God they took you off the case, huh?"

Jessie raked her fingers through her curls. "I'm actually back on it. Well, in a limited way, I guess."

"Oh," Donna said, but it was more question than statement.

"I'm not sure what I'll be doing," she said, deciding not to share that she'd been asked to observe Tim's questioning today. "But you're right. I think I'll have to tell Sam about the emails. I printed a few out on Friday and took some budget papers, too. I was going to look at them this weekend. They were in my bag at Foley's and I… I lost them."

She could hear Donna's sharp intake of breath through the line. "Oh, no," she finally murmured.

"I know. I know. I'm sorry. This is all on me. Don't worry."

"Did you call Foley's?"

"I did. They don't have them."

"Oh, no," she said again.

"Listen to me. It will be alright. Those papers, those emails won't mean a thing to anyone else. There aren't any HIPAA violations, at least. I'm the one who screwed up. I'll tell Sam. I'll let him know we just found the box, too. Don't worry. This is my fault, not yours."

"Maybe we should just give him the box and not say anything about the emails. He must have them anyway, and we don't need any trouble."

"I'm going to see him shortly. I'll play it by ear, but don't worry."

"Okay. I won't," Donna said, relief in her voice. "Call me, okay?"

Jessie hung up and sank to the couch, her eyes glued to the news anchor and the picture of Sheila Logan in the corner of the screen. "The body found in the Neponset River last week has been identified as Sheila Logan, the beloved nurse manager of the Boston City Hospital Emergency Room. The staff are reported to be devastated at the news. It had been believed that she'd left on an extended vacation, and news of her unexpected death has hit the tight-knit staff quite hard. A cause of death has yet to be determined, but it is listed as suspicious. The police ask that if you have any information, to please call the number scrolling at the bottom of the screen." And then he was on to the weather. "More snow expected," he said, and Jessie groaned and clicked the television off.

She'd just turned her coffee maker on when her phone rang again. Certain that it was Donna, who'd likely seen the same news report, she hit *accept*. "I know," she said, laughing. "Beloved, right? Where do they get this stuff?"

"Umm, Jessie?"

Jessie's brow furrowed. "Angela? I'm sorry. I thought you were someone else."

"It's okay. I just wanted to let you know my flight leaves in an hour and we'll be boarding in a few minutes. I'll try to come back soon, but I just wanted to say one more time that I love you, Jessie. Thank you for seeing me yesterday. You'll never know just how much it means to me."

Jessie's eyes fogged over with an unexpected blur of tears. "It was nice to meet you, too," she said, still wondering if the story was true, afraid to say more until she knew for sure.

"They're announcing my flight. I have to go. I love you."

The next sound was the dial tone, and Jessie leaned forward, her head in her hands, a silent moan escaping her lips. So much had happened in the last twenty-four hours, but she couldn't allow herself to be distracted. She had to focus on what mattered right now, and that was finding Sheila Logan's killer. She washed her face, slugged back a cup of coffee and pulled on jeans and a sweater as her phone pinged with a text message from Sam.

Change of plans. I'll pick you up in 5 minutes.

Jessie nudged her feet into her boots, still stiff with yesterday's snow, grabbed her jacket and headed outside, where the early-morning air crackled with the cold. Jessie shivered and wrapped her scarf a little tighter. She was bouncing on her feet when she spied Sam's Crown Vic turning onto K Street. She stepped to the street and slid in as soon as he slowed.

"I saw the news," she said. "There are reporters by headquarters."

"Good morning to you, too," he said, glancing quickly her way. "Yeah. The family was tired of waiting. They called the press, who are now all over us. Top story, but at least it's Sunday. People will sleep in, maybe miss it."

"What about Merrick?"

"He's still coming in, but I've told his lawyer to bring him in through the back. I don't want the press seeing him before we've spoken to him." Headquarters was almost hidden behind a group of news vans, their dish satellites pointed skyward, reporters queuing up, microphones in hand, setting up their shots. Sam grunted and swung the car around to the back entrance. "You go in there," he said, pointing to a door. "I'll be right in."

The icy wind hit Jessie again as she hurried to the door, pulling it open and stepping into the building. A uniformed officer approached. "Can I help you?" he asked, his coal-black eyes watching her warily. "This isn't a public entrance."

"I'm with Sam Dallas. He's parking. I'm Jessie Novak," she said, offering her hand and her red police ID.

"Nice to meet you, Jessie. I'm Otis. Sorry for the greeting. The press are coming out of the woodwork."

"I noticed," she said. "They're like a pack of wolves out front."

"There you are," Sam said. "Morning, Otis. Anyone else in yet?"

"Ralph Thompson's here."

"Let's get up there," Sam said, leading the way up the stairs to his office.

"Good morning," Ralph said, glancing at Jessie before catching Sam's eye.

"Who's going to question Merrick?"

"I am. Detective Barnes will assist, and Jessie will watch in the viewing room and let us know if we're missing anything. Any word from Merrick's lawyer?"

"On their way. If you're all set, I'm leaving."

"Okay. On your way out, will you ask Eddie to get the coffee ready?"

Jessie watched him leave before turning to Sam. "Why isn't Ralph involved in the questioning?"

"I need a seasoned detective with me, and Ralph, though great, is still fairly new to homicide, and anyway, he's heading back to Natick to get a clearer idea of what's missing from Sheila's apartment. We know her computer, checkbook, and tax information are missing. But that doesn't make sense. It's not like she was an international financier, so we need to get a closer look."

"Can't you get all that information anyway, once you have a warrant?"

"In the works," he said. "But sometimes things move at a snail's pace." His phone buzzed. "Hey," he answered. "Are they here?" There was a pause while he listened to the caller. "Okay. Give me five minutes and then bring them to the interview room. Get them settled and tell them I'll be right with them." He ended the call. "Let's get you settled too, Jessie."

He led her to the viewing room and clicked the monitor to life. They watched as Tim Merrick, clad in a black wool overcoat, was ushered in, his attorney, carrying a sleek leather briefcase, close on his heels. "Detectives Dallas and Barnes will be with you shortly," the patrolman said as he pulled the door shut.

Tim shrugged out of his overcoat to reveal a deep gray suit, crisp white shirt and a red tie. He swiped a trembling hand across the glistening beads of sweat that dotted his forehead. His eyes darted around the room, searching, she was sure, for the cameras and microphones that would catch every word, every movement, every nuance of the interview. He pulled out a hanky and patted his face and hands. She remembered how anxious she'd felt when she'd been sitting where he was now.

"Doesn't look too good, does he?" Sam asked.

"He's nervous," she replied.

"Or maybe guilty," he said, raising a brow.

CHAPTER 25

A chill hovered in the room, and Jessie pulled her coat in close and leaned forward to watch. On the monitor, Sam and Detective Barnes, an older man with graying hair and a suit as sleekly tailored as Tim's, appeared. There were introductions, and then everyone took a seat and Tim was asked to confirm his name, age, occupation, and place of work. Instead of the hardy, confident tone he struck at work, his voice cracked and broke. He stammered his way through Sam's probing questions, and he slumped in his seat when Sam asked him to describe his relationship with Sheila Logan.

"Well…" And he recited again the story he'd told Jessie. "We parted on amicable terms in, hmm," he said, "must have been September." He nodded as if agreeing with himself.

Detective Barnes raised a brow in mock surprise and slid a sheaf of papers over to Tim. "Really? These emails seem to indicate things were a little more intense and went on a little longer than that." He tapped the paper. "November twenty-third. She'd planned to see you before she left for Ohio. Ring a bell?"

Tim leaned forward, his skin blanching as he recognized the emails. He turned to his attorney, who stood. "A moment?" he asked, picking up the emails.

Sam nodded and gestured them to the room across the hall. When they'd left, Sam directed his gaze to the camera. "Jessie, I'll be right down to see if you have any thoughts." He and Barnes began to speak, too softly for Jessie to make out what they were saying. But from the set of Sam's jaw and Barnes's rigid posture, they seemed to be moving in on Merrick. Jessie stood and paced, wishing she could see Tim Merrick and tell him to relax, give them what they needed to know and just go home.

The door opened, a rush of cold air sweeping in before Sam. "Don't you guys have any heat in here?" she asked.

He laughed. "So, what do you think? Anything jump out at you?"

"Yeah, he's nervous as hell. It's tough to see him like that."

"Like what?"

"A suspect. You're treating him like he's a suspect."

"We're treating him as though he's a person of interest. Which he is."

Jessie crossed her arms and tilted her head. "He's a surgeon. I don't think he'd kill someone."

"You haven't seen the emails between them. Pretty intense. And he wouldn't be the first surgeon to kill a lover." His eyes were a cold steely gray, the usual dazzle and sparkle gone.

"I have..." she started to say, and caught herself before she told him she'd not only seen them, she'd printed some of them out and then lost them, "not seen them," she continued. "But emails? Come on, Sam."

"We're going to be asking him for DNA and fingerprint samples. See if they match what we've collected in the apartment."

"If they were having an affair, wouldn't he have left both there anyway?"

"Yes, but the question is—will his prints or DNA be on the furniture and lamps that were broken or rifled through?"

"You must have other persons of interest. My money's not on Merrick."

His eyes flickered to the monitor where Tim and his lawyer had just reappeared. "I'm going to go back. Keep watching. I'll check in with you again later."

And with that, he was gone, the door closing softly behind him.

The questioning in the interview room began anew, Barnes and Sam taking turns battering Tim with questions.

"How long had this been going on?"

"Did your wife know?"

Tim had slumped in his seat, his humiliation as clear as the red splotches on his face. Jessie sighed, her heart pounding in time with the rapid-fire questions.

"My wife and I were estranged and in the midst of divorce proceedings. I'd thought we were finalizing that, but—"

"You live with her," Barnes said, loosening his tie.

Tim sighed. "We're working on things."

"What did she want when she showed up in the ER looking for you?"

Tim raked his hand through his hair. "ER? Oh," he said as if remembering. "That was Lily. Money," he said wryly. "She wanted money."

"You still support her?"

"I try not to. She has a job, but she has expensive tastes and she sometimes hits me up. I'm trying to keep our relationship as amicable as I can, and so I occasionally give her money."

"Does she know about Sheila?"

"I don't think so."

"When was the last time you saw Sheila?" Sam asked, leaning back in his chair.

Jessie realized they weren't doing the good cop, bad cop thing; instead, they were all over the place, from one line of questioning to another, to make him squirm. It was working.

Tim turned to his lawyer, who nodded. "Go ahead," he said.

"I'm pretty sure it was late October. I saw her after that but only at work, and even there, I tried to avoid her. I told her I was still married. I didn't tell her we were only talking about divorce, not acting on it."

"What about November twenty-third? Did you see her?" Sam asked.

Tim shook his head. "I never went to her house that night. I never called, I never replied to that email."

"Was she trying to blackmail you?" Barnes asked, folding his arms across his chest, flipping the line of questioning once again.

Tim sat back. "Emotional blackmail, I suppose," he said reluctantly. "She resorted to the age-old lie. She told me she was pregnant. She wasn't, but she tried to frighten me with that. She knew that a lie like that could ruin my career."

"How do you know it was a lie?"

Jessie's chest tightened with the question, and she moved closer to the monitor. If Tim said he'd learned that from her, that would be the end of her job with the ME and Homicide. Maybe in the ER, too. Why couldn't she learn to keep her mouth shut? She closed her eyes and waited for what seemed like ages for Tim to answer.

"I just knew," he finally answered. "She was too old to be pregnant. At least, I hoped she was."

Sam raised a brow. "Did you tell her she was too old?"

"I did. She wasn't too happy with that."

"Where were you on Tuesday, November twenty-third?" Sam asked.

"At work, I'm sure. I'd have to check my schedule, but I can assure you, I did not see her that day."

"What about the twenty-fourth, the day before Thanksgiving?" Barnes flipped the line of questioning once again.

"Working," he said and, watching him, Jessie squirmed in her seat.

"You didn't go away for the holiday?"

"No. I stayed at the hospital. My wife," he said, "wasn't leaving for Florida until Thanksgiving morning. We'd had an argument. I thought it best just to avoid her."

Jessie blew out a plume of air. He was lying. She still remembered that day. It was her first day back in the ER after Sheila had banished her to the ICU for a week. She'd done a double shift, and though the ER had been busy, she hadn't seen Tim, not in the ER nor the ICU, and if he were working, he'd have been in one place or the other. She was sure of that. *Why was he lying?* The first seeds of doubt sprouted in her mind.

"We'll be checking your alibi, of course, and speaking with your wife," Barnes said. "And we'd like you to stay available for more questioning. Got any problems with that?"

Tim shook his head. "You won't release my name to those reporters, will you?" he asked.

"No," Sam said, "but we'd like to get your fingerprints and a DNA swab."

Tim's eyes grew wide with apprehension. "Why?"

"That information can rule you out as a person of interest, Dr. Merrick."

"But I've been there. My prints and DNA are all over the place. It doesn't mean I killed her."

"Did you go to her apartment any time after she was first reported as missing?"

"No," he said. "I didn't even know she was missing until Jessie told me. That was last week, I think. I had just assumed Sheila had given up on me and left her job. I was pretty darn relieved."

"Did you have a key to her apartment?"

"No. I wasn't there often enough."

"And you never broke in to get anything you might have left behind?"

"No," he said, a familiar arrogance in his voice. He'd clearly had enough. He stood, adjusted his tie and reached for his overcoat. "Are we done?"

"For now," Sam said. "Though I've asked a forensics tech to meet you downstairs for your prints and DNA. You okay with that?" he asked as he stood.

Tim nodded and shoved his hands into his pockets. "I guess I have to be." His lawyer held the door open and Tim strode toward it.

"My card," Sam said, passing one to the lawyer and one to Tim. "If you think of anything, please call me. I know that you're as anxious to solve this crime as we are."

Tim rolled his eyes and left the room, slamming the door behind him.

Down the hall, Jessie laughed. Dr. Merrick was himself once again.

CHAPTER 26

"What did you think, Jessie?" Sam asked.

"He was nervous, but besides that… I hate to say it. But he lied."

"About everything, or just one or two untruths?"

"About working the day before Thanksgiving. He wasn't there. And that's when she was killed, right?"

"That's not all he lied about," Sam said.

A bubble of unease made her catch her breath. Did Sam know she'd told Tim that Sheila wasn't pregnant? "What else?" she asked, her voice shaky.

"Nothing I can tell you right now. Want to get lunch? My treat."

"He lied, and you're going to leave me hanging?"

"First rule in this business, Jessie. Everyone lies."

She raised a skeptical brow. "*Everyone?*"

The silver flecks in Sam's eyes glistened under the glare of the fluorescent lighting. "Second rule in this business. Everyone makes mistakes."

"Hard to argue with either of those."

"Lunch?" Sam asked.

"When have I ever turned food down?"

"No shop talk, agreed?" Sam asked as they looked over their menus at the Victoria Diner.

"Oh, come on," Jessie said, lowering her menu. "You're going to keep me in the dark?"

"You ready to order?" A young waitress appeared, notepad and pen in hand, and slid two glasses of water onto the table. She snapped her gum. "Or I can come back?"

"No, we're ready. Right, Jessie?"

She nodded. "I'll have a pastrami on rye, a side of fries and a Diet Coke."

The waitress smiled and turned to Sam. "And you?"

"A Greek salad and coffee."

"Cream, sugar?"

"Both," he said, tucking his menu back behind the napkin dispenser.

"So, if we can't talk about Merrick, what can we talk about?" Jessie asked.

"The case, the other emails. We'll need your help to figure those out. Okay?"

She huffed out a sigh and nodded.

"And I wanted to ask about your friend, Kate."

Jessie bristled at her name. "She's not my friend. She's a travel nurse in the ER."

"Sorry, I didn't realize…"

"No. I'm sorry. She seems to really like you."

Sam laughed, a deep, hearty chuckle, his eyes shimmering. "I think she likes my job."

Jessie shook her head. "She was flirting like crazy at Foley's. Didn't she leave with you?" She pushed back while the waitress passed them each their drinks.

"Food will be out in a few minutes."

"I gave her a ride to that hotel she's staying at. That was it."

"Well, she was flirting even if you didn't notice it."

He poured cream into his coffee and followed that with four packets of sugar. He stirred it in and looked back at Jessie. "Believe it or not, I know when someone is flirting with me. And she wasn't. It was my job and this investigation she was interested in."

"I think that's her way of getting close to you. Ask about your job, bat her eyelashes, and boom, before you know what hit you, she's moving in."

"I don't think so. If she's interested in anything, maybe it's *your* job. I'm not kidding. She had a lot of questions about what happens in an investigation—how we make a case, what we look for." He paused for effect. "What it is that you do."

The waitress returned and slid their plates onto the table. "Here ya go," she said. "Need anything else?"

Jessie eyed the full ketchup bottle and reached for it. "I'm all set," she answered, squirting a large circle beside her fries. She picked up a fry and as soon as the waitress was out of earshot, she curled her lips into a scowl. "I think Kate should learn how to do her own job before she tries to take mine." She turned back to her food, running the fries through the ketchup.

"Tell me how you really feel," Sam said, dipping his fork into his salad.

Jessie laughed. "Sorry. I'm a work in progress. Still working on myself."

"You're fine just the way you are, Jessie," Sam said through a mouthful of lettuce.

Her irritation at Kate melted away. Sam seemed to have a great perspective on just about everything. She'd never seen him really angry or rude. He had an even-handed manner; he was never abrupt; he gave everyone the benefit of the doubt. She'd do well to be more like him, but she wasn't there yet. "One last question about the investigation, and then I swear, I'll keep my mouth shut. What about those foster kids? Any word?" She hadn't had the courage to use her credit card to pay for the telephone number origination information, leaving virtual fingerprints. Sam didn't know she'd heard those messages, but she had and she didn't want them to just focus on Tim. That caller, that ex-foster child, seemed a far more likely suspect.

"Ralph's already on that, trying to track them down. Hope to have something today. We have a telephone number from Sheila's voicemails. And the calls from the public have started coming in now, too, since she's been identified in the press. A man called and said he saw a couple arguing in late November on the riverbank. Our caller says he'd been drinking and just never thought of it again until he saw the news stories. It was dark, he said, so he didn't get a good look at them, but even in the dark, he could tell the woman was a blonde."

"Hmm, if she was in trouble, wouldn't she have shouted to him to help her?"

"Maybe, but maybe she didn't see him, or didn't think she was in trouble, and maybe it wasn't even Sheila. This is three months later, he's calling. It could all amount to nothing, but remember, this is just the beginning. There'll likely be others who come forward. Murder brings out the nuts who want to be a part of the whole thing. We'll have to sort this out like a puzzle—piece by piece."

Jessie bit into her sandwich, wiping the dripping mustard from her chin and watching as Sam speared an olive and tomato with his fork. "Are you on a diet?" she asked, dabbing her mouth with a napkin.

"Why? Do you think I should be?" he asked, sitting a little straighter.

"No, you look great. As usual. You're just not eating much."

"I'm trying to cut back on the junk meals I eat. So, tell me what's new."

"Since Friday night?" she said, a trace of sarcasm in her voice.

"Yeah. Since Friday. Any more incidents?"

Her cheeks flushed red. She'd almost wondered if he knew about Angela already, but of course he was asking about the attempted purse snatching. This was the perfect time to tell him about Angela and ask for his help, but she'd given him so many conflicting stories about her mother, she wasn't sure where to start, or if she even should. She swallowed the large chunk of pastrami she'd stuffed into her mouth and sighed. "No more purse snatchers, but, well…" She curled her fingers around her drink, the cold somehow soothing.

"Are you going to keep me in suspense?" Sam motioned the waitress for another cup of coffee.

"It's about my mother." She offered a half-smile, wondering why he'd never questioned her varied stories—*she ran off, she died.* Jessie had lied so often, she'd gotten tripped up, forgetting who knew what.

"What about her?"

"It's complicated. I lied to you and Ralph when I said she'd died. My father told me that she ran off when I was two years old, so she was always dead to me. I spent a lifetime hating her." She took a long sip of her drink, twirling the straw in the dark liquid. "I was wrong. She didn't abandon me. My father threw her out and lied to me about it. I spent the last twenty-five years blaming her." She shook her head. "It kind of explains my perpetual anger and rush to judgment, don't you think?"

He slipped his hand over hers. "So, how did you learn the truth? And when?"

Jessie told him about seeing Angela Novak last week at L Street, and then in front of her house talking to Rufus. "I'm embarrassed that I was so awful to her at first. But she called, and we spent yesterday afternoon at L Street, where she filled in the gaps in my life with stories and photos. I'm just not sure if it's true." She swallowed the lump in her throat.

"Wow," Sam said. "Where is she now?"

"On her way back to her home and job in Texas."

"Why didn't you say something earlier? You could have skipped this morning's interview and spent the time with her, taken her to the airport."

"She had an early flight, and I'm still processing all of it. I've been a motherless child for my whole life. I'm used to that. But this…"

His hand gripped hers. "Anything I can do?"

She slid her hand away. "I'm glad you asked. Will you check her out for me? See if her story is true?"

CHAPTER 27

Day 9—Monday

"Another staff meeting?" Jessie muttered, wiping the sleep from her eyes.

"Don't shoot the messenger," Donna replied. "Administration called it. They said mandatory attendance for every ER staff member. No exceptions. It's about Sheila."

"Of course, it is." She sat up and swung her feet over the side of the bed. "She's still at the center of everything." She ran her fingers through her tangle of curls. "I'm sorry. That sounded heartless. I suppose she will be at the center of things until we find her killer."

"True enough. I'll see you at ten. The press are camped out by the ambulance bay, so come in through the tunnels that run under the hospital. They won't be down there."

Jessie took a quick shower, pulled on jeans and a sweater, packed scrubs in case she was assigned to the ER instead of Homicide, and headed out. At the corner store, Sheila's photo adorned the front pages of both the *Herald* and the *Globe*. The headlines echoed the television news stories from yesterday: *Beloved Nurse Leader Found Dead.*

"The usual?" Patrick interrupted her reading.

She turned. "Yeah, and both papers too."

Patrick caught sight of the headline. "You knew her?"

Jessie nodded and tucked the papers into her backpack.

"Sorry about your loss, love. That's tragic, huh?" He slipped a warm muffin into a bag and passed it to her along with a large coffee.

"Very sad," she answered, deciding that was the best response. Once they were gone, people were always remembered in the best light, but Sheila Logan hadn't really had a best light, at least not with the ER staff, or even—it seemed—with Tim Merrick. Jessie offered a half-smile. "But I didn't really know her well."

"Ahh, then," he answered, his brogue thick as cotton today, "so that's something to be grateful for."

"Patrick, you're a good man. I'll see you tomorrow."

She navigated the lingering rush hour traffic, pulling into the garage at a quarter to ten. She raced through the tunnels, took the back stairs to the ER and made her way past the registration desk to the large conference room. She'd last been here for a tense debriefing shortly after a tragic murder, and Sheila Logan had simply disappeared not long after. No one had imagined that she'd been murdered. That stuff happened on television, not in real life to people you knew.

She picked up her pace as she rounded the corner and stopped short. There was a throng of people spilling into the corridor, all wearing suits and sour expressions. Those men and women, she knew, were part of Administration—the usually faceless, nameless group who ran the hospital but who knew little about its inner workings. One of them, a tall, thin-lipped woman with close-cropped silver hair and large diamond earrings, turned toward Jessie and smiled. "Are you one of the nurses?"

Jessie, rendered suddenly speechless by her friendly tone, could only bob her head in reply.

The woman moved back and nudged the men on either side of her. "Please let her by. She's one of the nurses."

They moved aside and Jessie slipped through the crowd, finally catching sight of Donna, Susan, Elena and Kate.

Donna raised her hand and waved. "Here, Jessie," she said, pointing to an empty seat next to her. Jessie clutched her bag and squeezed through a row of unfamiliar faces before finally plopping into the chair, an uncomfortably hard wooden one like they had at Homicide. She dropped her bag to the floor and looked up, catching sight of Sam. He winked and she smiled in turn.

A tall, bespectacled man with a head of thinning gray hair stood. "I'm Steve Alexander," he said, "the hospital CEO. I've met many of you." He paused to look around the room, and Jessie fought the urge to laugh. He'd never met any of them. "We are sure you've all heard of the tragic and unexpected passing of our beloved Sheila Logan, and I know you are especially hard hit..."

He continued, but Jessie's mind had begun to wander. Her gaze landed on Kate, who was sitting close to Sam, her adoring eyes only on him. Jessie wanted to vomit, but she bit her lower lip and looked away instead. The staff she recognized all had that glassy-eyed stare of people who are trying to appear as if they are paying close attention, but like Jessie, they were likely daydreaming. Jessie's thoughts turned to Mary Stewart, and she wondered if there had been a meeting like this in the nursing home where she'd worked.

"It's imperative," Mr. Alexander raised his voice as if he knew he'd lost the crowd's attention, "that you do not speak of this incident outside of this hospital, or even among yourselves. If you have anything to say, please see my assistant or the detective on the case, Sam Dallas." He glanced Sam's way, and Sam jerked his head back. He'd been daydreaming too. Jessie coughed to hide the laugh that had bubbled up. "Would you like to say something, Detective Dallas?"

"Detective Sergeant," Sam corrected him as he stood. He cleared his throat and gave a quick rundown on Sheila Logan's death. "Ms. Logan was murdered." A few loud gasps interrupted him. "Sorry to be so blunt, but it's important that if anyone here has any information, anything at all, you please call us. If you heard something—a heated conversation between Sheila and anyone, a bit of animosity that you noticed, even gossip might hold a key—please call us at Homicide. Whoever did this is still out there, and we'd like to catch him. Or her."

The air seemed to be sucked right out of the room. Even the suits, usually so garrulous and full of themselves, were suddenly silent. You could hear a pin drop. Jessie sank into her seat and wondered if anyone else had witnessed that argument in the hallway between Sheila and that man, and if maybe he was the foster child who had threatened her. A hand shot up, and Jessie leaned forward to hear. It was one of the X-ray techs.

"Are we in any danger?" the woman asked, her voice cracking.

Sam shook his head. "No, we don't believe that anyone here is in any danger at all. We suspect that Ms. Logan was targeted, or was perhaps in the wrong place at the wrong time."

"How was she killed?" a voice in the crowd asked. Jessie craned her neck but couldn't see the questioner.

"We're not releasing that information at this time," Sam answered.

Another hand was raised. "Excuse me." It was Kate. "I'm glad that we're not in danger," she said, "but is there anything we can do to help you with this investigation?" A low murmur of approval rippled through the group of men in suits who'd collected by the doorway, probably ready to make a quick escape.

Sam cleared his throat. "Well, it's been several months since Ms. Logan disappeared, so we are interested in anything you may remember about the days before Thanksgiving, when we believe she disappeared. And again, please don't discuss this case with anyone. Remember, any rumors you hear are likely just that—rumors. Please don't repeat them, but do feel free to call me for confirmation. I'll leave my cards here on the desk."

Mr. Alexander stood back up. "One other thing. We'd like you to know that Dr. Tim Merrick, our head of Trauma Surgery, has decided to take a leave of absence. His decision has nothing to do with Ms. Logan's disappearance or murder, and we do not want any speculation regarding that. Dr. Merrick has had some personal health issues that he must attend to at this time. We expect discretion and respect from all of you. Here at Boston City Hospital, we are family, and we look out for each other. And finally, please do not speak to the press. That's it. Have a good day." He smiled, the fluorescent overhead lights bouncing off the patches of shiny scalp that poked through his thinning hair.

The crowd began to scatter, though Jessie could see Alexander at the door nodding to staff as they left. She watched as Kate sidled up to Sam and laid the flat of her palm against his back. He stiffened. "Sam, can I speak with you?" Jessie swore she was actually batting her eyelashes, the violet flecks almost sparkling. She didn't even know Sheila, or Tim for that matter. Kate smiled again at Sam, wider this time. What could she possibly have to add?

Sam seemed to shake her off. "I'm kinda busy right now," he said, his voice dripping with barely concealed irritation.

Jessie couldn't help but smile. Kate's ploy to get attention from Sam didn't seem to be working.

"But it's important," Kate replied, a pout on her lips. "It's about this." She inclined her head toward the room, almost empty now as staff filed out, eager to be away from the topic of murder and this meeting.

What is she talking about? Jessie wondered, her shoulders tensing as she remembered Kate walking into Donna's office while she was studying and printing out Sheila's emails.

Sam exhaled noisily. "Jessie, will you wait for me?" he called.

She nodded, picked up her bag, and headed for the doorway.

"Jessie Novak, right?" the CEO asked, holding out his hand. "Good to meet you. Will you stay for a minute? I'd like to speak with you and the detective. I know that you also work with the Police Department. Correct?"

"Yes, Mr. Alexander," she said, feeling suddenly tongue-tied. *How did he know who she was?* Had Sheila complained about her to Administration?

"Please, call me Steve. I understand you've been in the ER for a few years. I'm hoping you can help bring our perspective to the investigation." He smiled, one of those practiced grins that powerful people use to put the regular stiffs at ease.

"Our perspective?" she asked.

"Yes, the hospital's best interest. An investigation like this can affect our reputation, and ultimately cut into our patient base and our bottom line. The impact can be devastating if not handled with kid gloves. You understand?"

Sam appeared at her side. "I can answer that, sir," he said. "We want to find a killer, and we do not intend, in any way, to harm the reputation of this hospital which, as you know, is the hospital of choice for the Boston Police Department. Your staff," he turned to Jessie and smiled, "have helped to save the lives of more than one of our officers. I promise you that we will do our best to keep the hospital's reputation intact." He offered his hand to Alexander, who shook it vigorously.

Jessie marveled at Sam's ability to make whomever he spoke to feel as though he heard and understood every word that was said. And more than that, they always believed him. Sam had more than silver flecks in his eyes—they danced in his words as well.

And once again, Jessie was spellbound.

CHAPTER 28

"From what Steve Alexander said, I'm guessing he agrees that you're back on rotation with us, which is perfect. Mrs. Merrick is coming in this afternoon. I'd like you to watch again. See what you think," said Sam.

He walked through the door and along the hallway to the ER. Jessie kept stride, relieved that she'd officially be back to rotating between the ER and Homicide. "Just give me a couple of hours. Despite what Alexander said, I think people here are going to be skittish. I'd like to hang out, see if I hear anything, or see anything."

Sam smiled. "You're developing the mind of a detective, Jessie," he said, resting a hand on her shoulder.

"Thanks. That might be the nicest thing you've ever said to me."

He raised a brow. "I hope not." With that, he picked up his pace and headed toward the ambulance bay.

Jessie turned and went in search of Donna. She found her standing by the pediatric ER, talking with Kate.

"Hey," Donna called when she spied Jessie. "Are you with us today?" she asked.

Kate turned, her eyes crinkling, a half-smile on her lips. "Jessie, it's so good to see you. Will I be able to work with you today?"

"No," Jessie replied tersely. "I'm only here for a little bit. I'll be heading to police headquarters shortly."

"I wish I could follow you around over there."

"You'll be with Susan Peters today," Donna interrupted. "She's waiting for you on the acute side."

Kate's smile faded. "I guess I'll get going then. See you later."

When she was out of sight, Jessie shook her head. "I don't know about her."

Donna laughed. "She's trying, and she's ours for at least the next three months."

"My advice to you is never use that agency again. What was the name anyway?"

"Rosehall something. I can check."

"No, that's alright. I want to take Sheila's box of documents and stuff today. I think we need to hand everything over to Sam."

Donna nodded in agreement. "Are you going to tell him you lost a few of those papers?"

"I should. I know I should, but I'm not sure. I'll see how today goes." She followed Donna to her office and caught sight of Susan, her brow raised in frustration, trying to explain the EKG machine to Kate. She laughed and stepped into Donna's office, closing the door behind them. "Can we have a quick look at some of the documents in that box before I take them?"

"Sure." Donna reached down and slid the box out from under her desk. "What did you make of the Tim Merrick announcement?"

"Poor guy. I feel sorry for him. The police are really looking at him closely."

Donna's eyes opened wide. "You don't think…?"

"No, no. And please don't repeat what I just said. I have to learn to keep my mouth shut."

"I won't say anything." There was an edge to her voice. She was feeling hurt, or maybe insulted by Jessie's words. With her foot, she pushed the box over to Jessie.

"I'm sorry I said that. I know you'd never say a word. This whole thing is just such a mess—Tim Merrick a suspect, the staff afraid, people suspicious of everyone." She leaned over and began to rummage through the papers, not sure at all what she was looking for. She could hear Donna tapping away on her computer. "Hey," Jessie said, pulling out a stack of stapled papers. "What did you say the name of that agency was?"

"Rosehall."

Jessie sat up, the papers in her lap as she read through them. "And they contacted you?"

"Yeah, why?"

"Looks like they worked with Sheila on more than staffing." She scanned the papers quickly. "Seems they provide ER aftercare equipment and follow-up. Ever hear of that?"

Donna shook her head.

"Me either. Yet here it is in black and white. Well, the bills at least. Looks like Sheila signed off on them. You've never been asked about follow-up?"

"No, we refer patients to visiting nurses, the VNA or their own doctors for follow-up or equipment. Same as always. We don't provide aftercare. Jeez, we do enough as it is."

"Hmm," Jessie said. "I'll have a look through this stuff and her emails. See if they match up. Strange, huh?"

"What isn't, these days?" She stood. "I gotta get out there and do rounds. I'll catch you later."

Jessie stood quickly. "Are we alright? I'm sorry about what I said just now."

Donna pulled her into a quick hug. "We're alright, Jessie. No worries."

"Will you keep your ears open? Let me know if you hear anything? I'll stop by later."

"Yes. I'm as curious as you to hear what people are saying, and despite what the CEO said, you can bet the rumors are flying out there."

Jessie lifted the box with a grunt and stepped into the hallway, walking right into the path of Kate.

"What have you got there?" she asked.

"Just some documents." She adjusted the box on her hip and forced a smile.

"Can I help you? It looks heavy."

Kate moved closer, her gaze focused on the documents as if she was trying to read them, or maybe Jessie just imagined that. "No, I'm all set. Thanks anyway. I'm heading to headquarters." She tightened her grip on the box.

"Please give Sam my best." She winked.

She turned away. Kate was baiting her; she wanted Jessie to think there was something going on between her and Sam. And she began to wonder if maybe there was something going on, and Sam was just being quiet about it.

At headquarters, a patrolman saw her wrestling with the box and offered to bring it in for her. "Where are you going?" he asked.

"Sam Dallas's office." She followed him as he lugged the container up the stairs and down the hall to the detectives' area.

"What ya got there?" Sam asked, reaching to take the carton and dropping it into a chair by the desk.

"Sheila's documents. They've been under Donna's desk for months. She forgot all about them. I thought I'd look through them, compare them with the emails. It's likely a dead end, but I just thought…" She shrugged. "It's worth a look at least."

"You can sit at my desk. Her emails are there under the tab Logan. I'm gonna see if we're ready for Mrs. Merrick."

"Hey, before you go, it's probably none of my business, but what did Kate want to speak to you about?"

Sam chuckled. "She wanted to tell me that she'd heard a rumor that you hadn't liked Sheila Logan. Said she heard you make some disparaging remarks about her."

"Of all the two-faced… That's a lie! I never spoke to her about Sheila except to tell her not to talk about her death. I'm going to have a word with her."

"Don't, Jessie. Not worth getting into an argument. I told you, she wants your job. She probably knew I'd tell you. Or, who knows, maybe she thought I'd believe her. Either way, forget it."

"That reminds me, she asked me to give you her best," Jessie repeated Kate's words in what she hoped was her most sultry voice. "I think it's you she's after, Sam. Not me." She puckered her lips and made a kissing sound.

"Everyone's a comedian. I'll be back for you when we're ready to interview the Mrs."

Jessie shrugged her coat off, slid into Sam's chair and turned her attention to the computer, bringing up the tab for Logan, Sheila and clicking on *Emails and Correspondence.* She sank into her seat. There must be thousands of emails, inter-office correspondence and notifications. Where could she even start? She rubbed the back of her neck and leaned forward. She'd start by creating new folders—one each for emails, correspondence and another for notifications. Once she'd done that, she began organizing by date, and then filtering by sender and subject. She was still huddled over the computer when Sam reappeared.

"You're still at it? Find anything?"

"Still trying to put things in some kind of order. There's so much here." She pushed back and stretched.

"We're ready for you," Sam said. "Mrs. Merrick and her lawyer are settling in. You can just sign out of that." He nodded toward the computer. "Want some coffee, water, donuts?"

"All of the above," she replied, standing and rubbing her back. "I didn't realize how long I'd been sitting here." She looked at her watch. "It's almost one. No wonder my stomach is rumbling." She followed Sam to the viewing room and peered outside. It was snowing again, the flakes—heavy and wet—hitting the window and melting into streaks of water.

"I got coffee, water and three donuts for you."

"Thank you," Jessie said, turning back to Sam. She watched while he hit buttons on the wall, the screen lighting up, the interview room coming into focus.

"Ahh, there she is," Sam said, his eyes on the screen.

Jessie turned to see a fresh-faced young woman, mid-thirties maybe, her long blonde hair secured with an elastic, her eyes wide, her lips parted. "Here?" the woman asked softly, pointing to a chair.

"Who is she?" Jessie asked.

"Mrs. Merrick."

Jessie shook her head. "That woman is not Mrs. Merrick."

CHAPTER 29

Sam's jaw dropped. "What? She's the one living with him. Her ID says that's who she is."

"She's not the Mrs. Merrick who came looking for him in the ER last week."

"Oh, hell," Sam ran his fingers through his hair. "Are you sure?"

"I am. She's not Mrs. Merrick."

"I'll be right back," Sam said.

Jessie watched the screen as Sam entered the interview room, his jaw tight, his brow furrowed, his eyes on the woman, seated now, her hands placed demurely in her lap, the overhead lights bouncing off the large diamond on her ring finger. "Mrs. Merrick?"

She looked up, her hand covering the ring as though she knew it was causing a glare. "Yes?" Her voice was soft, not the harsh voice of the other Mrs. Merrick.

Sam sat and leaned forward. "Do you mind showing me your ID again?"

She fished through her bag before passing an ID to Sam.

He nodded and passed it back. "Sorry, it's just that... well, is there another Mrs. Merrick?"

She rolled her eyes. "Only in her mind. Lily. She's the first Mrs. Merrick. Tim divorced her fifteen years ago. She just about cleaned him out. We married six years ago. I'm the current Mrs. Merrick and, I hope, the last one." She twisted the ring on her finger.

Jessie's jaw dropped. She felt a surge of sympathy for this woman. Tim clearly had a roving eye. He'd asked her out only last week, but why? His wife, at least from where Jessie sat, was attractive and seemed like a nice young woman.

Sam went over the introductory and now familiar questions. Mrs. Merrick answered them demurely. "My name is Melanie Merrick. I'm thirty-six years old." She worked as an administrative assistant at the Museum of Fine Arts. They had no children, though they still hoped to start a family in the future once this was behind them. "I know why I'm here," she added. "I know that Tim has been unfaithful, and this is embarrassing, to say the least, but he's a good man." Her eyes seemed to tear up, and she pulled a tissue from her pocket and dabbed at them.

Sam apologized for having to question her. "But it's important that we understand everything about this case. Please tell me what you know about your husband and Sheila Logan."

She wadded the tissue in her hand and took a deep breath. "I know that Tim had a fling with her, and I know that she wasn't the first, though she's the first one whose name I know." She pushed a loose strand of hair behind her ear. Her hand was trembling.

Sam probed gently. Jessie had never seen him approach an interview so delicately. "Can you tell me about this last Thanksgiving? Did you spend it with Tim?"

"No, we'd been having problems. I knew about the affair, but not who the woman was. I had no idea he'd worked with her and probably saw her every day. He'd promised me it was over, and we'd planned to spend the holiday weekend in Florida with my family. It was going to be a fresh start. At the last minute, we argued. He said he had to stay to cover the trauma service for another surgeon. What could I say? His job is important. He drove me to the airport on Wednesday morning."

"How was he? Was he nervous, out of sorts?"

"He's always a little on edge, that's what makes him such a great surgeon, but I didn't notice anything unusual."

"Did you speak to him over the weekend?"

"Not until late Saturday. He'd been on call, he said, and it was busy. He said he missed me." She smiled at the memory. "He picked me up on Sunday evening at the airport, and he was fine. Tired, but fine. And before you ask, he wasn't nervous or hiding anything. We went straight home and Monday, we both went back to work."

Sam's gaze narrowed, the sparkle in his eyes gone, the color indistinguishable under the too-bright lights. He was getting down to business. "Did you ask him about the holiday, about where he spent it?"

"Of course. He was at the hospital. He had one of those awful rubbery turkey meals they serve, and he stayed there pretty late." She seemed to stiffen just a little. "That's what he told me."

Sam cleared his throat. "And these last few months, how has he been? Tense, preoccupied?"

"No. Well, that's not true. He's always a little anxious about work. He worries about his patients. He'd wake up at two in the morning and call the ICU to see how someone was doing. Sometimes he gets up and drives back to the hospital to check on a patient." She smiled. "He's the best at what he does, and that's why I love him, why I'm hoping we can work things out. He's intense but focused, and he tries hard, maybe too hard, to please everyone. I think that's how he gets into these situations."

Sam raised a brow. "Situations?" he asked.

"Trusting people, even women, not seeing that they might be using him. And I think he's always looking for affirmation. He needs to know that he's the best at everything, not just surgery. It's not enough that I say it—he needs to hear it from everyone. He's insecure that way."

"Has he ever been violent?"

Melanie Merrick reared back as though she'd been slapped. "No," she almost shouted. "He's a good, kind man. What an awful thing to ask."

"We're investigating a murder," Sam said drily. "Murder is generally violent."

She pushed back in her chair as if trying to move away from Sam. Her lips parted as if she was about to speak, but instead she looked away, her face drawn tight as though she'd slipped behind a veil.

"Can you think of anything that might help us in this investigation?" Sam asked softly. "Anything at all."

She shook her head. "My husband was not involved in this," she said firmly. "I know that beyond all doubt, and not just because he's my husband, but because he's a man of unquestionable integrity."

Sam stood, his back stiff as a board. "Here's my card," he said, handing it to Melanie. "Please call if you think of anything, and please keep yourself available. We may need to speak with you again."

She slipped the card into the pocket of her down jacket and nodded. "No offense," she said, "but I hope we don't have to meet again."

Sam held the door open as she passed through. His phone chirped with a message and he lifted it from his pocket, his eyes growing wide as he read. Finally, he looked into the camera. "Jessie, I gotta take care of something. I'll meet you in my office. Okay?"

She nodded before realizing he couldn't see her. She gathered her things, cleared away the coffee cup and empty water bottle and swept the donut crumbs into her hand, depositing everything into a basket in the corner. She stopped by the window for another look. The snow continued to fall, heavier now, the flakes accumulating on the sidewalks and street. Jessie sighed. This winter would never end.

She headed to Sam's office where he sat, his phone to his ear, his jaw clenched. "It's Ralph," he mouthed, pointing to the phone.

Jessie rolled her eyes, sat down and bent to the box she'd brought from the ER, pulling out a pile of papers. At least she could go through Sheila's stuff while she waited. Maybe something in here could help Tim, or maybe point the finger further in his direction. There were so many inconsistencies in his story. A thread of doubt blossomed in her brain, and she wondered if maybe Tim had been involved in this whole mess after all. She began to sort through the paperwork, making small piles on her lap and along the edge of Sam's desk. He grunted and set his phone down. "What is it?" she asked, scanning the documents in her hand.

"That was Ralph," he said. "He's still in Natick, tracking down some leads on Sheila Logan. And it seems we now have another body."

CHAPTER 30

Jessie clutched the papers. "Another body?" she asked. "Who? Another nurse?"

Sam rubbed his forehead and leaned back in his chair. "No, not a nurse. A neighbor. She'd called the Natick police a few weeks back to report that she'd seen two people—a man and a woman—taking things from Sheila's apartment. This was after Sheila had disappeared, but before her body was found. Anyway, the neighbor, an elderly woman, had called to report the incident.

"She told them the woman was a blonde and the man was average. Said she thought she could identify the two in a lineup if need be. The dispatcher took the message and her number and passed it to the detectives, where the report sat on a desk. They gave it low priority, apparently assuming that maybe Sheila had turned up, or her family was getting her things." He raked his fingers through his hair.

Jessie tapped her fingers on his desk. "So, someone killed her? The old woman?"

Sam nodded sadly. "Yeah. Once Sheila was found and identified, and the police discovered that her apartment had been ransacked, they remembered the call and tried to get in touch with the woman. She didn't answer her door or her phone, and when the super let them in, her apartment was empty. They just found her body in her car in a far corner of the building's underground garage."

Jessie's mouth flew open. "Oh, no!" she said. "How awful. What happened?"

"I don't know. It looks like she was strangled. With her own scarf. Maybe she was surprised by someone hiding in her car. Anyway, they're bringing her into the ME's office, so I'll definitely want you there for the autopsy."

"Today, you think?"

"I guess that's up to Roger, but we'll definitely need him to get to this ASAP."

"Of course. That's awful. Poor woman. And you really think it's related to Sheila?"

"I think it's a hell of a coincidence if it isn't. I mean, she calls and reports the incident, a robbery or whatever, says she can identify the perps, and before anyone can follow up and speak to her, she turns up dead."

"Hmm." Jessie nodded and began to gather the papers, placing them back into the box. "I guess I can get to these later," she mumbled to herself.

"What are those, anyway?" Sam asked. "Remind me."

"Some papers and forms that Sheila kept in this box. It's been under Donna's desk. I just thought maybe I could check this stuff against the emails, see if there's any connection, anything that could help."

"Jeez," Sam said. "I can feel my eyes glazing over at the thought. Knock yourself out. You can leave them in here to keep them safe."

Jessie swallowed the lump of unease in her throat. Should she tell him she'd taken some and lost them at Foley's? "Thanks. This box is too heavy to lug around." *And I definitely don't want to lose any more of them.* "So," she said, standing and slipping her arms into the sleeves of her coat. "Can I ask you something?"

"Sure," he replied, his eyes crinkled at the corners, a trace of a smile on his lips.

"Does another body take Tim Merrick off your list of suspects?"

He shook his head. "No yet. The male was described as average, and the woman as a blonde of medium height. Sound familiar?"

Jessie closed her eyes. It wasn't the best description, and it was a stretch to say it pointed to Tim and his wife, but… She inhaled deeply and turned. "What about those threatening calls from that man who'd been taken from his mother because of Sheila? He seems a far more likely suspect."

"Ralph has him on his radar. Got a name and address late yesterday. His given name is Rock Powell. *Rock.* Street name for crack cocaine. His mother named him for her first love. That's mother love for you, huh? With that name, he probably never had a chance. He's in Walpole Prison right now. Not sure yet how long he's been there, and that might be his alibi, but Ralph's going to see him later today."

"And his siblings?"

"Sisters. One died two years ago from a drug overdose. The other one seems to have escaped the family's pull. She's married and living in California. We'll talk to her eventually but she's not on our radar right now."

Relieved that Tim wasn't the only suspect, she smiled. "I'll let you know about the autopsy. Will you give Roger a call and tell him I'm on my way?"

The morgue was humming with activity when Jessie swiped her ID and gained entrance. She raised her hand in greeting toward a couple of the techs who were just heading out. "Hey," she called. "Do you know if the body arrived from Natick yet?"

"Yes," the taller of the two answered. "Dr. Dawson and Tony are just getting started."

"Thanks," Jessie said, racing for the stairs. Once on the second floor, she went to her locker, changed quickly into scrubs, and donned her PPE. She made her way through the first room where bodies lay in wait for their final examination, and pushed open the door to the autopsy suite. Tony and Roger, clad in their own PPE, stood beside the body, chatting.

"Ahh, here you are," Roger said, "we've been waiting for you. We've done the X-rays and photos, so we're all set. Ready?"

Jessie nodded and moved to the other side of the metal table.

"Edith Grigsby," Roger began, "is an eighty-year-old female found slumped over in the front seat of her car in a garage in Natick. Mottling and lividity are evident to face and lower extremities. She has heavy bruising and large hematomas over the strap muscles of her neck. Her hyoid and cricoid cartilage appear to be fractured. There are marks here," he said, pointing to her neck, "that are consistent with the ligature, a scarf, that was tied tightly around her neck. The bleeding over her strap muscles along with the fractures I mentioned indicate she was likely subdued with a chokehold from behind, and then strangled with her own scarf."

He lifted her hands. "Her nails are broken. She probably put up a fight. We've already taken some scrapings from under her nails." He went back to examine the skin of her neck and reached for a tweezer, plucking two floating dark hairs resting on her neck. Tony held out a plastic evidence bag. "Please label that hair," Roger said as he leaned down and collected several tiny pieces of fleece and downy feathers from the same area.

"Tony, please label these as foreign particles, not at all similar to the cotton housedress and sweater she was wearing. Perhaps left behind by a careless killer." He continued his narration, examining her as Tony arranged instruments on a side table. When Roger paused, Tony passed him a scalpel. They worked in perfect tandem, Tony ready with whatever Roger needed before he even asked.

Jessie watched as Roger made the now familiar Y-type incision from the woman's neck to the end of her sternum before continuing down her abdomen in a straight line. He moved quickly, removing and inspecting organs, taking small slices of her heart and lungs before examining her stomach and its contents. "A little bit of undigested food in the stomach," he said. "She'd eaten or perhaps just started to eat not long before her death."

These were the moments that made these victims come alive for her—the understanding that this lady had been doing something mundane, some everyday thing, never knowing that she was about to die. Jessie swallowed the lump in her throat and watched as Roger finished up.

"Clearly a homicide—she died of strangulation." He stepped away from the table and removed his face mask, taking in a deep breath of the coppery air that permeated the room. "Sad way for an old woman to die, huh?" he asked, pulling off his gloves.

Jessie pulled her own mask away. "Any time of death?" she asked.

"Based on decomposition, I'd say at least a week, more likely ten days or so. I'll have a better idea once I have a look under the microscope."

"Are we all set then?"

"Yes," Roger said. "It's getting late." He glanced at his watch. "Almost seven. You should just get going. We'll talk tomorrow."

Jessie changed quickly and jogged across the street to the garage, pausing when she saw Kate leaving the ER through the ambulance bay. She was smiling and waving, and Jessie began to wave back when she realized that Kate wasn't waving at her, and hadn't even seen her. Kate approached a fancy Lexus idling at the curb as the driver got out and went around to open the passenger door.

He and Kate exchanged a quick kiss. Jessie stepped behind a delivery truck to watch. The streetlights caught the man in a faint glow. There was something so familiar about him, not to mention the fact that Kate had mentioned more than once that she didn't know anyone in Boston. Maybe it was that friend she'd mentioned, and maybe she wasn't interested in Sam after all.

Jessie tapped the pedestrian light and waited for the walk signal, which came just as the Lexus made a U-turn and was forced to a full stop at the light. The man's eyes locked onto Jessie, his gaze unsettling, his face somehow familiar. Jessie bent into her scarf and hurried across the street, but she could feel his eyes boring into her.

A sudden blast of horns and angry shouts caused her to look up. The Lexus was moving forward slowly, the man pulling his eyes back to the road at the last minute.

Her scalp prickled. She was sure she'd seen that man, but where? It didn't really matter. She needed to get home and call Sam with Roger's findings. She jogged through the hospital's tunnels, took the rickety circular stairway to the top floor of the garage and walked toward her car. And came to a dead stop. Even from a distance, she could see her car door open, her belongings scattered about. Someone had broken into her car. Her eyes scanned the garage, but it was late. Most cars were gone. Her footsteps echoed eerily as she approached her car and looked inside.

The lock had been jimmied, the interior torn apart, the glove compartment pulled open—her vehicle registration and inspection papers thrown about, empty water bottles tossed onto the floor. She leaned in. Her radio was intact, her CD player and CDs still there. Nothing seemed to be missing—not that she had anything worth stealing anyway. She walked around the car searching for dents or scratches but, aside from a few old dings, there was no fresh damage.

"What the…?" she said, her voice bouncing off the cement walls.

And then she heard it—the unmistakable sound of soft footsteps. She froze. Someone was standing right behind her.

CHAPTER 31

"Jessie? Is that you?" a man asked, his voice raspy.

She spun around to see Eddie, her homeless friend from the ER. The knot of tension that had coiled inside her veins unraveled itself into a surge of relief. "Eddie," she said with a long sigh. "I've never been so glad to see anyone in my life."

"Is that your car?"

"It is, and someone broke into it, but God knows why. I don't have anything worth taking."

Eddie scratched his head. "I saw a man breaking in and he was looking for something. He was throwing things and swearing. I would've stopped him if I'd known it was your car, but to tell you the truth, I've been drinking. He seemed like a big guy. He woulda knocked me out."

"Oh, Eddie, it's okay. What are you doing here?"

"Just looking for a warm spot for the night."

She reached out and ran her fingers along the edge of the scarf he'd wrapped around his neck. "Glad you're still wearing this, and the hat and gloves." She'd given them to him months ago to help protect against the bitter cold of this never-ending winter. "I can drop you back at the ER."

"No, I'm okay. I can drink a little here and no one will bother me. The warm air vents are right over there." He pointed to a far corner where a pile of blankets lay.

Jessie sighed. "I wish you'd let me take you somewhere. Pine Street?"

He shook his head vigorously. "No shelters for me, Jessie. You go on home. I'll be fine."

"Are you sure?"

He nodded. "These places are home to me. I'm safer here than in one of those miserable shelters."

"Okay," she said, reaching into her bag and grabbing a twenty-dollar bill. "Here," she said, passing him the money. "Get breakfast in the morning."

He leaned over and stuffed the money into his sock. "Thank you," he said. "Now go home. You're keeping me up."

She laughed and slid into her car. "See you later," she said, grateful that the door still closed and locked. She pulled away, her thoughts drawn back to poor old Edith Grigsby and her awful death. She wondered about the woman's family as she navigated the roads to K Street and pulled into a parking spot. Her phone chirped with a new message. *Thinking of you Jessie, Love Mom.*

Jessie shoved the phone back into her pocket. She had other things to think about right now—the attempted bag snatching, and now her car break-in. It seemed too much of a coincidence just days apart, and she wondered if she was being targeted. But who would target her? What did they want? She locked her car and headed inside, where Rufus's front door was wedged open with his baseball bat.

"Rufus?" she called, moving the bat aside and poking her head in. "Are you here? Are you alright?"

He appeared in the dim light from his front-facing living room. "There you are. I was waiting for you. You're late."

"Anything wrong?" she asked, following him inside.

"No. Just wanted to make sure to catch you. A repairman was here asking to get into your apartment. I didn't know you were having anything fixed, so I wouldn't let him in. I'm happy to let people in if you'll let me know ahead of time."

Jessie swallowed the heavy lump in her throat. "I'm not having any repairs. Did he say who he was?"

"No, just said he was here to fix your stove."

"My stove is fine." *What is going on? Maybe there is someone after me. But why?* She shook her head. She had to call Sam. None of this made sense.

"Hmm," Rufus said, resting his hands on the back of a chair. "Well, maybe he had the wrong house. That happens sometimes. He seemed nice enough. Had one of those smooth southern accents. Didn't give me a hard time. He just left. Our house numbers are sometimes hard to see. Simple mistake."

"You're probably right, Rufus. Thanks for telling me, and I'll let you know if I'm having any work done."

"You got yourself a deal," Rufus said. "Have you had dinner? I can slip a frozen meal into the microwave for you."

"Oh, Rufus, I just love you, but no thanks. I need a hot bath first, and then a can of soup and a glass of wine will do the trick for me tonight." She wished him a good night and headed upstairs, her apartment locked up tight and secure, but her senses alert for trouble.

Once inside, she texted Sam. *Will you call me?* She hit *send* and waited for the three bouncing dots that would indicate he was replying. She waited. And waited. Fifteen minutes later, she gave up, and began to run water for her bath. She'd just have to settle for hot soup and chilled wine and an early night, which was just as well. A good night's sleep would help clear her brain of all her paranoia. The attempted purse snatching was easily explained by city life, the car was the same—that garage had car break-ins all the time, and the repairman had the wrong address. Simple.

Coincidences. That was all they were.

Or were they?

CHAPTER 32

Day 10—Tuesday

Jessie woke with a start, her bedroom still dark. She sat up and reached for her phone—no missed calls or texts from Sam, so unless he'd spoken directly with Roger, he didn't know about the autopsy on Edith Grigsby. And then she noticed the time. *Two thirty!* She fell back and curled into her pillow. There was nothing she could do about it just now. With that thought in mind, she closed her eyes and drifted back to sleep.

An angry and persistent car alarm pulled her from her dreams at seven thirty. She sat and stretched, easing the kink from her neck. She splashed water on her face and ran her fingers through her curls before pulling them back with a clip. She swiped rosy-colored lipstick on, pulled on jeans, a sweater, boots, grabbed her bag and keys and headed out just as her phone pinged with a message from Sam. *Hey, Jess. Just saw your text from last night. You on your way in?*

She wondered if he'd been out late on a date. Her shoulders sagged as she typed her reply. *Yes. See you soon. Got coffee and donuts?*

Always! he replied as Jessie pulled open her door and pounded down the stairs.

"Hey, Jessie," Rufus called from his open doorway. "It snowed again. Need help shoveling?"

She came to a full stop and pulled on her gloves. "No, I'll be all set, but thanks. God, will this winter never end? It's March already."

"Oh, now, come on," he said with a sly raise of his brow. "This is Boston. It's snowed in May."

"Dear God, don't even tell me that." She pulled open the door, her tension fading at the sight. The street was a winter wonderland, the snow only a couple of inches deep, but it was the clean, fresh smell lingering in the air that Jessie loved. She took a deep breath and turned back to Rufus. "It is pretty, isn't it? I guess I have to look for the bright side of things instead of pissing and moaning about the dark side."

"There ya go. That's my girl."

Jessie waved and set off to her car, parked only half a block away. The door lock rattled when she inserted her key, an unpleasant reminder of yesterday's break-in. Why would anyone choose her crappy old car over the fancy ones in that garage? And why would someone try to snatch her bag, or get into her apartment? All in the span of a few days. She shook her head. Maybe she needed some kind of protection. Probably not a gun, but something.

*

"Hey, Sam, good morning," she said as she walked into his office. His back was to her, his attention focused on the whiteboard in front of him. It was the board where detectives posted photos of victims, crime scenes, suspects, clues, questions, avenues to pursue, and anything relevant to a case. Standing in front of it allowed the investigators a clear view of what they had, what they needed and where to go next, though sometimes, Sam had said, it remained an almost blank space, with the questions taunting them. Today, Jessie could see photos of Tim and Melanie Merrick posted alongside Sheila Logan's.

"Hey," Sam said, turning back. "Have a seat."

She dropped into a chair. "Before we get started, I want you to know I've had more trouble. That purse snatching thing Saturday, and yesterday my car was broken into in the garage, and some man tried to get Rufus to let him into my apartment. Said he was there to fix my stove, but Rufus, God bless him, sent him away. I just…" She'd spoken in a rush of words, and when she paused, she took a deep breath.

Sam's forehead wrinkled as he sank into his chair. "You okay? Anything stolen? Do you have your car?"

"I have my car. It's fine. The weird thing is, I don't have anything to steal. Why not break into one of the fancy cars in the garage? And why try to get into my apartment? Or snatch my bag? I'm beginning to think it's all related. But why?"

"And nothing's missing?"

"No, and Eddie, one of the homeless guys from the ER, was there in the garage. He watched it all. Said it looked as though the guy was looking for something. He was just throwing things around in my car. Weird, huh?"

"Did Eddie get a description?"

"No, he only saw him at a distance. Eddie was there for the night. He didn't want to get into a scuffle, so he stayed hidden."

"Did you report it?"

"No. Nothing was taken, and I thought maybe he had the wrong car, but with the supposed repairman showing up, and the purse snatcher, it just seems like an unusual run of bad luck. I texted you last night to tell you about it." She leaned forward, resting her elbows on his desk. "I think I need something. I'm not sure what there is besides a gun."

Sam's eyes narrowed. "I'm sorry I didn't call. I was out, got in late."

Jessie wondered if he'd been out with Kate, and a sting of jealousy swept through her veins, but not for long. She had too many other things on her mind right now.

He ran his hands through his hair. "But you're right. This is more than bad luck. Anyone pissed off enough to try to put a scare into you?"

"No. No one. So, back to my request. What do you think? I need something, and I'm not sure what. Maybe a firearm?"

He raised a brow and offered her a half-smile. "Let's start with pepper spray, and maybe work our way up." He pulled open his drawer and took out a tiny spray canister, passing it to her. "You know how to use these?"

She folded the tube into her hand. "I do. Does this stuff really work?"

"It does. I'll get you the paperwork for a license for that, and here," he said, sliding a blank police report across his desk. "Fill these out. Let's get the details of these events on the record."

She scanned the empty lines and empty spaces on the papers in front of her. This would take forever. "I'll get to it later, if you don't mind."

"Okay, good enough. Now, fill me in on the autopsy."

Jessie described Roger's findings, and his conclusion that Edith Grigsby had died of strangulation, likely after she was put in a chokehold to overpower her. "But she fought back. He has scrapings from under her nails. Poor old lady."

"Oh, that's tough." Sam grimaced and shook his head.

"So, you think it's related?"

"I do. Once we find her killer, I'm pretty sure we'll find Sheila's as well."

"Roger got some hairs and fibers from her body. Maybe that will help. Any video?"

"Not in that far corner of the garage. The last video we have showed Mrs. Grigsby hurrying toward her car, keys in hand."

"Maybe she was going out?"

"She was dressed in one of those light cotton housedresses that older women wear. She had a sweater and a scarf but no coat. Why would an old lady go to a cold garage dressed so lightly? Her phone records show she got a call right before she went down. I think someone lured her down there with some phony claim that she needed to check her car right away. Whoever called her used a burner phone. No way to trace it."

Jessie scowled at the image and leaned forward. "Doesn't that take suspicion off Tim Merrick? I mean, think about it. For him to have been so angry about Sheila's threats that he killed her, ransacked her apartment, though he'd said he wasn't there often, and then went back and killed the neighbor? And used a burner phone to call her?" She shook her head. "Not realistic. It's more likely that Rock Powell was involved. Don't you think? He had it in for Sheila."

Sam sighed. "We'll see. Unless Logan had a secret life we haven't uncovered yet, they're both on our list. Merrick was egocentric enough to lie, and maybe even kill to cover it, and Rock Powell, well, you're right, he definitely had motive." He pushed back from his desk. "I'm going to meet with the DA. You can have a seat here and go through Sheila's emails and documents, see if there's anything of interest there. Okay with you?"

She nodded. "What time will you be back?"

"Not sure. I'm trying to get a warrant for her bank accounts squared away. I need to speak with the DA, see if we're all set. Want to come along? See how that end of it works?"

"Not this time. I want to go through this stuff." She pointed to the computer and sank into Sam's chair. "See you later."

Sam waved and closed the door, leaving Jessie alone. She spun the chair around and stared at the whiteboard, at Sheila's photo posted right next to the current Mrs. Merrick. She had to admit that Sam was right on one count. Why would Tim be so interested in Sheila Logan? *On the other hand, why'd he ask me out last week?* Was he that stupid? That arrogant? She huffed out a sigh, logged into Sam's computer and pushed the box with Sheila's documents to her side. Too many questions, too few answers. With luck, she'd find something here.

CHAPTER 33

Jessie checked the emails first, but she'd seen those before. Interesting that Tim's emails were the only personal ones Sheila kept, and that, Jessie thought, was probably so she'd have material to blackmail him with if it ever came to that. And maybe it had come to that. Tim hadn't responded to Sheila's last email two days before Thanksgiving, the last Tuesday in November.

> I'll see you tonight and we can talk. I'm leaving tomorrow morning and can be back by Saturday. Wish you could come with me. Next Thanksgiving, we'll be together. I love you! xoxo S

The tone of the message seemed to indicate that Sheila hadn't felt threatened by Tim. To the contrary, she seemed to think that things would work out, that he'd be with her soon. Jessie leaned back. Sam was right. There were too many inconsistencies in Tim's story, and he had no alibi for the next two days—the days when Sheila was likely killed. She tapped her fingers on the desk.

She just couldn't buy Tim as a murderer—first of Sheila, and then a little old lady. It was too easy. He's a smart guy; if he was a killer, wouldn't he have shown up at the hospital? Created a bulletproof alibi? She wished she could speak with him, but they'd both be in hot water if she did. And if Rock Powell was already in prison when Sheila was killed, she'd just have to find another possibility, another suspect, and maybe there was something in here that could point her in another direction.

Jessie leaned forward and clicked on Sheila's work emails next. There were hundreds. Most were from Administration about meetings, patient complaints, budget questions. The budget office sent several messages asking Sheila to sign off on the ER's final fiscal year budget. Jessie clicked on the attachment—a detailed Excel report that included a confusing array of ER accounts and expenses, invoices, bills paid, costs for staff, equipment, education, general upgrades—and there, at the end, the strange bills for ER aftercare services and equipment that Jessie had seen before when she'd glanced at the emails in the ER, and which, she knew for a fact, the ER did not provide. Was Sheila stealing money, or was this someone else's handiwork? Or maybe it was a pilot project that the staff didn't know about yet.

The ER aftercare services seemed to be provided by a company called Rosehall, Ltd. That was the name of the business that had sent Kate as a travel nurse to the ER. Jessie googled the company, and came up with a mansion in Jamaica, but no businesses by that name. Strange—why wouldn't this company have a public profile or a website available on the internet? Wasn't that how these companies got business, got noticed? But maybe things in healthcare corporations were different; maybe word of mouth among medical professionals and hospital administrators was how they made themselves stand out, and maybe they were new. The emails and bills went back for just the last year.

She pulled up all the emailed invoices and messages from Rosehall and dropped them into a new folder. Once she was sure she had them all, she started with the first one Sheila had saved. It was May eighteenth of the previous year. The bill was for aftercare services and was for $250,000. She remembered that last May, the ER had been severely understaffed. Overtime was kept to a minimum because of budget constraints, or so Sheila had said at the time, but why spend $250,000 on some kind of shadow services when the ER needed nurses? It was only when the union had stepped in and filed a grievance that Sheila had been forced to hire two new nurses.

Jessie continued to read, her mouth falling open at the escalating costs of these Rosehall services, whatever they were. Four hundred thousand the next two months, and then, in August and September, $700,000; by October the bill was for $1.1 million. She turned her attention to the documents in the box and began to rifle through the papers, searching for anything from Rosehall. Finally, almost at the bottom lay a pile of bills from Rosehall—all signed by Sheila and stamped *Paid.*

Jessie scanned the pages, but the bills were short on specifics. There were patient names, medical record numbers, birthdates and notations indicating that aftercare services and equipment had been provided. She ran her finger along the list of names looking for anything that sounded familiar. And finally, there it was—Eddie Wilson, her friend Eddie from the ER. A flush of heat ran along the back of her neck. This was a lie. He was homeless, and he never had any aftercare services. Her eyes widened—Eddie certainly did not have the electric wheelchair that had been billed to Medicare.

Then she remembered Mary Stewart—the news story had described her job as a case manager responsible for Medicare and Medicaid compliance, which Jessie knew included billing. She googled Mary Stewart once again, this time focusing on the nursing home where she worked—a facility called Sunny Days, just beyond Bluebell Creek, Mary's hometown. A quick check of Sunny Days revealed a glut of stories that the home was being investigated for billing discrepancies.

The director, according to the news report, had denied those reports, stating they had a very qualified nurse on staff who managed that work and that her integrity was above reproach. The story was dated six weeks before Mary Stewart's body was found. And the final story was one month after that, a buried story stating no evidence of fraud was found at Sunny Days.

In spite of that, Jessie began to wonder if maybe this was the connection between the two cases. She had to do something. She couldn't wait for Sam. She needed to speak with the West Virginia police. She leaned back in Sam's chair, her heart pounding. She googled the number for the West Virginia state police, called and asked to be connected to Homicide. Jessie explained who she was, where she was calling from and why, and she was quickly connected to a detective. She explained Sheila's death and asked if they'd had a look at Mary Stewart's computer.

"And you are?" he asked.

She explained again and said he could call her back if he liked so he could be certain she was calling from Boston police headquarters.

"No need," he said. "We have upgraded caller ID. I can see that you're calling from Sam Dallas's office, so go ahead and ask. If I can help, I will. I spoke with Sam a few days ago, so I know about the nurse up there who was strangled and found in a river. But between us, we couldn't come up with anything else that connected them."

"That's just it," Jessie said. "There is something. Mary's nursing home was investigated for Medicare fraud, correct?"

"Yes, but there was never any evidence. The Feds dropped it."

"But her computer. Did that show anything, any weird bills? Or a company called Rosehall?"

"Interesting that you ask that. The Feds took hold of her computer, but it had been wiped clean, so whatever had been in there was gone. And no, Rosehall doesn't ring a bell."

"But couldn't a forensics technology team still recover the computer files?"

"One would think so, but not in this case. That computer was scrubbed by someone who knew what they were doing, and the hard drive had been removed. The fraud investigation was stalled. If anything turns up, we'll certainly advise them, but right now, we have nothing on the murder or the fraud investigation. All we have right now is an artist's sketch of a man who was seen with Stewart shortly before she disappeared. I can fax it to you if you'd like."

"Yes, please," Jessie said, reciting Sam's fax number.

"Okay, sending it now. Please keep us posted on whatever you find."

Jessie scrawled his name and number on a notepad and hung up before retrieving the fax—a grainy sketch of an average face. He could have been anyone; there was nothing especially distinctive in the drawing. The description that accompanied the sketch noted brownish hair, brown eyes, no distinguishing marks. She sighed as a long, low rumble of hunger sprang from her stomach. It was one o'clock. *Where did the hours go?* She'd take a break, call Donna to ask about any current bills from this Rosehall company, and grab lunch at the cafeteria downstairs.

She sent a quick text to Sam. *Found some interesting stuff in Sheila's emails and invoices, and a possible connection to Mary Stewart in West Virginia. Talk later.*

Connection? Still waiting for my warrants, see you later, he texted back.

She dialed the direct line to Donna's office. "Got a minute?" she asked when Donna answered.

"Just barely. You stopping by?"

"Maybe later," Jessie said before adding that her car had been broken into.

"Really?"

"Yeah, a few other unsettling things, too. Got me a little skittish."

"Just be careful."

Jessie pulled the small canister from her pocket and rolled it in her hand. "I asked Sam about a gun. He gave me pepper spray instead."

"You wanted a gun?"

"What happened?" Kate's voice suddenly echoed on the line.

Darn. Jessie was on speakerphone. "Nothing," she answered curtly, shoving the canister into her pocket as though Kate or Donna could see it. "Someone broke into my car in the garage."

"Oh, no. Was anything stolen?"

"There's nothing to steal. I don't even know why he'd target my car. There are better cars there."

"How do you know it was a *he*?" Kate asked.

"Eddie saw him but was afraid to approach him. Just as well. He didn't take anything."

"Eddie?" Kate asked. "Our Eddie?"

"Yes, our Eddie," she said, emphasizing the *our*. "I actually called to speak with Donna, so if you don't mind…"

"I have to get back to work anyway," Kate said, a perky lilt to her voice. "Glad you're okay, Jessie. See you later?"

Jessie ignored the question. "Is she gone?" she whispered.

"Yes," Donna said. "Sorry, I didn't even think about the speaker being on, she just walked in."

"It's okay. Do you have a few minutes? I just want to follow up on some weird bills and invoices and strange things in Sheila's budget."

"Not right now. But call me later."

"I will. Maybe I'll stop in and check on Eddie."

"He isn't here," Donna answered. "I was just in the waiting room. No sign of him."

"I hope he's holed up somewhere warm. Maybe I'll check the garage later."

Donna was tapping her fingers on her desk, the beat thrumming through the line. "Maybe you should stay away from there."

"Maybe. I'll see you later. Okay?" She hung up as a text from Sam appeared.

I'm heading back to the office. See you there.

CHAPTER 34

In the outer office, detectives were clustered around Ralph, who seemed to be scolding a forensics technician about a piece of evidence that hadn't been signed out. "Do you understand how important it is to maintain the integrity of the chain of evidence?" The technician bowed his head and nodded. Ralph caught Jessie's eye and shook his head. "Sam's waiting for you," he said.

"Thanks, Ralph," she said, glad to avoid his line of fire. She discarded the last of her sandwich in a nearby basket, walked into Sam's office and sank into a chair. "Ralph looks unhappy."

"He's angry about a misplaced piece of evidence. And he's right. He's doing a stellar job. No doubt about it. He'll be running this place in a few years." He pushed his chair closer to the desk. "Have a seat," he said. "Tell me what you found."

She told him about the bills and statements from Rosehall that didn't make sense. "The bills were paid in increasing amounts—the last one was for over a million dollars. And it was for services that I know we didn't provide."

"Ahh," he said, tenting his fingers and leaning back.

"And Mary Stewart's nursing home was being investigated for fraud when she was found dead. She was the nurse who kept track of and approved those charges. Sound familiar?"

Sam began to type away, his eyes on his computer screen.

"So, I should tell you that I already spoke with the West Virginia police," Jessie continued. "The federal fraud investigation was halted after Stewart's computer was scrubbed clean. The hard drive was gone and there was no paper trail. All of it had vanished. And they realized that only after her body was found." She caught his eye to see if maybe she'd overstepped, but he only nodded. "I wrote the detective's name and number down. He faxed us a sketch of a man who was seen with Mary Stewart before she disappeared. They're both on your desk." She tilted her head in the direction of the paper. "You spoke with him earlier, but that was before I saw the connections—those bogus bills and charges."

"Interesting. The warrant I got today was for Sheila Logan's bank accounts. She had three, and each of them had an impressive balance—over one million altogether. Most of that was deposited in the last eight months. Pretty impressive for a nurse manager, wouldn't you say?"

Jessie's jaw dropped open. "With Mary Stewart's hard drive missing, I'm wondering why no one got to Sheila's computer before we did."

Sam's brow furrowed. "Maybe they tried."

"Do you know where the money in Sheila's accounts came from?"

"They were separate direct deposits. I don't have the sender yet, still waiting on that information from the banks."

"What about Rock Powell?"

Ralph appeared in the doorway, his tie loosened, a satisfied smile tugging at the corners of his lips. "He's a tough character. He was fostered out beyond Springfield in a little mill town whose best days were long past. He was one of eight kids the family had taken in, probably for the income. He started using, and then selling drugs when he was ten years old. Spent three years in juvenile detention, back to foster care and bounced around like that until he was seventeen, when he was arrested for assault with a deadly weapon."

Jessie leaned forward. "So, he's our guy?"

Ralph shook his head. "Not likely. He's been in Walpole for four months, so he's off the list. He was genuinely surprised that she was dead, though that might have been an act. He might have set her up. His rap sheet is four pages long. Runs from minor drug charges to assault to attempted murder. He's one bad guy but being in prison is a fairly good alibi." He sank into a chair. "I'll still look into him. He may have connected with someone at Walpole to go after Sheila."

"We have something else," Sam said, and filled him in on the money in Sheila's accounts and the question of fraud, and the possibility of Mary Stewart's murder being connected. "How much money are we talking?" Ralph asked.

"Over a million," Sam said.

Ralph whistled.

Jessie caught his eye. "Sheila was signing off on bills that didn't seem to be based on the ER's work. Exorbitant bills for services and equipment that we don't provide, and listing real patients including Eddie, my homeless friend. I know for a fact he didn't receive any of those services. He was even billed for an electric wheelchair. There's a whole list of patient names, hospital numbers and Medicare and Medicaid numbers." She paused to take a deep breath. "I googled the company and couldn't find anything."

"Interesting. What's the name?" Ralph asked.

"Rosehall."

Sam's fingers raced across his keyboard. "Rosehall, you said?" She nodded.

"You're right. Nothing. Jessie, will you try to follow that up tomorrow? Check at the hospital? I'll ask the SIU to look into the money angle. It might not be related to her murder."

"SIU?" Jessie asked.

"Special Investigations Unit," Ralph replied, clearly relishing his role as teacher. He swiveled in his chair toward Jessie. "They cover fraud, banking, shell companies. They can dig pretty deep."

Sam turned and scribbled the information about Sheila's bank account on the whiteboard, drawing a line and a question mark between Sheila Logan, Tim Merrick, and Rock Powell. "Ralph, will you check on Rock, see if he had any connection to the money?"

"Will do," he said, straightening his tie.

Jessie huffed out a sigh. Sam was on the wrong track. She was sure of it. Sheila's money didn't come from Rock or Tim Merrick, and that money was at the center of this. "If we're all set here, I think I'll head home. I've barely eaten today," she said regretting the last bit of sandwich that she'd discarded. "My brain is about to shut down." She stood and slipped into her coat and grabbed her bag.

"Hey," Sam said, standing and reaching for his own coat. "I'm hungry too. Early dinner?"

"Yes," she answered almost too quickly. It would be good to get out, and not just to Foley's after work. She spent too much time alone wishing things were different, that there was someone to come home to.

"It's a date," he said, his eyes shimmering.

Jessie smiled, catching herself before she said something sappy, which was a good thing because Sam turned to Ralph. "How about it? You coming?"

Ralph looked at his watch. "Not this time. My wife's expecting me home for dinner. Another time, count me in."

A swell of relief swept through Jessie. It wasn't that she didn't like Ralph. She did. But this way, she could be alone with Sam, see if he'd had a chance to look into Angela Novak's story.

"I'm going to check to see if anyone's still in SIU. Be right back," Sam said as he strode through the door.

"Jessie," Ralph said softly as Sam disappeared. "We never get a chance to talk. How's it going for you?"

"Good, I think. At least I'm back. I heard you're doing great."

"That's nice to know. I heard the same about you. We should connect now and again. As rookies in Homicide, we should stick together."

She smiled and held out her hand. "Deal."

"Deal," he said, gripping her hand tightly. "Next time, drinks are on me."

"And don't think I won't hold you to that," she said with a wide smile.

"Enjoy your date with Sam." Ralph winked at her and hurried out.

*

Sam and Jessie wound up at a local restaurant and slid into a booth, the seats covered with plush red leather, a flickering candle on the table between them. Jessie tugged her coat off and reached for the menu, her color fading at the prices.

"Whoa," Sam said, his eyes glued to the open menu. "I had no idea this place was so pricey. You can pay next time, Jessie. This one's on me."

Jessie was too relieved to be proud. "Thanks, Sam. This is a little rich for me. Next time, I promise, I'll pay." She glanced at the menu again; the least expensive item was a chopped salad, whatever that was.

The waiter, clad in black pants and starched white shirt topped off with a red bow tie, arrived with glasses of ice water and a cheery smile. "Our specials today are a six-ounce prime rib served with mashed sweet potatoes and broccoli for $39.95, and a fresh haddock filet sautéed in lemon butter and served over rice with a side of asparagus at $32."

He paused to see if they were paying attention. Jessie nodded. "Can I get you a drink while you decide?" he asked.

"Water's good for me," Jessie replied, afraid to even guess at the wine list prices.

"Really?" Sam asked. "I'll have a Pinot noir. The house selection will be fine."

The waiter nodded and backed away.

"I don't feel comfortable staying here," Jessie whispered, reaching for her water. "I'm almost afraid to drink this. I bet there's a charge."

Sam laughed and tapped his own glass against hers. "It's okay."

Jessie shook her head. "It isn't. This is supposed to be an early dinner, not this." She flicked her finger against the menu. "This is a little highbrow for me. And it's only Tuesday."

Sam smiled. "All the more reason. Let's enjoy Tuesday, and anyway, we deserve this. I have a feeling we're close on the Logan thing. Just enjoy it. I'm getting the prime rib."

Jessie cringed inwardly. She knew he was focused on Tim Merrick, or maybe Rock, but she just couldn't see it yet. When the waiter returned with Sam's wine, they ordered—the prime rib for Sam, the fish for Jessie. "And a glass of white wine," she added.

Over dinner, Sam declared a work-free zone. "We can talk about the case tomorrow. Right now, let's just enjoy the food and some conversation. Agreed?"

She nodded reluctantly. She wanted to talk about Sheila's emails and the hospital bills that didn't make sense. She wanted to ask what else he had on Merrick.

"So, what should we discuss?" Sam asked as he sliced into his rare cut of beef, the blood oozing out.

She started on the fish special she'd ordered, and smiled. "I hate to ask. I know you're busy, but have you had a chance to look into Angela Novak?" she asked, reaching for her napkin and catching a drip of butter that rolled down her chin.

"Oh, hell, Jessie, no. I'm sorry. I've been so wrapped up in this case, but I promise I'll get to it."

"There's no rush," she said. "I've waited for years. A few weeks or more won't hurt." She sipped on her wine to hide the almost numbing disappointment she felt. Most people, she'd learned, had happy memories of their childhood, but Jessie could only remember her loneliness and her father's anger. It had shaped everything in her life, and she wanted to change that. And, maybe, Angela Novak could help.

"Have you spoken with her?" Sam asked, interrupting her thoughts.

"No, just a text here and there. That's all. I don't want to get wrapped up in her story if it's all lies. It's strange to find out *now* that I had a mother who says she loved me all along."

Sam's expression, so often unreadable, softened, his eyes crinkling at the corners. He placed his hand over hers. "Anything else I can do?"

"No, not yet. I'm just trying to adjust to this—to maybe having a family, and you're the first person I've told. The weird thing is, I've hated her my whole life, and if it turns out her story is true—that my dad kicked her out—well, I don't know what I'll think. She said she's been trying to reach out to me for years. She's not the monster I'd imagined." Her eyes teared up and she heard her father's warning. *Never let them see you cry.*

He might have been wrong about other things, but that advice had carried her this far. Why change now? She blinked away her tears. "It's all good. I'm just not used to having a mother. If I do. I just want to be sure." She almost mentioned the half-sister, but she wasn't even sure that was true either. She'd just keep that to herself. For now.

"Hey, I know this is important. This week, I'll check her out." He squeezed her hand before pulling away. "How are you otherwise? We never really get to talk, do we?"

"No, we don't. At least, not privately. This is nice." She rested her fork against her plate and lifted her glass of wine, signaling the waiter for another. He hurried over with a second glass of wine.

Sam smiled, the light catching the silver flecks in his eyes, and Jessie wondered, not for the first time, why she hadn't chosen him when she'd had the chance. But that horse had already left the barn, and if she'd learned anything, it was that good choices don't come around twice.

He tapped his glass against hers. "I'm relieved that Ralph didn't come. I wanted to ask you something, and if you're not interested—no harm, no bad feelings. Okay?"

"What is it?" she asked, seized by a sudden dread that he wanted her off the case again. But she'd proved herself, hadn't she? She took a long swallow of wine.

He leaned across the table, taking both of her hands in his, the candlelight catching the deep pools of silver in his eyes. She decided to simply savor the swell of contentment she felt when she was with him.

"I… I don't know how to ask this," he said, gripping her hands tightly. "I just wanted to know if you think that maybe you and I could go out sometime? On a date. A real date? Instead of all this pretending and dancing around each other."

A spark of joy bubbled up from deep inside, and Jessie opened her mouth to speak but the words wouldn't come. Instead, she laughed softly.

"This is embarrassing. I'm sorry, Jessie," Sam said, slipping his damp hands from hers. "Forget I asked." The shimmer in his eyes faded, leaving a flat-as-glass emptiness in its wake.

"No, no," she said. "You misunderstood. I laughed because I was surprised. And happy. Your question made me happy. That's all. And the answer is yes. Yes."

He leaned over to her, brushing his lips against hers. A sudden swarm of butterflies danced in her chest. Had she ever felt this totally unexpected kind of joy before?

CHAPTER 35

Day 11—Wednesday

It was the wind rattling her windows that nudged Jessie from sleep. She rubbed her eyes, slipped from her bed and opened the blinds to have a look. A sprinkling of icy frost on her window blocked her view. She held her warm palm tight against the window and watched as the frost melted away, creating a small porthole view to the street. She groaned. It was snowing again, the picture-perfect flakes piling up quickly, the drifts burying cars and thoughts of an easy commute. She checked her watch—five a.m. There was still time for plows and sanders to clear the streets, and nothing she could do at the moment anyway, so she crawled back under the covers, pulling them over her head and snuggling into her pillow, an image of Sam filling her dreams.

It was almost eight when her phone pinged with a new message. Jessie sprang up. She'd been deliriously happy and had simply forgotten to set her alarm when she'd gotten in last night and hadn't noticed when she'd risen at five to see the snow. It was from Sam. *Oh, no!* She was going to be late today. She swiped to see the message and smiled.

I'll pick you up at ten. Roads are a mess. Sam

She was grateful, at least this once, for the vagaries of a Boston winter. She took her time showering, brewed a pot of coffee, scrambled some eggs, and by ten a.m., she was dressed and ready and standing outside amid the swirling gusts of snow. She'd shoveled the front steps and sidewalk so that Rufus wouldn't have to, and she stood shivering, her hands deep in her pockets, her scarf pulled over her face.

The snow had slowed to a soft drift of lacy flakes. She breathed in deeply, inhaling the smell of winter—cold air, cold concrete, all of it fresh, as though the arctic air pushed out the usual city scents of misery, of rotting food and lost dreams. A slice of sun shimmered through the gray sky and Jessie smiled to herself.

It seemed an eternity before she saw Sam's Crown Vic turn onto K Street and slide to a stop in front of her place. The door creaked when she pulled it open, a gust of warm air enveloping her as she slipped inside.

"Ooh, you have heat?" she asked. "I thought it didn't really work."

"Morning, Jessie. I let the car warm up while I shoveled. And shoveled. So yes, we have heat. For now." He passed her a coffee and nodded to a box on the floor. "Stopped at Dunkin's and got us coffee and donuts. In this weather, who knows if anyone else will make it in."

"Really? Detectives won't be in?" She wrapped her fingers around the cup, letting the heat seep into her hands. "Thanks for this, you're the best."

He shrugged. "They don't have to be physically in there if they're actively working a case. Snow generally makes it easier for us to track down suspects at known addresses. I'm going in because Tim Merrick is supposed to be coming in with his attorney and his financial records, and you're coming in because I'm hoping you can have a closer look at Sheila's emails and bank records, see if there's anything related. And maybe, once that's done, we can begin to plan an evening alone, away from work."

She slid down in her seat, a rush of happiness, of hope, sweeping through her. "So, first order of business—figure out who killed Sheila Logan and Mrs. Grigsby. And maybe Mary Stewart."

He rested his hand on her thigh, her skin tingling at his touch. The car began to swerve sideways and Sam, his eyes firmly on the road, lifted his hand away and gripped the steering wheel tightly, righting the car and slowing his speed. "Let's just get there in one piece, and then we can work the case."

Despite the weather, headquarters was busy as always—the parking lot crowded, the hallways a flurry of activity, the hum of chatter filling the air. "Hey, Sam," someone called. They stopped, and Sam turned. "We lost power this morning. Computers are still down. IT is working on getting everything back up, but just so you know, it might be a while."

"Damn it," Sam muttered, taking the stairs two at a time, Jessie trying to keep up. The outer office held only one detective, his feet on his desk, a newspaper in his hands. "Nothing working, Sam. Just so you know."

"I heard, Larry. Anything in today's *Globe*?"

"A story about Sheila Logan, nothing else."

Jessie lifted her lips into a half-smile. "Let me guess—a saintly nurse who met a tragic end?"

Larry laughed. "That's it in a nutshell, except for the dig at Boston's finest for not solving the case yet."

"Nobody reads that old rag anyway," Sam said. "Any word from Tim Merrick and his lawyer?"

Larry pulled his feet off of his desk and sat up straight. "They cancelled. Sorry, I thought you knew already."

"No problem," Sam said, walking into his office and trying to reboot his computer. But Larry was right. It was down. "I guess you can look through the rest of Sheila's papers," he said. "Anything there?"

"A few things of interest, but I wanted to cross-reference them with her emails." She leaned down and plucked a sheaf of papers out. She shrugged her arms from her coat and lay the papers on the edge of Sam's desk. She scanned the papers and huffed out a long sigh. "Without the emails, these don't tell me much."

She picked up one of the Rosehall invoices, found the contact information and dialed the number listed from Sam's desk phone. Her call went right to voicemail. No introduction, no mention of Rosehall, just one of those generic voicemail announcements. She tried again, certain that she'd dialed wrong, but the result was the same. She grunted to herself.

Sam, true to form, sensed her frustration. "We got a call," he said, standing over her desk. "Just so we don't waste the day, want to go out? See what it is? Probably not a homicide—it's a guy found frozen in a snowdrift, but we can go have a look. You can see what it's like on the street. What do you say?"

She couldn't get her coat back on fast enough. She was longing to be outside, to get moving, to see what this job was really all about. "I'm coming," she shouted, racing after him as he headed out the door. "So, what do we do when we get there?"

"We're just going to have a look. I wouldn't ordinarily go to something like this unless there were suspicions of foul play, but I think it'd be good for you to see what it's like to see a body in the street, maybe start to get used to it. It's different from the ER, that's for sure."

She nodded and sat quietly as he drove past the hospital and down Albany Street to an area under the expressway, where Sam parked the car and they got out. She could see the lights of an ambulance and a police cruiser, and people standing around. She pulled on her gloves, adjusted her scarf, and followed Sam, the air crackling with the cold. "First, we're going to scan the scene as we approach, look for anything in the landscape that seems out of place. Sometimes, we can pick up important evidence right by the scene, and you could miss it if you're not paying attention. Once we're by the body, stop and look at it from every angle—the position of the body, the face, and especially for you, the wounds, if there are any…"

And though Sam continued to speak and to move forward, Jessie stopped in her tracks, the sound of his voice fading. Just ahead, poking out through the snow, was the cap and scarf that she'd given to Eddie not so long ago; she raked her mind to remember if she'd seen him since he was huddled in the garage the night her car had been broken into.

"You coming?" Sam called, standing by the body.

She swallowed the lump in her throat and moved closer, and then she saw him. It was Eddie, curled into himself as though he'd been trying to keep warm. He had on the gloves she'd given him as well, but none of that had helped. He was dead: a layer of frost covered his face, his eyelashes white with snow. She felt tears prick at her eyes, and for the first time in her life she forgot her father's old adage—*never let them see you cry*—and she fell to her knees and wrapped her arms around him, her tears falling like icicles onto his frozen face. She could hear the concerned hush of murmurs behind her, but she didn't care.

A hand touched her shoulder. "Jessie?" Sam whispered. She shrugged him away and took off her own coat to wrap around Eddie. She wasn't sure how long she knelt there when she heard the crunch of fresh footsteps in the snow.

"I'm here for him," Tony said softly, squatting down beside her.

She shook her head, her tears running along her cheeks, her eyeliner trailing down her face. "No," she said. "Not this way, Tony. Let the ambulance bring him into the ER. It was his home. Just let me take him there one last time so everyone can say goodbye. Please."

Sam leaned down and ran a hand along her back. "They'll take him," he said, pulling her to her feet so the EMTs could gently lift him onto their stretcher.

Sam and Jessie followed the ambulance, sirens blaring as they headed back down Albany Street and into the ambulance bay. Jessie jumped from Sam's car and led the ambulance crew into the ER. "Trauma One," she directed them, calling Donna on the intercom.

"Ooh, Jessie, I'm sorry," Donna said. "I'll let everyone know so they can say goodbye."

And one by one, the staff who'd taken care of him came in to say a prayer, kiss his cheek, or just stand quietly. Eddie had been one of them, a family member, almost. Jessie gently wiped away the last traces of ice and snow from his face, and when Tony came for him, she was ready to let him go. Tony pulled the sheet over Eddie's face and Sam suddenly appeared. "I'll help," he said to Tony, and he turned then to Jessie. "And I'll be outside whenever you're ready." He pulled her into a hug.

She leaned into him and let herself sink into the comfort of his embrace. Aside from losing her father, she'd only witnessed the grief of others. She'd forgotten how all-encompassing it was—the sadness, the what ifs, the last images that flickered through her mind. He pulled her closer and kissed her forehead. And that gentle touch was enough to trigger another bout of weeping, her shoulders heaving as she cried. Sam held her tight through all of it, through the swell of tears that dotted his shirt and jacket, never once pulling away.

Finally, her sobs subsided, she sniffled and stood back from him, turning to reach for a tissue to wipe her nose. "I'm ready," she whispered, and Sam nodded. Jessie took one last look at the trauma room before pressing the intercom. "Housekeeping to Trauma One," she said, her voice cracking.

CHAPTER 36

"You okay, Jessie?" Sam asked, wrapping his arms around her as they settled into his car. "I can just take you home." He wiped away her tears with his fingers and brushed his lips against hers. "Whatever you need."

She nestled into his shoulder. Sam was exactly what she needed right now. "I don't want to go home and cry. That won't change anything, it won't bring him back. Right now, I just want to get back to work, to Sheila's emails, and figure this mess out. That will help take my mind off Eddie, and right now, that's what I need."

Sam released her from his arms and eased the car back into traffic, the streets cleared, the cars hugged close together. And as Sam drove, Jessie noticed how the snowdrifts had left no room for the usual hordes of homeless who'd taken over these streets with their tents and blankets and shopping carts, but today, they were gone, only a stray cart poking out of the snow indicating they'd been here at all. She sank further into her seat. "Sam, do you think Eddie was outside because he was afraid to go back into the garage after the break-in to my car?"

"I don't have any idea. Sorry, Jessie."

"I know he hated the shelters. I was just wondering why he wouldn't go to the ER on such a bad night."

"That storm came on pretty fast. He might have just been caught unawares, and maybe he was already curled up fast asleep when the snow and cold came. That's the best way to think about, isn't it? There's nothing you could have done for him."

*

At headquarters, they were greeted with the news that the internet was working once again. "Who knows? A power surge, maybe," a uniformed officer said.

"I need to follow up on some warrants in another case, so I'm going to set you up out here," Sam said, pointing to an empty detective's desk. He stepped into his office, emerging with the box of Sheila's documents. "I'll download Sheila's emails and bank statements so you can have a look and check them against them the paper bills in here." He set the box on the floor. "Give me a shout if you need anything." He strode back to his own office and disappeared inside.

Jessie pulled a pile of bills and invoices out and spread them on the desk. She was determined to throw herself into work, as there was nothing she could do now for Eddie. Once she clicked onto the file she'd created with Sheila's bills, she opened the file on the bank statements. Sheila had had three accounts, and each of them with a lot of money—$400,000 in one, $325,000 in another and $280,000 in the third.

Jessie whistled. Sheila Logan had over one million dollars in her accounts. That money had been deposited in the last six months before her disappearance, and aside from her weekly salary—$1,600 after taxes—the deposits were all from Rosehall, Ltd, the company whose name was on the dodgy bills and invoices for the non-existent aftercare services.

Jessie spread the bills from Rosehall across the desk. They were vague on details, but clear on amount due: $250,000 in May of last year, $400,000 in both June and July, $750,000 in August and September, and $1.1 million in October, the month before she'd disappeared. She pulled up the calculator on her iPhone and added the numbers—her eyes wide as she saw the total—the staggering sum of $3,650,000. Sheila had signed off on each invoice and the financial office had stamped *Paid*. The direct deposits to Sheila's accounts were each made weeks after the bills were paid. *She was stealing!* And right under everyone's nose.

"Sam," she called, jumping up. "You have to see this."

He appeared at his office door and made his way to the desk. "What do you have?"

"This," she said, pointing to the invoices from Rosehall and the corresponding deposits from that company to Sheila's accounts.

Sam leaned in for a closer look and whistled. "Three accounts, so the deposits wouldn't look too suspicious."

"And look at this." Jessie pointed to the account that held the $280,000 total. "This was the account where her hospital pay was deposited. It looks like she opened the other two later, so that the account connected to her job wouldn't raise suspicions if she were ever questioned." Jessie ran her hand across the pile of bills. "The deposits to her accounts came in within weeks, sometimes days after these were paid. It looks as though she was getting a third of the total paid out. And she has confirmation emails from Rosehall including routing numbers and deposit confirmation. She had some kind of dicey partnership with this company."

"And this is the group that doesn't show up on the internet, right?"

Jessie nodded. "They don't exist. I think it's some kind of shadow company skimming money from the hospital. These bills, though—they're so real-looking, I don't think the discrepancies would have been caught but for Sheila's death."

Sam ran his fingers through his hair. "SIU is working on a warrant so we can dig deeper, see where these deposits originate, try to follow the routing numbers and see if we can trace Rosehall that way. And—"

"Hey, Sam," a young woman called from the entryway. "Dr. Merrick is here to see you. He's downstairs."

"Tell him I'll be right there." He raised a brow and turned to Jessie. "Well, that's a surprise. I'll set you up in the viewing room so you can watch. Okay?"

"No. Doesn't this stuff with Sheila and Rosehall absolve Tim? I mean, why question him again?"

Sam's jaw tightened. "It doesn't absolve him at all. I want to see his bank statements, too. Maybe he's a part of this Rosehall group."

Jessie's throat tightened, but she kept her mouth shut. She wasn't in the mood to argue with Sam just then. She'd just have to prove that she was right. She followed him down the hall and watched as he adjusted the monitor and audio buttons, the empty room coming into view. She sat and picked at her cuticles until she heard voices on the monitor.

She looked up to see Dr. Merrick, a folder in his hand, take a seat. He looked almost disheveled in wrinkled jeans, a crisp white button-down shirt open at the neck revealing mottled splotches of red dotting his pasty skin. He jerked his head in a slight nod toward Sam as he placed the folder on the desk, his fingers trembling. Jessie's heart broke for him, for the humiliation this thing with Sheila had brought him.

"These are our bank statements, mine and my wife's. We each have our own account, and there's one joint account. I've brought our credit card information and income tax forms as well."

Sam slid into the seat across from Tim. "Where's your lawyer? Is he coming?"

Tim shook his head. "He canceled earlier because of the snow, but when the roads cleared, I just wanted to get this over with. I called him, but he couldn't make it. He knows I'm here. He thinks it's a mistake. I don't. I have nothing to hide."

"Alright. You're on tape saying that."

"I understand. Here's the information you asked for."

He slid the folder toward Sam, who opened it and began to scan the documents. "And this is it? No other accounts? Nothing hidden from your wife?"

A blush of red flooded Tim's cheeks. "Only the short-lived affairs, which I will regret forever. Our finances are shared. Neither of us hides anything that way."

Sam offered a wry smile. "Ever heard of the Rosehall company? They offer aftercare services, or something like that."

Tim scratched his chin. "Never heard of them, but I don't have anything to do with discharge planning or home care services. The nurses take care of that. What is Rosehall?"

"I'm not entirely sure yet. Did Sheila ever mention them?"

"Not that I remember. We didn't spend that much time together. We didn't have long conversations. I'm embarrassed to admit that our trysts were for sex only. At least on my part. For Sheila, as I've told you, it was much more. I honestly had no idea she was like that—vengeful and hateful."

"And even though she threatened to report you, which potentially could have ruined your career, your marriage, your life, you never harmed her? Even by accident?"

Tim sat forward, his expression tight, his eyes narrowed, his voice suddenly forceful. "Never. I'll take a lie detector test if you'd like. I never harmed her. By November, I was doing my best to avoid her. And that is the truth."

"I can keep this?" Sam asked, lifting the folder.

"Yes, those are for you. As you can see, I'm not rich, but I work hard and I just want to get back to that, to my wife and the hospital and the things that matter. You see, even in death, Sheila is exacting her revenge."

CHAPTER 37

Jessie waited until she was pretty sure that Tim had left. She didn't want to run into him and cause him even more embarrassment than this whole thing had given him. She moved toward the window and pressed her face to the frosty glass. The snow had stopped but the wind had picked up and swirled the drifts high into the air. The streets were clear, the traffic was filling in, but the homeless were still missing. She wondered if they'd gone to shelters, though she knew that, just like Eddie, the hardcore homeless shunned the shelters as dangerous.

"Jessie? Are you okay?"

She spun at the sound of Sam's voice. "Yeah, why?"

He shrugged. "I've been standing here a few minutes. You never heard me come in. I know it's been a tough day, with Eddie and Tim Merrick, and all."

"I'm okay, really. Just wishing I'd seen Eddie yesterday. Maybe I could have…"

He placed his hands on her shoulders and looked into her eyes. "You couldn't have done anything for him. He wouldn't have let you."

Jessie smiled faintly, remembering him curled up in the garage just days ago, refusing to go to a shelter. "He did live by his own rules."

Sam released her and dropped into a chair. "He did, and I don't think he'd have done it any other way."

Jessie bowed her head and slid into a nearby chair, inhaling deeply.

Sam stayed quiet as if to allow her time with her thoughts. She caught his gaze and smiled. "Thanks, Sam. I'm ready if you want to get back to work."

He nodded and pointed to the monitor. "What did you think of Dr. Merrick?"

"I think he's right. Surgeons have nothing to do with discharge planning or visiting nurse services. All he'd care about would be the surgical wound, and follow-up for that."

"But it sounds as though that's what Rosehall provides, doesn't it?"

She shook her head, her shoulders tight. "Except that Rosehall doesn't seem to exist."

"The SIU is already on it. They're going to need that box full of documents." He glanced at his watch. "It's almost four. Want to call it a day?"

"Can we stop at the ER? I'd like to ask Donna if Rosehall has been in touch. It seems to me they sent our travel nurse, Kate, so maybe a part of the company is legit. It will only take a minute."

Sam stood, the chair creaking as he did so. "Okay. Let's go."

They headed back to Sam's office to collect their things. Jessie eyed the documents she'd been going through, scattered on the desk she was using. Her brows knitted, remembering how she'd already lost some of those documents. She knew she should tell Sam what had happened and get it over with, but she couldn't bring herself to do that. Not yet.

She knew that lying—about anything—never ended well, but she needed to work this out herself. She watched as he turned and went into his office, and she hurriedly pulled out her phone and took photos of the Rosehall invoices and bills. She didn't want to wait for the SIU to come up with something. She wanted to figure this out now. "Ready?" she called, putting everything back in place just as he reappeared and reached for the box.

"Everything in here?" he asked. "I'm just gonna drop it off at SIU. This stuff will make much more sense to them." He lifted the box and stepped into the hallway. "I'll see you downstairs."

She made her way to the staircase, pulling on her gloves and hiking her backpack over her shoulder. "All set?" Sam asked, catching up with her.

She nodded and matched his stride as they walked to his car, which was covered with a fresh coating of blowing snow. They brushed the flakes from the windows and headed to the ER. When Sam pulled into the ambulance bay, Jessie threw open her door and jumped out. She didn't want Donna to slip and mention the emails and documents that they'd found and had kept from Sam and his team. "I'll just run in and check. Be right back."

"No problem," he said, sinking back into his seat. "Maybe the heat will come up by the time you get back."

Jessie entered through the ambulance bay and turned right into Donna's office, but it was empty, the lights switched off, the computer powered down.

"Hey, Jessie," Kate called. "She went home about an hour ago. I'm going now."

Darn. She'd have to ask her tomorrow. "Thanks," she said, as Kate retreated toward the ambulatory exit. She was about to ask if she needed a ride when she remembered the man who'd picked Kate up days before, and the strange way he'd seemed to keep his eyes on Jessie. He'd seemed so familiar, as though she knew him from somewhere. She decided to follow Kate to see if that man was there again. Maybe this time she'd remember where she'd seen him. She followed at a safe distance, pushing open the wooden door to the waiting room as Kate stepped through the glass exit doors.

The Lexus she'd seen before pulled up and Jessie hurried to the doorway to catch a glimpse of the driver. He turned and smiled at Kate as she slipped inside, and then suddenly his eyes, dark and brooding, lifted toward Jessie. She stepped back quickly, out of his line of sight, her breath catching in her throat.

She hurried back into the ER and made her way to the ambulance bay where Sam was waiting. "That was quick," he said, sitting forward.

"She wasn't there. I'll check tomorrow."

"Want to stop for a drink, or a quick bite?"

"I'd love to, you know I would, and any other time, I'd say yes, but tonight I just want to go home, think about Eddie, maybe call Angela Novak." *And see what I can learn about Rosehall.* Though she'd keep that to herself for now.

"You want me to pick you up tomorrow?" Sam asked as they pulled onto K Street. "Your car is probably encased in ice."

"Oh," Jessie groaned. "No, I don't want to have to rely on you. I'll have to dig it out sooner or later. Will you just drop me off at my car?" She fished through her bag for her keys. "I'm just up there," she said, directing him.

He pulled alongside and whistled. "I'll help," he said. "I have a shovel, and we can get this done quickly." He pulled over and reached in back for a collapsible shovel.

While Sam shoveled out, Jessie started her car and scraped the frost and ice from her windows. In no time, they were done, her car free of the icy snow that held it tight in place. Sam leaned down and kissed her lips as the first drops of rain began to fall. He laughed, holding his hand to catch the drops. "Sweet dreams, Jessie. I'll see you tomorrow," he called over his shoulder.

She watched him walk away, grateful that she was in a relationship, though still so new, with him. At least now she knew that he was as interested in her as she as in him. She took a deep breath, the icy air and raindrops chilling her to the bone.

She let herself into her apartment, heated a can of soup and settled on her couch, her thoughts on Eddie, and what she might have done differently. She knew that Sam was right. Eddie had chosen his own path; she was lucky that her life had intersected with his for a time. She only wished it had been longer.

She finished her soup and picked up her iPhone. To get her mind off Eddie, she tapped on the photos she'd taken earlier of the Rosehall account statements, and focused in on the contact information. Or what there was of it. All she could find was a phone number. No names, no mailing address, no email address, not even a fax number. She couldn't even tell how the bills were actually paid. Did the money go through Sheila? That didn't make sense. Though managers controlled their department budgets, they signed off on bills and then the finance department paid out. At least, that was what Jessie always thought.

She zoomed in on the telephone number that she'd called earlier from Sam's office. It was an 800 number: maybe it was on the West Coast and it had been too early. It was worth another try, she decided as she pressed *call*. And listened to a distant ring once again. Just as she was about to hang up, a man's voice came on the line.

"Hello?" he asked, clearly disgruntled.

Jessie hesitated, wondering if she'd dialed the wrong number.

"Hello," he said again, his voice gruff. "Who is this?"

"Is this the Rosehall company?" she asked tentatively. There was silence for what seemed forever until he spoke again.

"Who wants to know?"

"I'm actually calling for Sheila Logan."

The man on the line didn't answer, but she could hear him breathing. He hadn't hung up. At least, not yet.

"Who?" he finally asked.

"Sheila Logan. You've done business with her at Boston City Hospital." She'd decided not to tip her hand, not to say that Sheila was dead.

"The name doesn't ring a bell. Sorry."

And before she could tell him she had the emails, he hung up. A small thrill ran through her veins. She dialed again, but this time there was no answer and no voicemail either. Someone had taken the time to disconnect any message service. She was on to something. She had to be.

No doubt about it.

CHAPTER 38

Day 12—Thursday

She woke with a start. *Foley's!* That was where she'd seen that man, with Kate. She sat up, pushed her hair back from her face and sighed. That only confirmed Kate's story that she'd gone to Foley's to meet people. Aside from his brooding eyes—and maybe they weren't even that—he was average, nothing remarkable about him. Nothing memorable, anyway.

She slipped from bed and peered through her blinds, her lips curling into a smile. The morning sun was bright, the snow had melted with last night's rain and only shrinking mounds, created by shovelers and plows, remained. The street and sidewalk glistened with the last traces of slush. She pulled her window open, leaned forward and took a deep breath. She'd almost believed it wouldn't happen this year, but the air carried the clean, unmistakably sweet scent of spring. She knew that in the first week of March, it was only a tease of things to come. But a tease was exactly what she needed just then. Her thoughts drifted to Eddie. She laid her forehead against the windowpane and swiped away the tears that tracked along her cheeks. If only he'd been able to make it another day, he'd be safe now.

She paused before pulling back from the window. Seven thirty. She could get in a quick run and clear her head, maybe ease her sadness, before making her way to the ER and headquarters.

She sent a quick text to Sam. *Can't resist a run. See you after I go to the ER, and maybe the morgue to check with Roger about Eddie. Okay?*

His reply was swift. *Morning Jessie. See you when you get here.*

Smiling, she drew her hair back with an elastic, pulled on her running gear, laced up her shoes, slipped money and her house key into her sweatshirt pocket and made her way outside, where she blinked away the burst of full sun and considered, for only a second, going back for sunglasses. No need, she decided. This would be a quick run along a familiar route. She stretched briefly, warmed up with an in-place jog and finally took off running down K Street to Columbia Road and Day Boulevard, gulping in air, her arms pumping, her feet flying over the surface of the sidewalk, her mind lost in the pure joy of an unexpected chance to run.

Her thoughts wandered from Eddie to the investigation and then to Angela Novak. Her chest tightened momentarily. *Mother*—a word she'd never imagined in her vocabulary or her life. A car horn interrupted her musings, and she stopped short at the intersection as cars sped by, jogging in place to keep her muscles warm.

When the traffic slowed, she headed across the street to the center island, and when the coast was clear, she set her feet into the road and began her run. She slowed at a sudden screech of tires but the sound was coming from behind her, and by the time she turned her head for a look, it was too late. The sun was directly in her eyes, but she could make out a car picking up speed and headed right for her. A jolt of pain burst in her hip as she was hit and thrown to the street, her knees and hands and face skimming along the concrete until she skidded to a stop. She heard a shout and felt a whoosh of air as the car sped away.

She lay there motionless, afraid to move, her hip on fire, the skin of her hands and face scraped and bleeding, her leggings torn.

A hand reached down and touched her back. "Miss, are you okay? I've called an ambulance. Can you move?"

Her hand went to her right hip. "What happened?" she asked, her fingers surveying her hips and legs to feel for any bone injuries, but she seemed intact. She turned over and pulled herself to a sitting position, her eyes sweeping up to her rescuer, another runner, she thought, by the looks of his clothing and slim build. "Did you see what happened?" she stammered.

"Only the last bit. A car hit you and then burned rubber to get away. It looked like he sped up when he saw you." He bent to his knees and put his arm under hers. "We should get you off the street. Come on, put your arm around my shoulder." He helped her to the grassy center island, the whoop of sirens filling the air. A police cruiser and ambulance, their lights and sirens slowing, pulled up beside Jessie and her rescuer.

"Jessie?" a familiar-looking EMT asked. "What happened? Let's get you into the truck and to the ER."

She shook her head. "I'm not going anywhere. I'm okay."

The EMT pulled on gloves and ran his fingers along the side of her face, the stinging there a white-hot volley of pain. She pushed his hand away. "The skin is all scraped," he said. "Looks like on your hands, too. You have gravel embedded there. You should come in and get it cleaned, at least. You know, better than most, how quickly wounds like these can get infected."

But she wasn't paying attention. Instead, she'd turned her head to listen and watch as the runner who'd helped her relayed to the police and the other EMT what he saw. He pointed to the street, describing what little he knew. "I was running on the other side of the street, my mind a million miles away, when I heard tires screeching. I looked up to see the car hit that girl."

He jerked his head toward Jessie and smiled. "It looked as though she'd just stepped off the curb and into the street. And I just have to say, my first impression was that the car headed right for her. I know it sounds ridiculous, but that's how it seemed. I shouted and the car veered. It hit her but not full on. She fell to the ground and the car sped away. And I mean sped. And that's it." He rubbed his own hip as if in sympathy with Jessie.

"Get a description of the car? Plate number?" the patrolman asked.

The man shook his head. "Sorry, it all happened so fast."

The policeman frowned. "Color of the car, at least. Maybe a make?"

"It was a sedan of some kind, and it was dark-colored, but I don't really know cars. Sorry." The runner turned back to Jessie. "The officer has my information if you need it. I'm glad you're okay." And then he was off, his feet pounding hard as he crossed to Day Boulevard and the route along the beach.

"Thank you," Jessie called, hoping he heard her over the buzz of traffic and city noise.

The EMTs gave her some antiseptic and bandages, and pulled back onto Columbia Road, sirens at full volume as they raced off to another emergency. The patrolman approached her, took her information and insisted on driving her home. "Detective Sam Dallas would have my badge if he thought for a minute that I didn't get you home safely."

Jessie nodded gratefully. Her hip was at the very least bruised, the skin on her hands and knees scraped raw. Every step she took sent a searing pain shooting through her body. She poked at her face, wondering how bad she looked and hoping she'd still be able to work. She moved slowly toward the patrol car when the officer's cell phone pinged with a call.

"Officer Lincoln," he said, his head nodding at what the caller was saying. "Yes, sir," he said, pushing the phone toward Jessie. "For you," he said. "Detective Dallas."

Jessie smiled, despite the pain the effort caused. "Hey, Sam," she said.

"Are you okay? Are you going to the ER?"

"I think I'm okay. I'm going home, but—"

"I'm on my way," he said. "Be there in ten minutes." And before she could reply, he'd hung up. She passed the phone back to Officer Lincoln.

"Thanks," she said as she opened the back door to his car.

He closed it softly and directed her to the front seat. "Up here, Jessie. I don't want you sitting back there."

She slid in, lifting her right leg gently as he closed the door. For the first time since the car had hit her, she took a deep breath and felt a flood of tears collect in her eyes.

Never let them see you cry. And for the second time in just days, she didn't care, and she leaned forward and let her tears fall.

CHAPTER 39

Once home, Jessie peered into the bathroom mirror to have a look at her wounds A long, angry scrape ran along the left side, and just as the EMT had noted, tiny pieces of gravel and dirt were stuck to the raw skin. Jessie splashed warm water over her face, wincing at the sting but grateful to see bits of grit falling into the sink. She patted her skin dry and gently picked out the remaining traces of debris before squeezing a soothing antibiotic ointment onto the scrapes.

That chore completed, she peeled off her clothes and had a good look at her leggings—the fabric shredded at the knees and likely beyond repair. She stepped into a warm shower, turning her face from the stream but holding out her hands and then her legs to get the cuts and abrasions clean. Once she was satisfied that the wounds were as clean as she could get them, she twisted to examine her hip, and found a fresh bruise spreading over the place where the car had hit her. She flinched as she grabbed a towel and dried off.

Her doorbell rang as she was pulling on sweats over her sore legs. "I'm coming," she shouted, running her fingers through her hair.

When she pulled open the door, Sam stood there, his tie askew, his forehead creased with worry. "Oh, Jessie, what happened?"

He reached out his hand to touch her face, but she pulled away. "Sorry, Sam, but it hurts like crazy."

"Sit down," he said, his voice soft as a whisper as he took her elbow and guided her to the couch. "Tell me everything while it's still fresh in your mind." A muscle twitched in his jaw.

She eased herself onto the couch. "There isn't much to tell. The guy who helped me told the officer what he knew, that he saw a dark car that sped up and swerved to hit me. I think I heard it, too, or maybe it was the runner's shout. The car veered at the last minute but not before it grazed me and knocked me to the ground." She swiveled to her left to take the weight off her aching right hip.

"It hurts, huh?" he asked, crinkling his eyes, but all Jessie could see were the shimmering flecks of silver.

"What?" she asked.

"It hurts?"

"Yeah, but I'm okay."

"I think you need to get checked at the ER, and then we need to figure this out. This is what—the fourth incident in less than a week? A purse snatcher, a car break-in, a phony repairman, and now this." A cloud crossed his face. "I'm worried," he said. "I think someone's definitely targeting you."

A faint chill ran along her spine and she wondered if it was about the documents she'd lost and the Rosehall connection. Someone did seem to have it in for her. It was clearly time to fess up. She tried to sit up straighter, but shrank a little at the effort. *Might as well just dip her toes in first.*

"Do you think it's related to the whole Sheila investigation?" she asked.

"I don't know. It might be."

She shook her head and, true to form, she spoke before she thought. "I think it all started that night at Foley's."

Sam's eyes narrowed. "What are you talking about? What does Foley's have to do with anything?"

And suddenly the pain of her injuries was replaced by a tightening in her chest.

Sam tilted his head and fixed his eyes on Jessie. "What's going on?"

She swept her eyes down to avoid his gaze, but it was no use. She could feel his stare as though he were looking into her soul. "I… I was going to tell you."

He slumped back in the couch, his hand whisking beads of sweat from his forehead. "Are you in trouble? Are you connected with this in any way?"

She sat a little straighter and laid her hands palms up on her legs. "No, and I'm not in trouble. But I did see some of Sheila's emails before you did."

He jerked his head back. "Oh, Jessie…"

"Wait," she said. "Donna discovered she had them on her computer, and I just wanted to have a look."

"Why didn't you ask me, or at least tell me you'd seen them?"

"I was off the case by then, if you remember. And besides, I only saw Tim Merrick's emails at first."

"So, you knew about Merrick and Sheila?"

"I'd only just heard the rumors, and then Tim came to me when word of Sheila's death leaked out. He wanted to know what he should do."

"And you told him to do what?" Sam asked, his jaw clenched tight.

"To speak with you guys—I told you that at the time. I thought he'd call you right away."

"And instead, he avoided us. You gave him time to come up with a cover story, a plausible alibi."

"No, I didn't. Besides, he doesn't have an alibi. You already know that."

Sam sighed and sank further into his seat. "Anything else?"

"I printed a few of her emails—the early, confusing ones from Rosehall—and I took a couple of documents from her box. I'd planned to look at them at home over last weekend. I thought maybe I could put some things together. I stashed them in my backpack and met you guys at Foley's that night, and the next day

I discovered they were gone. I called Foley's, and they said they weren't there. I just hoped someone had thrown them out. They wouldn't mean anything to anyone else, right?"

She paused and tried to read his expression, but his jaw was set, his lips tight. She was already in; she had to plow ahead. "There's more. I called Rosehall last night when I got home."

"And?"

"A man answered. Said he'd never heard of Sheila Logan, and then he hung up. When I called back, no one answered. I think I spooked someone, and I think Rosehall's at the heart of this."

Sam shook his head slowly as if deciding what to say. Jessie looked at her hands, the raw skin, the sprinkle of blood, the swelling that was just beginning. She wiggled her fingers. Sam reached out and caught her hands in his.

"You should have told me about the documents. Maybe they weren't lost at all. Maybe somebody took those papers from Foley's, and they think you have other incriminating documents, and you know too much." He looked her straight in the eye. "You just can't go off and do this stuff on your own." He tilted her chin up with his hand, his brow wrinkled, the shimmer gone from his eyes. "It's dangerous, Jessie. And risky."

"I had to do something. I couldn't just wait for SIU."

Sam stood. "It's too late now, but clearly, you can't stay here. You're not safe. Get some things together, and we'll decide where you should stay. And not a word to anyone. Understood?"

"I'll have to tell Rufus."

"Okay, I'll talk to him."

"And I need to stop at the ER and the morgue. I still have to ask Donna if she knows anything about Rosehall. And I want to speak with Roger, especially now, after everything you pointed out. What if Eddie didn't freeze to death? What if he was killed because of what he saw at the garage?"

CHAPTER 40

Jessie sat stiffly in Sam's Crown Vic en route to the ER; it wasn't just that she knew he was disappointed in her. It was the throbbing pain in her knees and hip and hands, and even her face. "Will I be in trouble, Sam? I really thought I could help."

He glanced her way momentarily, his mouth a tight line, before he drew his eyes back to the road. "No. I wish you'd shared this with me earlier, or maybe I wish we'd kept you on the case from the start, but either way, no, you're not in trouble. Truth is, you seem to have broken this case wide open. Just remember you're on a team. We work things together, not separately." He dropped her off in the ambulance bay. "I'm going to see that CEO, what's his name?"

"Steve Alexander?"

"Yeah. That's him. I have a few questions for him. See if he knows anything about Rosehall. I'll meet you back here in thirty minutes. Text me if you're going to be late."

She nodded gratefully.

"And get yourself checked out. I can't have you out injured yet." He winked. "You're not trying to avoid going out with me, are you?"

She laughed and then winced with the pain. "I could think of easier ways to avoid a date, but I have no plans to avoid you."

"Jessie," someone called as she hobbled through the ambulance bay doors and stepped into the ER. It was Donna. "Hey, what happened? The EMTs told me about the car, and they said you refused to come in to be seen." She grabbed her elbow. "Come on. We'll get you checked now."

"I'm fine," Jessie said, gently pulling her elbow away. "It's just scrapes and bruises."

"You look awful and you're limping. You need an X-ray."

"I don't. Honestly. But I won't say no to some more antibiotic ointment and non-stick bandages."

Donna sighed. "Come on. I guess we can do that."

They walked toward the supply room, where Donna filled a small plastic bag with a few essentials. "Need anything else?' she asked, pushing Jessie's hair behind her ear.

"Actually, I came here to ask what you know about a company called Rosehall. I remember they sent Kate, but does the ER do any work with them? Have you signed off on any bills?"

Donna crossed her arms and leaned against the supply cart. "Yes, that's the nursing agency that sent Kate. I have those invoices in my office, but aside from that, I don't think I have anything else from them. I can check," she said, motioning to her office. "Why are you looking at them?"

"Seems Sheila had been doing business with them. Fraudulent business."

Donna's brows shot up. "Sheila? Really?"

They turned for the hallway in tandem, and as they stepped forward, they saw Kate, her face flushed, her eyes flickering with surprise.

"Do you need something?" Donna asked.

"Umm, supplies," Kate answered, pointing to the supply room.

They stood aside to let her pass. "Go on in," Donna said softly.

"Hey," Jessie called after her, "do you work for a company called Rosehall?"

Kate turned, her lips parted, her brow knitted. "I... Rosehall, you said?"

"Yes. Rosehall," Donna replied. "That's the agency that sent you here. Right?"

"To tell you the truth, I don't know the name. I can check, I guess. I just used the same agency as a friend had. This is my first assignment."

"Don't they send you checks? Is there a company name on them?" Jessie asked.

Kate chewed on her lower lip. "I get direct deposits."

Jessie huffed out a sigh and turned back to Donna. "Can you show me what you have?"

Jessie closed the door once they were in her office. "Do you think she heard us talking about Rosehall and Sheila?"

"I think she was listening, but I don't blame her. If her agency is in trouble, what does it mean for her?"

Jessie nodded. "I guess you're right. Maybe she's worried about her job. How did you find Rosehall anyway? Was it through Sheila's contacts?"

"No," Donna answered. "They emailed me just when I'd gotten approval to hire a travel nurse to cover your hours. I'd been looking into travel nurse agencies, and I was shocked at the price. They wanted over twenty-five hundred a week, though the nurse only gets half of that. I wasn't sure Administration would approve it, and that was when Rosehall emailed me out of the blue. You can see it right here," she said, tapping her finger on the computer screen.

Jessie moved to her side and read aloud:

Dear Nurse Manager,

I represent Rosehall, a well-known and respected nursing agency that offers both short- and long-term assignments to help cover your needs. To introduce you to our services, we are able to offer you an ER nurse for a two- to three-month *assignment, according to your requirements, at a cost to you of just $1,000 a week. This of course is an introductory rate, but I can assure you we hire only the most qualified RNs. I hope to hear from you.*

B. Dixon, RN, Director of Hospital Relations, Rosehall, Ltd.

"Can you print that out for me? And how did you reply?"

"I emailed back that same day and asked for an experienced RN for three months."

"Did they send a résumé?"

"No, they sent her Wisconsin license, and a note explaining that she'd recently graduated but had been working in an ER in Madison and came with superb references."

"Did you ever check those references?"

Donna shook her head. "I was so excited to get an experienced RN at that cost, I never thought to check. And Administration was so pleased with me, I didn't give it another thought. I guess I really screwed up."

"No, you didn't. And think about her. Maybe she's been a pawn in this too. Maybe they used her to get into the ER, hoping that they could run the same scam with you that they ran with Sheila."

"They haven't been in touch since she came. They never even ask about her hours. It's only been about three weeks, so I assumed that maybe they'd send me forms to complete at the end of the first month."

"Will you print out all of your communications with them, for me? I'll check her license myself at headquarters."

"You don't think she's involved in this scam stuff, do you?"

"Not really, but I'd like to know how they hired her. Maybe Rosehall runs a legit nursing agency as a front. Who knows?" She collected the emails from the printer and stuffed them into her bag, that was already filled with toiletries and a fresh change of clothes. "I've got to go. I want to check with Roger about Eddie and, not that I have to tell you, but don't share this information with anyone. Okay?"

Jessie limped across the street and swiped her ID on the electronic reader to gain entry to the morgue. She smiled, remembering what Tony had told her about needing an ID for the morgue. "This place is popular, Jessie," he'd said. "Everyone is dying to get in." And she'd laughed at his hokey humor. But today there was nothing to laugh about. She took the stairs one step at a time, her hand on her hip as if she could press away the ache.

"Hey," Tony said as she rounded the corner to the autopsy area, "what happened to you?"

"I fell," she answered, deciding that was the best way to avoid more questions. "And before you ask, I'm fine. Scrapes always look worse than they are."

He leveled his gaze at her. "You forget, I'm an autopsy tech, and Dr. Dawson's right-hand man. I know wounds and what causes them, and I don't believe you for a second, but I won't ask you if you don't want to tell me."

"Thanks, Tony. That's why everyone loves you, isn't it? It's not because you're an outrageous flirt, it's because you're such a good guy."

"It's both," he said with a lopsided grin. "Ya gotta admit, I am a great flirt."

Jessie laughed. "You are that, but today I'm here to see Roger. Is he in?"

Tony inclined his head toward the autopsy suite. "In there. He just finished up with that homeless guy you know."

Jessie pushed open the door and poked her head in. "Roger?" she called. "Got a minute?"

He was at the back by the sink drying his hands. "Be right with you, Jessie. You're here about Mr. Wilson?"

She smiled. That was the first time anyone, including her, had referred to Eddie as Mr. Wilson, a sure sign of respect. Seemed the morgue was full of good guys. "Any sign of trauma?" she asked.

He placed the towel he'd been using on a rack by the sink and walked toward her. "None. He froze to death, but if there's any consolation in that, it's that he'd been drinking and probably just fell asleep and passed away quietly. Likely never felt a thing."

Relief swept over her. At least he hadn't suffered. "Thanks, Roger. I appreciate that."

He took off his eyeglasses and studied her face. "May I ask what happened to you?"

"I fell," she answered, the lie slipping so easily from her lips she almost believed it herself. "I have to go. I'll see you later."

The walk to the ambulance bay took more time than Jessie was used to, but Sam was there, sitting in his car, reading something on his iPad. "Hey," she said, pulling open the door. "I have more interesting stuff on Rosehall. What about you? Anything?"

He nodded. "Turns out Dr. Merrick signed off on some of the Rosehall invoices. He's definitely in the running in this."

CHAPTER 41

At headquarters, Jessie felt her anxiety deepen with every step she took as she followed Sam to his office. "You can go in and get started," he said. "SIU wants to see me. I'll be back in a few minutes."

If truth be told, she was grateful to be alone, and to gather her thoughts. Sam had to be wrong. Tim Merrick wasn't involved in any scam, and he wasn't a killer, but the possibility that he had been involved still rattled her. She took in a deep, steadying breath. The outer office was empty, and Jessie pulled up a chair in front of the computer she'd used yesterday, and logged in. When she searched for her files with all of Sheila's emails, the folders were gone. *Darn!* She'd never thought to save them in a new folder. The SIU had probably got everything, since they were taking over the Rosehall part of the investigation.

Though her access to those documents was closed, she wasn't ready to give up on that side of the case. Maybe a search for Kate Wagner would reveal something. She knew that in Massachusetts, you could verify a nursing license online. She searched for the Wisconsin Board of Nursing and typed in Kate's name, hoping they would be as open with that information as most states were. Of course, she'd always thought the downside of that was that your license information was available to anyone and could be easily stolen. It hadn't ever happened that she knew of, but it seemed to her it was only a matter of time.

She typed in Kate Wagner's information and a license appeared. She peered at the report, blinked and then looked again. This couldn't be right. The Kate Wagner who was licensed by the State of Wisconsin had been an RN since 1992, which made her about forty-nine or fifty. She wiggled the stiffness from her fingers and googled Kate Wagner, RN in Wisconsin. A burst of documents filled her screen. She clicked on a local news story.

Kate Wagner had just been given an excellence award for her work in the ER at St. Mary's ER in Madison. The story included a photo. Jessie clicked on the image, enlarging it for a closer look. The photo showed a smiling woman, her gray hair pulled back in a tight bun, her smile open and warm. But maybe there were other Kate Wagners there, too. She searched again and again, but Wisconsin had only one nurse named Kate Wagner and she certainly wasn't the Kate Wagner who had come to Boston City Hospital.

"Hey," Sam said, interrupting her search. "SIU is taking over the Rosehall investigation. They have everything. It's looking like Medicare and Medicaid fraud, so they'll be turning it over to the US Attorney's office."

"What about the murders of Sheila and Mrs. Grigsby?"

"We still have those. I'm circling Tim Merrick."

"Don't be so sure of yourself." She turned the computer screen to face Sam. "Have a look. The Kate Wagner who was sent to the ER was sent by Rosehall." She pulled out the emails she'd printed and spread them out on the desk. "Donna thought it was a real agency, but when I checked her Wisconsin nursing license, only one Kate Wagner comes up, and this woman," she said, pointing to the image on the screen, "is not the Kate Wagner in the ER."

Sam's jaw went slack. "Wow," he said. "This complicates things."

"And our Kate Wagner is blonde, just like the woman who was seen at Sheila's apartment taking things out."

"But where's her accomplice? She's here alone, right?"

"No. That's what she says. But I've seen her twice with a man in a dark Lexus. I saw him at Foley's the night she was there. Whoever this Kate Wagner is, I think she's involved, and probably him, too."

"Do you think she's involved with Merrick?"

Jessie shook her head in exasperation. "Stop pointing your finger at Merrick, and while I think of it, do you have the bills he supposedly signed, or did SIU take those, too?"

"I have them, so we can do a handwriting check."

"Can I see them?"

"Sure."

She followed him into his office and watched as he rummaged through his in tray and pulled out a folder. "These are scanned copies. I found them in Sheila's documents before SIU took them." He passed her the folder and Jessie flipped through the pages.

"That's not his signature," she announced.

"How do you know what his signature looks like?"

"I don't, but I know a stamped signature when I see one." She held a paper out to him. "See how the signature is kind of thick and bleeds at the edges? The hospital uses stamp signatures for things like equipment and VNA orders. Just to move things along. Physicians don't have time to sign every letter or equipment order. You found these in Sheila's box? I think this was her way of dragging him into her web of lies."

Sam whistled. "I guess it's back to the hospital to get his signature stamp, and maybe talk to Kate Wagner."

Jessie smiled. "I think that's a good idea."

Sam sped through traffic, his tires screeching as he pulled into the ambulance bay. "Hey," a security guard shouted. "Hey, Detective, you can't keep parking there. We have a gunshot on the way in."

Sam threw his keys to the guard. "Take care of it. I'll find you when we're ready to leave."

The guard caught the keys in one hand. "Okay."

They hurried through the entry, and Jessie stopped at the center desk and hit the overhead microphone. "Donna to the ambulance bay, please," she said.

Donna poked her head out of Trauma One. "We're getting a gunshot, and we're short-staffed. What do you need?" she snapped.

"We need to…" Sam started, and then paused as the wail of sirens drowned out his words.

The EMTs hurried by, a young man in a wheelchair clutching his foot, a small bandage wrapped around it. "That doesn't look like trauma room material," Jessie said, wryly. "Trust me, Donna will be out any minute."

And sure enough, before Sam could respond, Donna was pulling off her gloves and heading toward them. "What is it?" she asked, a trace of aggravation in her voice.

"Sorry to bother you," Sam started again.

"It's not you guys," Donna said. "It's just been one of those days."

"We have a couple of questions," Jessie said. "First one is, do you have one of those signature stamps for Tim Merrick?"

She smiled. "I can't believe you're asking that. I found one a couple of months ago in Sheila's desk. I had no idea why she had it, but I thought maybe I'd need it, so I held onto it, but I was just thinking yesterday I should get rid of it."

"Oh, no," Sam moaned. "Please tell me you didn't throw it away?"

"I didn't. I'm a bit of a hoarder. Come on. I'm happy to give it to you."

They followed her to her office, where Donna searched through a drawer and retrieved the stamp. "Here you go," she said, handing it to Sam.

"Thanks. Mind if I stamp something just to see what it looks like?"

Jessie slid a blank notepad to him and watched as he used the stamp, his eyes growing wide. "It's exactly how you described it,

Jessie. Bleeding at the edges and thick. And companies accept these?"

"Of course, they want the business. But we don't use signature stamps here in the ER," Donna said. "I didn't understand why Sheila had this one."

"Where's Kate working today? We need to speak with her," Jessie asked.

Donna's mouth twisted into a hard line. "She went home sick not long after you were here, Jessie. She said she had to leave."

"She didn't look sick to me."

"Not to me either, but nothing I can do. I can't force someone to stay."

"Darn! She heard us talking about Rosehall," Jessie said, her arms crossed tight over her chest. "Maybe we can catch up to her. Do you have an address for her?"

Donna shook her head. "She never provided one and I never asked. The nursing agencies that send the travel nurses provide housing, and I remember her saying that she was in a hotel, not an apartment."

"Sam," Jessie turned her head. "You dropped her off last week after Foley's. Where'd you take her?"

"The Lenox," he said. "I remember thinking that travel nursing must be a pretty good gig."

"Let's go," Jessie said, starting for the door.

"Wait," said Sam, turning back to Donna. "Do you have any photos?"

"A copy of her ID," she said, pulling open her drawer and rifling through a file box. "Here you go," she said, handing over a small hospital ID encased in plastic. "We keep duplicates just in case."

Sam slipped it into his pocket as he and Jessie raced for the exit. Jessie motioned for the security guard to get Sam's car as Sam called headquarters, requesting back-up at the Lenox Hotel. "We're looking for a young woman, blonde, and a male." He turned to Jessie. "What did he look like?"

"Average. Brown hair, brown eyes, nothing special about him." She shook her head. "Sorry, he just had one of those nondescript faces."

Sam chuckled. "That's a hell of a picture to go on." He shared the brief description. "Tell everyone to stand down. I don't want to tip them off. No sirens, and only undercover cars if you can. Tell the uniforms to stay out of sight." Satisfied that his instructions were being relayed, he turned to Jessie. "Do you feel well enough for this? Do you want to stay here?"

"No way I'm missing this," she said. "I'm coming."

CHAPTER 42

Sam pulled up to the valet at the Lenox and showed his badge. "Official business. Please just keep it parked here." He slipped the man a twenty and he and Jessie entered the lobby. A large, lavish room, its marble floor was covered with ornate rugs, plush chairs and couches filling the open spaces. Open doorways led off to bars and restaurants.

"Pretty impressive spot for a travel nurse, huh?" Jessie asked.

Sam nodded and made his way to the registration desk. He held up his badge and asked to see the manager. "Yes, sir," the clerk said nervously.

He returned with a balding, middle-aged man with an obsequious smile and thick eyeglasses that almost hid his eyes. "I'm Josef, the manager. How can I help you?"

Sam nodded to the office behind the desk that Josef had just exited. "We'd like to speak with you privately."

"Of course," Josef answered, motioning for them to follow him. "What can I do for you, sir?" he asked.

Sam took Kate's photo from his pocket. "This woman is staying here, maybe under the name Kate Wagner. Ring a bell?"

"We're a large hotel. But this woman," he tapped the photo, "is someone I've noticed. She's been here for weeks. Goes out most days wearing hospital scrubs, which is unusual attire for a tourist. And she spends most evenings at the bar with her companion."

"And he is?" Sam asked.

"Let me get the ledger," Josef said, rising from his seat and heading back to the main desk.

Sam pulled a radio from his pocket and spoke softly. "Dallas here, everyone in place?"

"Yes, ready to go, unmarked vehicles and plainclothes officers in front and at the side. Uniforms up the street," a familiar voice said.

"Who was that?" Jessie asked.

"Ralph," Sam said with a smile.

"Here we go," Josef said, sliding the ledger open and running his finger along the pages.

"Ahh, here it is. Kate Wagner is in Room 438. She is registered with a Buddy Dixon in Room 440."

"Did you check his ID?" Sam asked.

"Of course we did," he answered haughtily.

"And they are still here?"

"Yes, Miss Wagner returned a few hours ago. She said she'd be leaving today, and asked to have the bill ready and a car for the airport."

"And Dixon?"

"He left this morning."

"Maybe she's meeting him at the airport?" Jessie asked.

Sam nodded. "Please call her and tell her there's a package for her here in the lobby and she has to come down and sign for it."

A trickle of sweat broke out on Josef's forehead as he picked up the phone and dialed her room. "Miss Wagner?" he asked, his voice a little shakier than Sam would have liked. "I have a package for you in the lobby. The driver says you have to sign for it. Can you come down?" He hesitated. "Ahh, fine, we'll see you then. Thank you." He hung up and swiped his hand across his forehead, whisking away the gathering beads of sweat. "She'll be down in ten minutes," he announced.

Sam pulled up his radio. "Ralph," he said, "give me three in plain clothes in the lobby, the rest by the front entrance."

"You got it," Ralph replied.

"I'm going to put my men at the desk. Please get your desk staff and have them stay away from the lobby. I'm going to use your office."

Josef scurried out to collect his staff and hurry them all away.

"Where will I be? And you? She'll recognize us right away."

"We're going to stay just inside the doorway to the City Table restaurant. We can see her from there. Let's go, make sure everyone is in place."

In the lobby, the staff at the desk had been replaced by three undercovers in suits, all looking polished and professional, and Jessie marveled at the ability of the police to turn on a dime and take up positions as though they belonged there. She knew that they carried guns, and were experts at what to do should trouble break out.

Sam nodded to the men at the desk and quickly advised them of the situation. "Her accomplice is already at the airport, we think. I'm going to ask Detective Thompson to alert the state police to be on the lookout. Though I don't know which terminal he's in, but I expect to have that information once we question Miss Wagner."

The men went back to looking busy at the desk as Sam and Jessie took up position in the doorway. Sam pulled out his cell phone and texted Ralph. "I don't want to use the radio now. I want us to keep a low profile."

Jessie watched as guests and staff walked through the area oblivious to the police operation happening around them. She tapped Sam's arm as Kate headed from the elevator to the desk. One of the officers looked up. "Miss Wagner?"

She nodded. "I have a package?"

"Yes, please come with me," he said, leading her into Josef's office.

Jessie and Sam raced to follow and slipped into Josef's office on Kate's heels. She spun around, her mouth falling open. "What are you doing here? What do you want?" She started for the door.

The undercover cop folded his arms across his chest and smiled as he closed the door. "Have a seat, Miss Wagner."

She sighed and fell into the chair. "I don't know why you want to bother with me," she said, her blue eyes as flat and icy as a winter sky.

"Ahh, Kate." Sam slid into a chair across from her. "We know you're working with Rosehall and are connected to the murders of Sheila Logan and Edith Grigsby."

The color drained from Kate's face. "I had nothing to do with any murders," she whispered.

"Where's your friend?" Sam asked. "Is he at the airport waiting for you?"

She sat silently, her gaze focused firmly on her hands.

"Is the US Attorney here yet?" Sam turned to the officer.

"On the way. FBI, too."

Kate squirmed in her seat. "You can't prove anything. And I haven't done anything wrong."

"But we can. For starters, we know you're wrapped up with Rosehall in a Medicare fraud scheme, and we know you're not Kate Wagner, RN. A check of your fingerprints will likely help us, so why don't you just tell us who you are?"

Kate swallowed hard.

"We can help you if you cooperate. And the first thing we need is the location of Buddy Dixon."

"That's not his real name."

Sam scooted his chair closer and looked Kate straight in the eye. "Tell me who he is and where he is. Now. The longer you wait, the more likely he gets away and this all falls on you. Your choice."

Kate's eyes grew round as saucers and she seemed to deflate. "I don't know his real name. He calls himself Buddy Dixon, but I've seen other IDs in his bag. Anyway, he's waiting for me at the Delta counter. Our flight is at four p.m."

CHAPTER 43

Sam glanced at his watch as Ralph opened the door from the reception area and stepped inside. "We all set?"

Sam's jaw tightened. "We have two hours to get this guy. Ralph, I'm putting you in charge here. Read Miss Wagner, or whoever she is, her rights, accompany her to her room to collect her things and then close that room off. Once that's secure, take her to headquarters. She can make her call once we have this guy. Let the state police crime unit, the FBI and US Attorney know that we have her."

Sam looked at his watch. "And please call the state police airport unit and tell them to get to the Delta counter and do a sweep of the area. Give them what we have, which isn't much—average-looking, brown hair and eyes and likely traveling by the name of Buddy Dixon. And I want these four guys to follow me to the airport. Got it all?" Ralph nodded and began to bark orders into his radio.

Sam turned to Kate. "Where is your flight headed?"

"Tampa," she said. "Home."

A satisfied smugness coursed through Jessie's thoughts. That was the first thing she'd noticed about Kate Wagner—her distinct southern accent, though she'd insisted again and again that she was from the Midwest.

"Hey, Jessie," Sam said, "we'll need you, since you're the only other person who can ID this guy. You ready?"

"Yes," she answered. "I am."

Outside, Sam directed the patrol cars, with sirens and lights on full, to lead the way to the airport. Jessie slid back into the Crown Vic and watched as the caravan sped to Kneeland Street and then onto I-90 and the airport exit. It seemed only minutes before they pulled into Terminal A, where Delta Airlines was located. The squad cars powered down their lights and sirens and blocked off all exits and entrances. The state police troopers were there waiting, the blue lights of their own cars spinning soundlessly.

"We have eyes on the entire terminal, and have closed off the Transportation Security Agency—TSA—security checkpoints," one of the troopers said sternly. "TSA records show that a Buddy Dixon passed through to the departure area twenty minutes ago. We have plainclothes officers and detectives just getting into that area." He nodded toward Jessie. "Is she the one who can identify him?" he asked Sam, as if she wasn't standing right there.

Jessie took a deep breath and vowed to keep her mouth shut.

"Jessie Novak, RN," Sam said. "She works with us in Homicide."

The trooper's brow knitted as if he wasn't sure he'd heard that correctly, but he held out his hand. "Nice to meet you, Jessie. I'm Derek Hudson."

Jessie took his hand, forced a crooked smile and nodded toward the entrance to the terminal. "Shouldn't we be in there?" she asked him.

Sam stifled a chuckle of his own and placed his arm on Jessie's back. "She's right. Let's go."

Inside, a cluster of uniformed Boston and state police stood in the center of the terminal. "People are starting to get anxious," the trooper said. "We've told them that this is a very quick security exercise and apologized for the inconvenience. We've held the uniformed guys out here, so we don't spook our guy."

Sam nodded his approval. "Okay. Once we get into the departure area, we should spread out. We don't want him to see a large group. It will only alert him that we're on to him. I'll also ask Detective Thompson to have our Kate Wagner text Dixon, see where he is." He sent off a quick text to Ralph and they all waited for his reply.

After what seemed an eternity, Ralph replied. *No response from Dixon and no delivered notice on her phone. Probably has his phone off.*

Sam huffed out an irritated sigh. "Okay. Jessie, stay with me." He turned to Hudson. "No radio use, please, the static and crackle of radios will announce our presence. Cell phone texts only." Trooper Hudson nodded. "I'll separate from you both once we get inside." They swapped cell numbers and passed quickly through TSA, the security staff there standing quietly to the side. The area was crowded with travelers, some sitting idly, others rushing to gates.

"We've asked Delta to announce early boarding on their other flights so we can keep the number of people here to a minimum. No reports yet of anyone resembling Jessie's description, but hopefully," Hudson said, turning to her, "you can find him for us. His flight departs from Gate Six. I'll be in that office," he said pointing to an enclosed area.

Jessie and Sam made their way toward Gate Six, noting the restrooms, restaurants, coffee bars, and shops along the way. "I think I should keep a distance from you," Jessie said. "No offense, but you scream police. I can just wander around alone and not attract attention. You can find the plainclothes guys who are in here and see if they know anything yet. Agree?"

Reluctantly, Sam grunted his approval. "Keep your phone in your hand. Call or text me immediately if you see anything. Just put 911 and your exact location. Got it?"

"Agree. See ya," she said, pushing away from Sam and walking toward Gate Six, where rows of chairs held travelers waiting to board. A digital sign above a check-in desk announced that the flight to Tampa was on time. Jessie wandered over and dropped into a chair in the last row of a bank of seats, designed not so much for comfort as for economy.

She'd pulled out her phone, hoping to look immersed in email while she surreptitiously scanned the crowd, composed of a perfect cross-section of people—young, old, tall, short, screaming children, an old man, his head bobbing in sleep, a woman beside him reading a book. Nothing suspicious, no one out of the ordinary. Jessie stood as if to stretch, and moved toward the full-length windows that looked out on to the runway. A waiting plane stood, its door connected to the jetway, a flurry of activity as workers threw bags onto the conveyor belt that led to the plane's cargo hold. She sighed—maybe he wasn't here. Kate might have lied, but then she remembered that TSA had said Buddy Dixon had gone through security.

She turned around, her gaze falling on a man who had just moved into a seat against the far wall. His head was bent forward, his eyes intent on his boarding pass. As though he knew he was being watched, he looked up. *It was him.* Her heart pounding against her ribs, Jessie leaned down quickly, pretending to check her shoe, hoping she'd avoided his glance. Hunched over her knees, she fired off a quick text to Sam: *911 sitting in back row at Gate 6.*

The little *delivered* word seemed to take forever. Jessie raised her head slowly, scanning the seats, but she couldn't find him. She stood gradually, bending from the waist, her head still angled down as she surveyed the seats and nearby stretch of terminal. He was gone. *Darn it!* He must have seen her. She raised her head and her gaze just in time to see the door at the end of the seating area slam shut. She raced toward it, propelling herself along the tightly connected rows, banging into legs and luggage as she went. "Sorry," she called more than once.

She pulled the door open and found herself at the top of a staircase. She heard another door slam below, this time accompanied by a whoosh of air and the sound of engines revving on the tarmac.

She stood just inside the doorway and called Sam. "I know I wasn't supposed to call," she said quickly, not giving him a chance to speak. "But he's outside on the runway by Gate Six. Hurry up. I'm in the stairwell. I'm going to follow him." Sam started to shout something—probably to stay put, but Jessie wasn't about to. Not now. Not after all this. She hit *end* and, her hip pain and injuries all but forgotten, she took the stairs two at a time.

Once outside, the cold wind slammed into Jessie, nipping at her cheeks and fingertips, but it was the noise, the ear-blasting sound of jets—some racing along the runway, others with engines roaring as they readied for takeoff—that forced her to turn away.

She pulled the collar of her coat high and turned back in time to see the luggage cart by Gate Six, with its driver and handler, heading back to the terminal, leaving several bags under the moving belt that deposited it all into the cargo hold. Behind it, a bevy of planes attached to departure gates by jetways stood, bellies open, some with bags being thrown out onto carts while others had handlers haphazardly tossing suitcases on board.

Jessie craned her neck to see beyond all the activity, but aside from moving luggage and food carts, mechanics scooting about in pickup trucks, their suspect seemed to have vanished. She inhaled angrily and hoped that Sam was on his way, or that maybe he was nearby, setting up a staging area to keep everyone informed and ready.

She turned toward the door, certain that Sam would be hurtling through, but he had yet to arrive. Then she pulled the door open, half expecting to see Sam and the state police troopers gathering there, but the stairwell was empty. *Where were they?*

She stepped inside and pulled the door shut. She was afraid that if she went in search of Sam, Buddy might somehow slip from their grasp. She pushed up against the concrete wall, her eyes glued to her phone, and sent another text. *911 I'm at gate six—the runway.* She waited for what seemed like an eternity, and still no reply.

Maybe she was in a cell dead zone. Anxious that she might miss Buddy, she pushed open the door for a quick look, and as she did, like a shy turtle checking his surroundings, he suddenly poked his head out of a nearby plane's cargo hold. His eyes darted every which way, and anxious to avoid being seen, Jessie jumped back inside, keeping the door slightly ajar with her fingertips.

She counted to ten, enough time for him to have made a move one way or another, and pushed the door open a crack, peering out in time to see him leap from the plane and make a run for it along the tarmac. *And still no police in sight!* But she knew that this guy had been through security, which meant he had no weapons; he was no real threat to her, but he could be to others if he got away. She took off after him, picking up her pace, her arms swinging, her legs pumping, her heart pounding, every ounce of her certain that this was the run of her life.

Darting in between, around and under hulking jets, she watched as Buddy slowed and then stopped by an unattached jetway, its yawning accordion shape still wide open. She turned briefly and watched as approaching planes descended and raced almost gracefully along the sleek, blacktopped surface before slowing and turning toward waiting jetways. When she looked back, Buddy had disappeared. She had lost him.

CHAPTER 44

As she considered her quandary—to stay, or to go in search of Sam—activity on the tarmac came to a sudden stop. Overhead, planes halted their descent before pulling back up into the sky, joining a line of jets in formation overhead waiting for clearance to land. On the ground, mechanics, luggage handlers, food cart and vehicle drivers were holding onto cell phones or radios, listening or reading intently. A fleet of official airport vehicles rolled onto the tarmac. They separated and went in different directions. From where Jessie stood, they seemed to be slowing at departure gates and jetways, speaking with workers.

It was only minutes before all of the workers hurriedly exited the area—some on foot, others hopping onto available vehicles—all leaving, and all, she assumed, heading to a place of safety, and likely ordered by Sam, which must mean he'd received her messages. She glanced at her phone quickly. He hadn't answered her, but he had to be nearby. She stuffed her phone into her pocket. She'd miss Buddy if she spent too much time messaging Sam.

She watched as every plane that was already lined up on the runway preparing for takeoff slowed and then stopped their forward movement, their engines still humming, their taxiing lights still blinking. One last plane rose slowly to the sky, soaring gently before disappearing from sight.

A convoy of state and Boston police cruisers appeared off in the distance at the intersection of several runways. The usually bustling airport had ground to a strange and unexpected halt. But the noise—of idling engines, wind whistling off the ocean, and police sirens in the distance—seemed to echo and bounce off the tarmac, increasing in intensity. There was no sign of Buddy. But she was sure he was hiding right there—in plain sight.

One official car stopped by Gate Six, the plane idle, nearby baggage and food carts abandoned. The driver, likely a plainclothes police officer, exited his still-running car and walked toward the plane, peering into the open cargo hold before walking along the lines of parked planes and peering inside. He was soon joined on the tarmac by several other official vehicles, all driving deliberately at a snail's pace. *They were looking for Buddy.*

A swell of relief surged through her veins and Jessie, afraid to show herself and disrupt their search, tucked herself safely out of view behind an almost full baggage cart sitting to the side of a large jet's open cargo hold. From there she had an almost three-hundred-and-sixty-degree view of the Delta terminal, flight line and taxiways. The floor-to-ceiling glass front of the terminal had been cleared of passengers who'd been crowded there to watch the drama unfold, but as Jessie watched, she realized that they were looking in the obvious spots—open jetways and gaping cargo holds. And that Buddy Dixon, she was certain, was too smart to be hiding there. Instead, he was likely tucked away in a plane's landing gear, or watching from a catering truck or one of those oversized cargo transporters.

Determined to find him, Jessie stepped out of her safe place, the ocean wind whipping around her, the arctic cold seeming to settle in her very bones, her bruised hip throbbing, and began to search the hidden nooks and crannies of the nearby planes. She ducked first under a hulking jet, peering into wheel wells and abandoned service trucks. Her first search came up empty—no trace of Buddy. She moved quickly to plane number two, her eyes watering and her throat and lungs burning in the raw sting of frozen air. It was then she realized that her exhalations were creating frosty plumes that seemed to hover around her, a neon sign announcing her presence. She quickly adjusted her scarf to cover her mouth, the warmth immediate and soothing against the stark, cold air.

As she bent to inspect the gap in the landing gear tires, she caught a movement behind her, so slight she might never have noticed it but for her isolation huddled underneath the belly of the plane. *The police had found her.* When she stood, a gust of cool air brushed against her neck, and when she reached back with an ungloved hand to pull her scarf in close, she felt a sudden rush of hot breath on her skin.

She began to turn, certain it was Sam, when a sturdy arm suddenly wrapped around her neck, pulling her into a chokehold and jerking her body back. She struggled to free herself, only to find herself deeper in his hold. A helpless kind of fear gripped her throat as firmly as his arm did. It was Buddy. It had to be. He'd found her before she could find him. She clawed at him to get free of his clutches, but his grip grew stronger as his fingers found the loose ends of her scarf and began to pull, tighter and tighter, cutting off the air until she couldn't breathe.

"I've got you now, Jessie Novak," he whispered. She tried desperately to pull away, thrashing against him, but it was useless.

Her heart hammering in her chest, fresh terror pulsed through her veins and seeped from her pores. The blood rushing from her head left her feeling dizzy and almost numb as she realized she was likely hidden from sight. Her eyes darted wildly, searching for a way out, but she knew there'd be no help, no last-minute rescue. A dreadful certainty swept through her—he was going to strangle her right there with her own scarf, just as he had the others. And there was nothing she could do about it.

CHAPTER 45

She tried to count the seconds—or was it minutes now?—since he'd grabbed her. The timeline for losing consciousness due to oxygen deprivation, she knew, was two to three minutes, but her airway hadn't been cut off completely. She could still feel tiny trickles of air seeping in and out through her nose. Images of Sam, Rufus, and the woman who might be her mother flickered through her mind. There'd be no first date, no more breakfasts with Rufus, and no chance to get to know Angela Novak.

Then, as swiftly as Jessie had been overwhelmed with panic, a kind of calm came over her. And she knew. *She wouldn't give up, not without a fight.* A sudden surge of adrenaline coursed through her. In one last push of waning strength, she squirmed against the ligature, her fingers clawing at his hands, desperate to breathe, her foot kicking back at him, but it was all in vain. He was using her own scarf as a garrote, just as he'd used Sheila's, Mrs. Grigsby's, and probably Mary Stewart's, to squeeze the last breath out of her.

Her thoughts racing, her heart pounding out what felt like its last beats, something connected in her brain and she remembered—the pepper spray that Sam had given her was still in her pocket. Her assailant, intent on choking the life out of her, failed to notice as she reached into her pocket, her trembling hand folding around the canister, searching for the spray release button. Her fingers secure and ready, she pulled the canister out quickly and, in one swift and shaky movement, she held it up and back and pressed hard on the little nozzle.

She could hear the hiss as the toxic spray spewed from the canister and when he loosened and then lost his grip, she knew it had hit him full in the face. She dropped to the ground, the scarf dangling from her neck. She scrambled to her feet and caught sight of Buddy, screaming in pain, his hands over his eyes. He fell to his knees and Jessie, gulping in the sudden burst of fresh air, sprinted for safety, looking over her shoulder, determined to keep him in her sights.

As she cleared the space under the plane and raced for the terminal, a sudden wail of sirens filled the air and Jessie turned to see Sam running toward her, the state police trooper on his heels. She slowed to a stop and bent forward, her hands on her knees, relief sweeping over her as Sam pulled her into his arms and held her tight.

"What happened? Are you okay?"

"I was looking for Buddy, but he found me first," she said breathlessly, her throat raw, her voice hoarse. She looked into Sam's eyes and he held her away from him, searching for signs of bruising around her neck and face.

He brushed his lips against her forehead and drew her close once again. "Where is he?" he asked, an urgency in his voice. She knew his eyes were darting about in search of Buddy.

She pulled away and pointed to the underbelly of the nearby plane. "I was in there by the landing gear and from nowhere, he came up behind me. He's still there, I think."

His hands reached to gently touch her neck, his eyes flashing with worry and then a steely resolve. "How did you get away?"

Then she realized she was still clutching the canister of pepper spray. Her hands trembling, she held it up, a faint smile forming on her lips. "You were right. This stuff does work."

But as she spoke, Buddy appeared, one hand rubbing at his eyes, as he raced to a still-running official car, jumped in and headed for the runway, the police vehicles just beyond, sitting idly. "That's him," she shouted. "They won't know who he is! Call them! Tell them to get him. He's…"

Sam was barking orders into his radio before Jessie had even finished speaking. Trooper Derek Hudson had joined them, his own radio in his hand. "Our suspect is crossing runway four left, heading toward runway nine. Sirens and lights on but stand down until we can be sure what he's up to. He's going the wrong way if he thinks there's an exit to the highway over there." It was then that another plane began its descent, heading for runway nine. Hudson was on his radio once again. "Where the hell are the controllers? Tell the tower to get that plane back up!"

Buddy sped along runway nine, apparently oblivious to the plane just overhead, but Jessie's eyes were drawn to the sky and the approaching disaster. Could the control tower reach the pilot in time? Jessie held her breath and waited. At what seemed the very last second, the plane shuddered and started to rise, the engine's thrust forcing a high-velocity explosion of air along the runway, the tornado-like blast of wind taking control of everything in its path. Buddy's car was thrown forward, the wind's power forcing it into a roll toward the runway's end and the ocean beyond.

Sirens and lights and the noise of activity pierced the quiet as police, ambulance and fire vehicles converged on the area. Hudson's radio squawked, interference cutting into the connection, but the message was clear. "Rollover with injured suspect on runway nine, ocean edge."

By the time they made it to the area, a group of EMTs, firemen, and police were huddled over Buddy, who lay on his back on the ground, his right leg under him. "They tried to kill me," he shouted to anyone who'd listen.

Sam stepped forward, glaring angrily at Buddy. Jessie, her fingers resting protectively on her throat, stayed behind and watched as the EMTs assessed his injuries, palpating his neck, his hip, and his injured leg. He screamed as his leg was straightened. "No c-spine tenderness, no bony deformities, distal pulses good," the EMT announced. "But he definitely has to go to the ER."

The EMTs placed a soft collar around his neck, splinted his leg and scooped him onto a stretcher as a trooper began to read him his rights. Jessie slipped through the small group. "Can we send him to BCH, to my ER?"

"We gotta go to Mass. General with him," one of the EMTs said. "It's closest."

Jessie sighed and turned back to Sam. "Are we going to follow them?"

"No. We'll let the state police arrest him and hold him. Professional courtesy, and we're on their turf. We'll be notified, and we'll get him once the hospital releases him and he's booked. And remember, SIU and the Feds are still interested in him, too."

Buddy started to shout. "I'm going to sue you for false arrest!"

"Famous last words," Trooper Hudson muttered.

Jessie turned away. "Can't we go to the hospital, Sam? Maybe begin to question him there?"

"No," he said. "First things first. We need to get you checked out. You've almost been killed twice today. No excuses. The second ambulance is taking you to the ER."

She might have put up a fight, but suddenly her legs felt wobbly, her vision cloudy, and her skin clammy. The runway seemed to sway, and she felt herself being sucked into a vacuum. She reached a hand out to steady herself, but it was too late. She heard Sam shout as her legs gave way.

CHAPTER 46

She couldn't be sure if it was the blare of the sirens or the way the stretcher jumped as the ambulance took a tight corner, but a hammering in her skull let Jessie know that she was awake. A flickering image of Buddy trying to strangle her flashed through her brain and her hands went instinctively to her neck, still raw and sore.

"Hey, you're awake. How are you feeling?" a smiling EMT asked.

"As though a train ran over me. Where are we headed?"

"BCH ER," he answered. "The detective told us you work there."

"I do. Any chance you can just drop me off at the bay? I'll take it from there."

The EMT bobbed his head. "I don't think so. Hear that other siren? The detective is in front of us, providing an escort."

Jessie groaned as the ambulance pulled into the bay. In the ER, she was wheeled into a cubicle on the acute side. "Please," she whispered to Elena. "Can someone just examine me quickly, so I can get out of here?"

"I heard that," Sam said from behind the privacy curtain.

"I'll ask the surgical chief to see you. How's that?"

Jessie sighed and lay back, pulling the sheet to her chin. She was used to being the nurse, not the patient, and she felt fine, just a little tired, but it was useless to argue.

An hour later, discharge instructions and a prescription of Motrin in hand, she pulled her sweater back over her head, suddenly aware that every inch of her body ached.

"Your X-rays were negative," the surgeon said, "but you have a concussion from that hit you took this morning, and your throat is bruised. Get plenty of rest and try to speak only when necessary."

She was just slipping her arms into her coat when Sam appeared. "The doctor told me that you have to rest, and—" He was interrupted by a ping from his phone. He looked down, nodding as he read.

"What is it?" she asked, her voice hoarse, her throat scratchy. "Everything okay?"

"Our Kate Wagner was booked at District Four, and she's on her way to headquarters. I'll go there now so we can get started on her. She just might be willing to roll over to save herself. Right now, she's facing two counts of accessory to murder in the first, and Medicare fraud. I think we have a chance to convince her to talk to us before Buddy does. He's still at MGH, by the way." He slid the phone back into his pocket, his eyes locking onto hers. "And you are going home to rest."

Jessie shook her head. "Please, Sam. I should be there. I want to hear what she has to say, and besides, I can rest while I listen." She cleared her throat as if to emphasize her willingness to be quiet.

He huffed out a sigh and shook his head dramatically. "Ahh, Jessie. I have a feeling you'll never take my advice. Or anyone else's, for that matter."

"I might, just not today. I need to hear what she says."

"I'm not going to win this argument, am I?"

She shook her head and smiled demurely. She knew she'd won when she caught the shimmer in Sam's eyes.

"Ready?" he asked.

*

"Hey, Jessie, I heard what happened. You okay?" Ralph asked, his brow furrowed, as they arrived at headquarters.

She smiled. "I'm okay." Her voice was a whisper. "I've lost my voice, though."

Ralph raised a brow and chuckled. "There's always a silver lining."

Jessie smirked and forced a smile. This kind of banter, she knew, was good. It meant she was one of them.

"Anyway, Wagner's in the interview room," Ralph said. "She's crying up a storm. Her public defender is with her—he's a little shell-shocked. Don't think he ever expected to pick up a case as big as this." Ralph rolled his eyes. "I told them we'd be right in." His gaze turned back to Jessie. "But let's make sure we have Jessie settled first."

Sam nodded and guided Jessie to the now familiar room where she could watch the questioning. He adjusted the monitor and sound and Kate Wagner, slumped low in a sturdy wooden chair, appeared on the screen. Her lawyer sat stiffly beside her. "You can adjust sound or resolution with these buttons. Okay?"

Jessie nodded. "Hey, before you get started with her, can you rustle up some coffee, and maybe a sandwich? I'm starving."

"Good to know some things never change," he said with a smile.

She pulled up a seat, wriggled out of her coat and sank down with a satisfied sigh. When Sam returned with a hot coffee and a limp bologna sandwich, she was too grateful to complain. "Thanks, Sam," she said softly.

"I'll be in and out. I'd love to have you in there with me, but I want you to rest your voice, so…"

She held up her hand and nodded in agreement.

"You're a quick learner, Jessie Novak."

She rested her feet on the table and sipped her coffee, her free hand rubbing the soreness out of her hip. She leaned forward, dropping her feet to the floor, and watched as Sam and Ralph entered the room and formally introduced themselves.

"I know who you are," she said curtly. "I don't know why I'm here."

"I think you do," Sam said. "How about we start with who you really are, with a name?"

"Did you get Buddy? Have you spoken with him?" she asked. Her lawyer placed a hand gently on her arm and shook his head as if to encourage her not to speak. She shook him off.

"We have him," Ralph said, "but right now, we're here with you. Where this case goes depends on you. Let's worry about Buddy later."

"I… I'm afraid to say. Buddy will kill me."

"He's in custody. He's not going anywhere," Sam said gently.

Kate's eyes fluttered and she looked at her lawyer who said, "You have to tell them who you are."

"My name is Brittany Lee," she whispered, her bluster fading.

"Are you a nurse?" Sam asked.

She shook her head.

"Why don't we start with Rosehall, then. Tell us what you know, how you came to work for them."

Brittany's eyes filled with tears. "I was a nursing assistant in Tampa, in a private doctor's office. He was the one doing business with Rosehall. I don't know exactly what Rosehall did, but every few weeks Buddy Dixon came in with forms for the doctor to sign. We got to talking one day, and he said I was too smart to work in a dead-end job, said I could make money working with them. I was interested. I mean, who wouldn't be?" She reached for a bottle of water on the desk and took a long swallow.

Ralph's impatience got the better of him. "And?"

She set the bottle down. "He asked if I could pretend to be an RN in a Boston ER. He said Rosehall was investigating some illegal activity and they needed a manager's documents. He said she'd been cheating them. It sounded exciting, almost like what Jessie Novak does—investigating crimes. I said I'd do it. He flew me up here and we stayed at the Lenox, and before you ask, we had separate rooms. Ours was a business arrangement only." She paused and ran her fingers through her hair, distracting herself momentarily.

"He took me to the ER at Boston City before I began to work there. He thought if we could get what he needed, I might not have to pretend I was a nurse. And that part was easy, at least at first. Anyone can get into that ER and just wander around. We found Sheila's office, but it was always locked up tight, so that seemed like a no-go. Buddy thought what he was looking for was probably at her apartment, so we went there, and Buddy just went crazy. We tore that place apart. Got her computer, IDs, bank books. But none of it turned out to be what he needed. And on top of that, an old lady saw us. She poked her head out her door and asked what we were doing. Buddy just sneered at her."

"And how did you get into the ER to work?"

"Buddy stole the nursing registration and license information of a nurse in Wisconsin. That part was easy, too. That stuff is available online. Anyway, he made sure she was an ER nurse in case anyone checked, but no one ever did. And, anyway, I'm a nursing assistant. I can do most of what nurses do."

Just down the hall, Jessie huffed out an angry sigh. She wanted to shout, but she had to save her voice, or what was left of it. She sipped her coffee and turned her attention back to the screen.

Brittany was still speaking. "I tried to get into the manager's office, but I never made it. A couple of times, Jessie caught me, and I just acted stupid. She thought I was stupid, though you can see I'm not. But she just didn't like me. It didn't help that I really didn't know how to do anything in the ER, but I thought we'd get what we needed and be out quickly, no more than a week or two. But as the days dragged on, and then that manager's body was found... well, I started to panic. I told Buddy we had to do something."

Her lawyer whispered into her ear. Brittany shook her head. "I haven't done anything wrong. Not really."

"Go on," Sam prodded her.

"Last Friday, I knew that Jessie and Donna were looking at emails and things on the computer, and when I tried to get a peek, Jessie ushered me out. I called Buddy. I said I was pretty sure that Jessie had some of the documents we were looking for. I saw them on the desk and later, when she thought I was gone, I saw her stuff them into her backpack. I called Buddy and told him they were all going to Foley's that night and we should go, too. And it was there I cozied up to you, Sam, so Buddy could go through Jessie's bag."

She turned to him, the violet flecks in her eyes shining through her tears. "I asked you to drive me back to the hotel to rattle Jessie, so that she wouldn't notice that her papers were gone. And it worked. Buddy got a few papers, enough to let him know there was more, and that he had to get the rest of what she had. The next afternoon, after the snowstorm, he followed her to that bar at L Street, and he waited until he saw her leave, and tried to snatch her bag. But I guess she fought back, and he didn't get it."

"That miserable creep," Jessie whispered to the empty room.

Brittany was trembling by the time Jessie composed herself and began to listen once more.

"When that didn't work," she continued, wringing her hands as she spoke, "he tried to get into her apartment when she was at work, but the old man wouldn't let him in. Buddy was furious, so he broke into her car in the garage. But that was another dead-end. She caught him off guard when she called the Rosehall number last night and said she was calling for Sheila Logan. He was convinced that Jessie was on to him. He said she'd seen him in the ER months ago arguing with Sheila, and he said she knew too much, and he'd just have to kill her. There was nothing else he could do. I tried to talk him out of it but he wouldn't listen."

She took another gulp of water and whisked away the beads of sweat that had gathered on her forehead. "He left the hotel this morning when it was still dark, and he kept watch for her. I thought about calling her and warning her, but I was afraid he'd come after me instead, so I kept quiet." She laced her fingers together and continued. "He said later he'd thought about breaking in, but then she appeared in the doorway and started on her run, and he made his way to that big main street. When she started to cross, he revved his engine and hit her. He said he was sure he'd killed her, or at the very least incapacitated her. That's why I was surprised to see her walk into the ER, and when I heard her mention Rosehall to Donna, I called him. He told me to get out. He said we were leaving. I came back to the hotel to pack, and that's when you guys showed up."

Sam looked at his watch. "It's late, almost seven. Let's take a quick break."

He headed to the viewing room, where Jessie sat fuming. "What do you think?"

"Miserable," she started, but caught herself. Her throat was burning. She wouldn't waste her voice hurling insults they'd never hear.

"Anything I'm missing?"

"Tim Merrick. I want her to admit that he's not involved. And ask her about Eddie, if Buddy had anything to do with his death."

CHAPTER 47

Sam gulped down a bottle of water and headed back to the room where Brittany sat, her arms folded, her legs crossed, one foot swinging back and forth.

"A few questions before we break for the night," Sam said. "Is Tim Merrick involved with you, with this?"

Brittany puffed out her lips. "No. He's not involved. Buddy said he liked to keep the circle small."

"What about Eddie Wilson? Did Buddy hurt him?"

She looked away, her eyes misting over. "I told Buddy that Eddie had seen him break into the car. He bought him a gallon of cheap whiskey and dropped him off underneath the expressway. Turned out that Eddie didn't have a clue who Buddy was, so he decided he didn't need to kill him. But the whiskey and the cold killed him anyway. I felt badly about that. I wish I'd kept my mouth shut. Eddie was a nice guy."

Tears streamed down Jessie's face and she buried her head in her hands. *She was the one who should have kept quiet.* He was dead because Brittany, or whoever she was, had overheard her telling Donna that Eddie had witnessed the car break-in. She sniffled and wiped her sleeve across her eyes, aware that the interrogation had started again.

"What do you know about Sheila Logan's death?" Ralph asked, his voice edgy.

Brittany shrugged. "Nothing. That was months ago. I was in Florida."

"Hard to believe," Sam said, "that Buddy never told you about it."

"He told me that he'd had trouble with her, that's all." Her voice cracked.

"He didn't tell you he'd killed her?"

She folded her trembling hands on her lap as if to still them. "He said she was planning to leave the ER and didn't want to be involved in Rosehall anymore. Said she had enough money. Buddy said he picked her up to talk about it and they got into an argument. He said she took off. That's all I know." She looked directly at Sam. "And that's the truth. By the time I realized Buddy was a killer, I was in too deep, and I was afraid for myself."

"What about the old woman who saw you both at Sheila's apartment?" Sam asked.

"What about her?"

"She called the Natick police. Said she could identify you and Buddy."

Brittany's eyes grew wide. "I… I… well, I guess we'll see. I already told you I was there."

"So, you don't know that she was killed?"

Brittany remained silent, and it was hard to tell if she was surprised or just protecting herself. She balled her fists and finally spoke. "He had me call her and say there was a problem, that someone had broken into her car. I told her we needed her to come down to the garage and have a look, see if anything was taken. He said he was just going to talk to her. I didn't think he'd kill her. I mean, she was old. I thought he just wanted to see if she remembered him. I'm sorry about that, too." She blinked away a tear and sank a little further into her seat. "I would never be a part of that, of hurting someone, especially an old lady. He told me only that she wouldn't be identifying us."

Sam sighed and loosened his tie. "Alright. For now. We'll leave the Rosehall questions to the SIU and the US Attorney. But we're not done with you just yet. We'll pick this up tomorrow."

"Where's Buddy?" Brittany asked.

"The state police have custody of him right now."

"What about me? Am I going back to the Lenox?" she asked, her eyes wide.

Sam shook his head. "You're going back to the lock-up at District Four." He nodded toward Ralph. "He'll make arrangements. See you tomorrow."

Sam strode into the viewing room where Jessie sat with her arms folded. "They're both in custody, so you can go home," he said. "You'll be safe but want to get a quick bite, maybe a bowl of soup, before I drop you off?"

She lifted her backpack, her nightgown and toothbrush peeking out. "Not tonight, Sam. I'm beat."

Sam wrinkled his brow, grabbed his coat and followed Jessie outside. "How do you feel? You okay?"

"Huh?"

"Brittany reminded us all that you were hit by a car this morning, badly enough that Buddy thought he'd killed you. And then he strangled you almost to death, so yeah. I'm a little concerned."

"I'm okay. A little stiff, but so glad this mess is over. And sad that Eddie had to die, and poor Mrs. Grigsby, and even Sheila."

He wrapped her in his arms, his embrace warm and comforting. She sank into him, her heart fluttering as he brushed his lips against hers. "Let's get you home," he said.

*

Once safely in her apartment, Jessie took a hot shower and a Motrin and settled into bed. She picked up her phone. With everything going on, this might be a perfect time to speak with Angela, the mother she'd imagined only existed somewhere deep in the tunnels of her mind. But it was late, she was tired, and there would be too much to explain. So instead, she placed her phone on her bedside table, turned it to silent, and slid underneath the covers, drifting quickly into the sweet abyss of sleep.

It was later, in the deep quiet of night, that the soft murmur of voices lifted Jessie from the fog of her dreams. She froze, and held her breath to listen.

There it was again.

CHAPTER 48

Day 13—Friday

Jessie sat bolt upright, took a deep breath, and reminded herself that her lock was secure. No one could have broken in. She swung her legs over the side of her bed, wincing as her sore muscles cramped up, reminding her of her brush with Buddy Dixon and his car just yesterday. She ignored the discomfort as she stood and padded to the living room, expecting to see the soft glow of the television, but the screen was black, though the hum of conversation was more insistent. She stood quietly, trying to connect the synapses of her brain and decide if the voices were real or leftover fragments of her dream.

But as she stood there, it came to her. The unmistakable sound of conversation was coming through the heating register from Rufus's apartment just beneath hers. His television, maybe? He was a little deaf, so maybe he had the volume turned up, but she hadn't known him to be a night owl. Maybe he wasn't feeling well. She'd have to go down and check on him, make sure he was okay.

She pulled on her sweats and headed down, aware of the old bones of the house creaking with each step she took. The house wasn't as quiet at night as she'd always imagined. She could almost hear it groan as the wind slipped through its gaps. She gathered herself and knocked softly on the door. "Rufus?" she whispered, her voice a croak, her throat still raw and sore. A rustle of movement and chairs squeaking from inside made her smile. She imagined him talking to his cat, rising slowly from his chair to answer the door. But aside from that, there was silence. She knocked again. "Sorry to bother you, I just wanted to be sure you're okay."

And suddenly the door was inched open and Rufus peered out, sweat beading on his forehead, the cat skittering out from behind him.

"I'll get him," Jessie said, scooping the cat into her arms. "Are you okay? You don't look well." She began to push past him and step inside, but he put up a hand and shook his head.

"No," he whispered, his head turned slightly, his eyes darting. "I'm good. Go home." He seemed hunched, and somehow smaller.

"But…" Jessie began. He raised both brows as if trying to tell her something other than what he was saying, and he began to shut the door.

"Well, if it isn't Jessie Novak, the girl who ruined everything," Buddy Dixon called from somewhere behind Rufus.

The hairs on the back of her neck stood up. *How the hell did he get here?* She stood her ground firmly at the doorway, her glance falling on Rufus's metal baseball bat still tucked into the corner by the door. Her thoughts racing, she tried to formulate a plan. But first she had to get Rufus out of here. She swallowed the knot of panic that welled up in her throat and willed herself to be calm, and to remember that she'd already gotten the better of Buddy twice. She could do it again.

In one swift move, she shoved the door open wide and stepped in front of Rufus. "Get out," she whispered. She saw the hesitation in his eyes, and she pushed him out behind her, putting the cat in his arms as she did and slamming the door with her foot.

"You bitch," Buddy snarled as he stepped from the kitchen clad in a hospital gown and a ragged coat and pants. Hospital slippers covered his feet.

Jessie reached her fingers back, feeling for the bat, just to make sure it was within her grasp. "How did you get out?" she asked, her voice still scratchy.

His odd, demented laughter came in a short burst. "Your throat still hurts, huh?"

Jessie remained perfectly quiet and perfectly still, her other senses on full alert—the stale scent that hovered in the hallway, the smell of cardboard and old newspapers, the sound of Rufus's wall clock as it ticked the seconds away. Out of the corner of her eye, she caught the light switch set on the wall just to her right.

"It looks like it's just you and me," he said, taking a step toward her, a glistening knife in his hand.

She swallowed the pain in her throat. "I can help you. You can have my car and get away," she lied, pasting a half-smile on her face. "There's still time."

He shook his head angrily. "Do I look stupid? I should have killed you when you saw me in the ER arguing with that sneaky bitch, Sheila. You spooked her, and everything that happened since then is your fault. You as good as killed her and that old woman. Not to mention your friend, Eddie." He drew his lips back in a snarl. "You shoulda minded your own damn business!" His face flushed red with anger.

The mention of Eddie fueled her anger and her resolve. She knotted her hands into tight fists ready to fight back if she had to, but what she really needed was time—to think what to do. And for that she had to placate him, appear to understand him, or at least want to. "You seem like a smart guy, Buddy. You had an almost foolproof system."

"Not almost. It was foolproof. Still could be." He shrugged.

Keep him talking about himself, she thought. "So, how did you do it? I can't even figure out how Medicare works, never mind how to get it to work for you."

The corners of his lips turned up in an odd kind of half-smile. "I was pretty good with computers. I hacked into my high school's system, changed grades, classes, even seating assignments. They knew they'd been hacked but they never figured out who'd done it. I got better at it when I took a few computer courses after high school, and when a hospital's billing department hired me, I learned how to sidestep their system and have money deposited into my accounts. Genius, huh?"

"I suppose so, but wouldn't a bank be suspicious? I mean, how old are you?"

He nodded, seeming happy to talk about himself. "You're right. I knew it would send up red flags, so I created online accounts and a bogus company called Rosehall."

"Rosehall? Does that stand for something?"

"Named for my mother, Rose Hall. She died when I was a baby."

His eyelids drooped as he spoke, and she knew she had him. A common thread would keep things going. "I didn't have a mother either," she said. "It's hard, isn't it?"

He tilted his head as if really listening for the first time. "Did your mother die, too?"

She fell back easily into her old familiar lie. "When I was two."

"Hey, me too. See, we coulda been friends, you and me. Now…" he began, but cut himself off. "Too late."

"It's not too late. We can still be friends. I can help you to get away."

"How?" he asked with a smirk.

"My car is right outside, and you can use Rufus's clothes. I have cash, too."

"How far do you think I'll get? Your friend Rufus is probably calling the cops."

"He's just waiting outside. He doesn't know who you are unless you told him. Maybe he thinks you're an old boyfriend." But she knew that Rufus was nobody's fool. She was sure he'd already gone looking for help. She just had to buy some time.

"You think it'll really work?" A muscle in his jaw twitched. "You'll have to come with me. For insurance. Understand?" He was already formulating a plan, and he stood a little straighter.

She nodded. "I'll have to go upstairs first, get my stuff."

"I don't think so," he said, walking toward her, the knife still in his hand. "We'll both go."

Her time was up. She had to do something, and do it fast. She leaned back, her shoulder catching the light switch, throwing the apartment into sudden darkness.

"What is this?" he shouted as he tripped over some of Rufus's clutter and fell with a thud, the knife clattering to the floor.

Jessie held her breath, and reached back, her fingers closing around the bat. Her eyes adjusting to the darkness, she could see him in shadow sprawled on the floor. He pushed himself to his knees, his eyes searching for the knife.

Running footsteps and raised voices filled the silence before the back door crashed open and Sam and the Special Ops team rushed in and surrounded Buddy, pulling him roughly to a standing position. A look of pure fear crossed his face. For Jessie, the whisper of relief she felt surged to her muscles, which went limp, the bat slipping from her hand. She leaned back, hugging the wall, and flicked the light switch on.

"Read him his rights. Again." Sam's voice was fierce, his eyes narrowed, a vein popping out in his neck.

"I need an ambulance," Buddy whimpered.

"Right outside," a policeman said as they pulled him through the door, dragging his feet along the floor, his last pathetic effort at resisting arrest.

Once they were gone, Sam pulled her into his arms. "I can't believe I'm asking this again, but are you okay?" he asked, the silver flecks in his eyes shimmering.

"Yes, but where's Rufus?"

He appeared in the doorway. "Right here, Jessie, and I'm fine, thanks to you."

CHAPTER 49

It was almost noon by the time Jessie had completed her statement at headquarters and was ready to head home. Buddy, she'd learned, had demanded an MRI when he was at the Mass. General ER.

"He was smart enough," Sam said, "to know that meant no handcuffs, no metal, no visitors in the room. The staff slid him into the MRI tube and when the technician was setting up, he slipped out, took another patient's jacket and pants, went outside and apparently stole a car. When the state police notified us, I was pretty sure he'd head back here. I actually sent you a couple of texts. We were just setting up outside when Rufus came out and told us he was inside with you." He shook his head. "I damn near lost it."

Jessie smiled. "What about Buddy and Brittany? What's next for them?" she asked.

"Justice. The US Attorney is going to take Buddy. He's committed his crimes across state lines, so they're going to charge him in a federal court with three counts of murder in the first, one of attempted murder—that one would be you—and multiple counts of Medicare fraud. He'll likely be in jail for the rest of his life."

He paused for breath. "Buddy admitted to killing Mary Stewart. Poor kid had no idea what he was up to, and when she figured it out, he killed her and moved his operation to Boston. He said it was almost too easy, so many hospitals to scam, so little time. He'd been operating in Florida, honing his skills before he decided he was ready for the big time, and moved on." Sam stuffed his hands into his pockets, and she couldn't tell if he was pleased that the Feds were taking the case, or if he was disappointed to lose it.

She nodded. "And Brittany? I almost feel sorry for her."

"Her story checked out. She was a nursing assistant in Florida, and he used her. She had no idea what he was really up to. She's genuinely sorry for everything, and she's agreed to testify against him. She's gotten herself into a mess, but she'll likely just wind up with a slap on the wrist. She wasn't involved in any of the murders. Not sure yet what they'll charge her with, but she will have a record. Either way, it's out of our hands. Kind of a relief."

"And what about Mrs. Logan? Will you call her?"

"I think she'd rather hear the news from you, Jessie," he said.

She nodded. "I guess I should just do it now, so she doesn't hear it on the news. Do you have her number?"

"In my office on the desk. Go on. I'll wait out here for you."

Jessie took a slow, deep breath, and a long swallow of water before she dialed. "Mrs. Logan? It's Jessie Novak," she began. "I have news." And once she'd shared the necessary facts, there was a long pause. "Mrs. Logan? Are you there?"

"I am," she answered, her voice stuffy with tears. "But why did he kill her?"

Jessie knew the full truth wouldn't help this dear woman recover from her grief, and so she did what she was best at: she held some of the story back. Mrs. Logan would learn it in time, but not just then, and not from Jessie. "He's a bad man, Mrs. Logan. I'm sorry."

"Well, that's my dear Sheila, isn't it? Always trusting the wrong people."

As they said their goodbyes, Mrs. Logan insisted that Jessie keep in touch, and she promised she would. Once she'd hung up, she leaned back in the chair and wondered again at the possibility that Angela Novak might be her own mother. It seemed a long shot, but it was worth checking. A knock on the door interrupted her musings.

"Hey," Sam said, slipping into his office. "Everything alright?"

She looked into his eyes, into the shimmer that always reassured her. "I was just wondering if you'd had a chance to look into Angela Novak."

Sam rubbed his chin, the fresh stubble there only adding to his allure. "I did."

Jessie sat straight up, her back suddenly rigid, her aches and pains and bruises forgotten. "And?"

"She checks out so far. Born in Boston, married your father in 1990, had you in 1993. And started a job in Texas in early 1996, after she had a baby."

Jessie's heart hammered against her ribs. "And the baby?"

"No other information. There was a closed adoption. The records are sealed."

She exhaled a long breath of air. "I have a mother," she whispered to herself as much as to Sam.

"Do you want to call her?" Sam asked as he pulled a chair close to her and sank into it.

She shook her head. "Not yet. I need time to get used to this, to the whole idea of it." She drew his hand into hers. "You might not have noticed, but I'm a bit of a skeptic."

He laughed out loud. "You don't say?"

She ran her fingers across the stubble on his jaw and looked into his eyes.

"What do you say, Jessie?" he asked. "A night out this weekend, if you're feeling up to it?"

She opened her mouth to speak, and stopped. There were too many what ifs to count. But only one mattered. He wasn't just her co-worker; he was her friend. Maybe her best friend, and she couldn't afford to lose that—to lose him.

"What if it doesn't work out?" she whispered.

"Ahh, Jessie," he said, running his finger over her lips, the silver specks in his eyes lighting up his face. "What if it does?"

A LETTER FROM ROBERTA

Dear reader,

I want to say a huge thank you for choosing to read *The Frozen Girl*. If you did enjoy it, and want to keep up to date with all my latest releases, just sign up at the following link. Your email address will never be shared and you can unsubscribe at any time.

www.bookouture.com/roberta-gately

As an ER nurse, I've always been interested in forensics and crime investigation, and I've thoroughly enjoyed researching and writing every aspect of this story. I hope you loved reading *The Frozen Girl* as much as I enjoyed writing it. And if you did, I would be so grateful if you could spare the time to write a review. It makes such a difference helping new readers to discover one of my books for the first time.

I'd also love to hear your thoughts about Jessie Novak, so please get in touch on my Facebook page or on Twitter, or through my website.

I hope that you'll follow Jessie Novak in Book 3, due in November of 2021. Thank you for your support!

Roberta Gately

robertagately.com

robertagately.com/mailing-list/

RobertaGatelyAuthor

RobertaGately

ACKNOWLEDGMENTS

I am enormously grateful to Cynthia Manson and Judy Hanson, my incredible agents and even better friends, for their extraordinary guidance, their cherished friendship and their unshakable faith in my ability to craft a story. I am more grateful than a simple thank you can ever convey.

To Maisie Lawrence, my brilliant editor—your edits and your encouragement have inspired me every step of the way, and have helped this story to come alive. To the wonderful team at Bookouture, including Noelle Holten, Kim Nash and so many others who have helped along the way, thank you. I am enormously grateful to be a part of the extraordinary Bookouture family.

Thank you to my good friend Kate Conway, who continues to provide me with the insider's view of South Boston, helping to carve out the perfect niche for Jessie Novak. And many thanks to Detective Sergeant James P. Wyse (BPD Ret.), for his technical guidance and tips into homicide investigations, and for his lifetime of service at the Boston Police Department. And thanks as well to Stan Bykowski for his behind-the-scenes airport expertise.

To my family and friends, who've always believed in me, my gratitude is endless.

Made in the USA
Las Vegas, NV
19 May 2021

23273471R00164